This novel uses some terms—such as "Negro"—that are offensive to many people today, myself included. I do not use these terms to condone them, but I believe it is the job of a historical novelist to reflect the past, including its uglier and more racist parts. In doing so, we are better able to understand the roots of our present and work toward a more equitable future.

Eleanor Shearer

This novel uses some terms [illegible] such as 'Eskimo' that are offensive [illegible] to many people today. I have included [illegible]. I do not use these terms to condone them, but I believe it is the role of a historical novelist to mirror the past, including its beliefs and mores, as [illegible] parts. In doing so, we are better able to understand the roots of our present and work toward a more equitable future.

[illegible]

FIREFLIES
in WINTER

Eleanor Shearer is a mixed-race writer and the granddaughter of Windrush generation immigrants. She splits her time between London and Ramsgate. Her debut novel *River Sing Me Home* sold in twenty territories. It was named as one of *Time* magazine's 100 Must-Read Books of 2023, was a finalist for the 2024 Dayton Literary Peace Prize Fiction Award, shortlisted for the Grand Prix des Lectrices ELLE 2025 in France and also shortlisted for the Prix Fragonard 2025 in France. It was a *Good Morning America* Book Club pick, and has been optioned for film by AL Films and BBC Films.

Also by Eleanor Shearer

River Sing Me Home

FIREFLIES
in WINTER

ELEANOR SHEARER

REVIEW

First published in 2026 by Headline Review
An imprint of Headline Publishing Group Limited

1

Cataloguing in Publication Data is available from the British Library

Hardback ISBN 978 1 4722 9146 2
Trade Paperback ISBN 978 1 4722 9147 9

Offset in 12.22/17.68pt Baskerville MT Pro by Six Red Marbles UK, Thetford, Norfolk

Printed and bound in Great Britain by Clays Ltd, Elcograf S.p.A.

Headline's policy is to use papers that are natural, renewable and recyclable
products and made from wood grown in well-managed forests and other
controlled sources. The logging and manufacturing processes are expected
to conform to the environmental regulations of the country of origin.

Headline Publishing Group Limited
An Hachette UK Company
Carmelite House
50 Victoria Embankment
London EC4Y 0DZ

The authorised representative in the EEA is Hachette Ireland,
8 Castlecourt Centre, Dublin 15, D15 XTP3, Ireland (email: info@hbgi.ie)

www.headline.co.uk
www.hachette.co.uk

For Cal, my first reader for the last time

Live in each season as it passes; breathe the air, drink the drink, taste the fruit, and resign yourself to the influence of each.

—HENRY DAVID THOREAU

FIREFLIES
in WINTER

The Trial

January 1798

Halifax County Court is a stage waiting for its players. The judge's place is empty, as is the dock, enclosed on all sides but one. This is where the accused will stand.

The room carries the weight of its past, all it has witnessed, leaving it hard and cold. Winter winds rattle loose window-panes. Dark wood-paneled walls remember the methodical dissection of every kind of crime. Killers and crooks, robbers and the robbed, victims and perpetrators alike have all wet the uneven floor with their tears, lifted their gaze to the rafters and prayed.

The public benches are almost deserted, but a young woman waits there. It is, of course, a waiting kind of place—for confessions, for verdicts, for justice. Her eyes dart between the clerk in the corner and the two white men who stand in hushed conversation at the front, a lawyer and his client. She cannot stay still, one moment leaning forward in her seat, the next sitting back and gripping the bench with both hands. She breathes with some difficulty, the sign of a chill settled on the lungs.

The door to the courtroom opens. Everyone falls as silent as the snow-covered streets outside.

As the accused is brought in, she keeps her hands behind her, as if bound, but when she reaches the dock, she holds its sides to steady herself. They have left her free for now, though red welts of worn skin at her wrists betray that she has recently been chained.

On the public benches, the young woman is on her feet. She says a name. The accused looks up. Their eyes meet. They cannot move from where they are, but their gazes cling to each other with the desperation of the drowning. All the accumulated history of the courtroom, the vast body of past crimes, recedes, and something vital and singular shines through. These two women. This case. The whole world might as well hang in the balance; the whole world might as well be awaiting the arrival of the judge, for the trial to begin.

WINTER

1796–97

1

The air smells of salt and fish on the edge of rot, their carcasses piled high and stinking in the market. But it is the noise that assaults Cora—the noise and the crowds, wagons trundling over mud and stone, shouts from the drunks crowding the taverns, the distant sound of drums and pipers as the militia parade up Citadel Hill. Squat wooden houses, peeling brown and yellow paint, flank the streets. Rising up the hill are grander buildings, made of slate; the morning's frost, now melted, turns them dark and foreboding. All the people have hard, weathered faces, and they walk at a tilt, angled into the bitter wind.

Cora passes stalls with slaughtered sheep and pigs. Barrels of oats. Shops—the tanner, the dressmaker, the dry goods store. Her trip here has been in vain, still no flour to be bought in the city. She misses home with a dull ache, everything in Halifax reminding her only of what has been lost: bright-colored fruits and crystal-clear mountain streams. She has forgotten how it feels to be warm. . . .

A hand seizes her by the lapel of her woolen coat. Cora starts but does not shrink or cower. She stares directly into the face of the white man who has stopped her, their heights almost the same.

"Quite a way from the Negro quarter, aren't you, girl?"

His features sharp, a mean set to his mouth.

"Papers," he says.

"Let go—"

"Papers," he repeats. "Where are your papers, girl?"

The eyes of strangers slide over her, indifferent to her plight. She swallows anger as she pulls herself free.

"Me no have papers."

The white man is thrown, briefly, by something. Perhaps her lack of deference; the way she has, all this time, held his gaze. Or perhaps it is the unfamiliar accent, the rise and fall of it where he expects broad, flat tones.

He is the one who looks away first.

"In that case—"

Cora puts a hand on her chest.

"Maroon," she says. "From Jamaica."

It hurts a little, the name in her mouth. Home.

The man still stands too close, slow to understand.

"Free," Cora says firmly.

It might not be enough. She has learned that the people in this place don't know what Jamaicans know. Can't always accept her status as something different than the others with skin like hers. But luck is on her side. A shout from close by. The man turns; a fellow inspector tussles with a ragged-clothed man, someone who looks more like the runaway type. Cora is left as the white man hurries to help with the arrest. She doesn't want to watch. She walks away and lets the market crowd swallow her.

———

She leaves the city empty-handed, huddled on the Dartmouth ferry, freezing; she still doesn't have the knack for this weather, is without a hat or gloves, her thin layers inadequate to warm her. Hard waves knock the sides of the boat. Impossible to believe that this water is the same as the water that breaks on the sands of home.

Will she ever return?

Cora oscillates between determination and despair. Some days, she thinks she would swim the distance if she could. That nothing could stop her from clawing her way back—that she would rather die in the attempt than resign herself to a life on these forbidding shores. But then there are the dark days, the days when she can hardly rise from her bed, when she lies motionless, listening to the roaring wind or driving rain outside, or when fog presses close around the windows, and she cannot imagine ever seeing her island again.

2

The problem is that she is not paying attention. Taking a shortcut, off the main road from Dartmouth toward Preston, but her mind is following the forest paths of Trelawny Town in Jamaica, retracing old steps. The cold draws her into herself—cutting off the feeling in her fingers and toes, a spreading numbness as though the inessential parts of herself are falling away and she will be left with only her core. And the core of her has always been the forests of home.

Lost in the past, she does not realize she has taken a wrong turn until it is too late. Until, looking around, she thinks that these spruce trees are not as they should be. The uncanny feeling of familiar shapes turned slightly strange—just enough to make the world around her feel unreal, like the illusion of another distorted landscape in the surface of rippling water.

She stops. Looks around, inwardly cursing. But not so bad, surely. She can retrace her steps, she is sure of it. She looks up at the gray sky, trying to calculate the angle of a sun half-hidden by cloud—and that is when she feels something land on her face. A pinprick of cold.

The winter's first snow.

Cora stands for a while and watches it fall, the flakes so slow it makes the heavy, pounding rains of Jamaica feel like a distant memory.

Overhead, the sky seems lower. Cora recalls a folk story, of a time when people could reach up and pick pieces of the sky like ripe fruit and eat it, so no one ever went hungry. The story can't be her mother's, but Cora imagines for a moment that it might be. That somehow, twenty years ago, a woman laid a hand on the swell of her belly and whispered things, making herself heard through layers of skin, speaking of lions and trickster gods and the very beginning of the earth.

The flakes settle on her face and hair fleetingly before they melt away. The paths are beginning to disappear under the dusting of white. She is already lost. How will she find the right way now?

Some, at this point, would start to panic, but Cora's is not a mind so easily unsettled. She prides herself on taking things as she finds them. Has little patience for those who worry, where getting to work will do. So, nothing for it but to walk.

She sets off, back in the direction she came.

———

By the changing quality of the light, Cora guesses that another hour has passed, maybe more. Her feet, at least, do not ache, too frozen for feeling. But her shoulders, hunched around her ears, are stiff, her coat fighting a losing battle to keep out the cold.

This new, muffled world does strange things to sound; her heels kick up snow as she walks, and it is easy to imagine that the soft noise as it lands is something else creeping behind her, close as a shadow. She looks around. Nothing. She is alone.

Her rational mind keeps fear at bay. What use, after all, is fear? But there is an animal part of her that is heightened by the thick silence, that hears every snapping twig like a gunshot, that turns the whistling wind into some creature's call. She finds herself walking a little faster, releasing silver clouds of breath. Paying more attention to the forest, until her eyes are drawn to something and she cannot, at first, make sense of it. A break in the trees, a vast expanse of whiteness. She moves toward it until she understands. A lake, the ice covered with snow, creating the illusion of solid ground.

She stands and shivers. The desolate beauty of it. The ache of loneliness, the quiet. Easy to imagine nothing living out here but her.

She closes her eyes the better to regain control of herself, of her racing heart.

When she opens them again, there is something out there.

A shape in the distance. She had taken it to be a tree stump on the distant shore, but now it is moving, a slow shuffle across the ice.

Wolf? Bear?

Cora's chest tightens. She dare not breathe.

It is dark and bundled in fur, too distant for her to make out anything but the strange movement of its limbs, ghostlike in the weak afternoon light.

Cora has, without realizing, been drawn out from the tree line and to the lake's very edge. Another step, and she is on the ice; underneath her feet, it groans, an awful noise that sends her back into the thick of the war and the sounds of people dying.

The creature turns to look at her. It cannot be possible—she is too far away—but she feels, in that moment, that she can see its eyes, black, devoid of anything like feeling or life. Neither animal nor human. Eyes that do not belong in this world.

All at once, the hold she has kept over her terror breaks; cold panic leaks through her body as she stumbles back, slips, tumbles to the shore. The creature moving again with startling speed. Cora turns and runs.

Crashing through the pines. Roots poke treacherously from the earth to trip her. Snow still swirling, a storm of white, one hand held out ahead of her to shield her face, the thudding of her heartbeat matched to every stride—

When the forest falls away and Cora tumbles out into the road, she smashes headlong into something as solid as a wall. The impact knocks the breath from her. From the ground, dazed, she looks up—sees all kinds of strange apparitions until finally, the shape looming over her resolves itself. An ox, white, camouflaged in the snow. Its keeper, a man, gazes down at her. With his hood drawn, a shadow falls across his face, but she gets an impression of calm curiosity, his skin as dark as the ox is white.

She takes the man's proffered hand and gets to her feet. Neither of them speaks, but his look conveys a question—is she hurt? Cora, stiff but unharmed, glances back toward the forest, the tangle of pines and cedars and bare-branched maples, birch trees the color of bone. The fall has knocked her to her senses, giving everything a surreal quality. The creature on the ice, the running. What was she so afraid of?

Cora and the stranger assess each other. He seems steady, surprisingly unruffled by an unfamiliar girl hurling herself out of the trees at him. The ox waits patiently, blowing clouds of steam from its nose.

"Thursday," the man says.

Cora frowns. "Monday today."

He does not laugh or smile, but his shoulders open a little in a way that conveys amusement.

"No," he says. "My name. Thursday."

"Oh," she says. "Cora."

She isn't sure what to make of him. He must be one of the Americans. She has heard of them, seen a few around Halifax. Like the Maroons, war brought them here, though she is not sure of the details.

"You all right?" he asks. His gaze sliding behind her, to the woods, the way she has come, as if in case of a pursuer.

She nods; a few snowflakes come loose from her hair. Rationality has returned now, and she would be too embarrassed to try to explain. Not to this man—so real and solid, big and made bigger by his bulky coat.

"Lost," she says finally. "Looking for Preston."

Thursday considers this. Cora stares back, her expression polite but firm—she will account for no more than this. He is willing to accept it.

"You ain't far. Just up the road here. I can show you."

Thursday pats the ox once and says, "Gee up." The animal plods away, Thursday beside it, while Cora follows. She watches the way the ox's bones move under its skin. Each heavy step produces a jolt, a sense of crushing and crunching—a fleeting image of herself caught under its hooves.

Cora, not usually one for shyness, finds it hard to know what to say, so they walk in silence.

They come to a crossroads; Thursday speaks a command and the ox responds, turning left with a slow grace. It moves with its head bowed, as if braced against something heavy, though currently it is yoked to nothing at all.

Thursday must see her looking.

"Name's Abel," he says.

"Abel," Cora repeats. The road is wider here, so she can come alongside him.

"Like the Bible."

Cora doesn't know the Bible, so says nothing.

"Two working on the farm. One's always Cain. One's always Abel. Cain on the left, Abel on the right."

Underneath the hood, what little she can make out of his face shows it to be broad, moving slowly and deliberately from expression to expression.

"What you mean, 'always'?" Cora asks.

"One Cain dies, train the next," he says. "Same with Abel."

He gestures toward the ox.

"This'll be the fifth Abel."

Gradually, imperceptibly, the snow has slowed and then stopped. Now there is a little low afternoon sunlight from behind the clouds; it makes the snow glitter.

"So you a farmer?" Cora asks.

"Work for one."

This makes her wonder. . . . In Jamaica, as far as she knew, there was only white, slave, and Maroon. This place is harder to understand. Here there are rich whites and poor whites and whites without a penny to their name, and there are free Blacks and there are slaves and there are people who seem to hover somewhere in between.

Eventually, the wondering gets too much. She has to ask—

"You free?"

Thursday doesn't lose the rhythm of his strides, but the surprise registers on his face. The question seems straightforward enough to Cora, but he takes his time considering it.

"Yes," he says. "And no."

"No?"

"Farmer Nash got me some years yet. No choice about the work. So he owns me, I reckon." A glance toward Cora, and he must be able to tell that she doesn't quite understand. "It's called indenture."

Cora repeats the word slowly.

"Like a contract," Thursday says.

"So you choose it?"

Under the hood, she catches the flicker of sadness.

"You might say that."

Even though he is a stranger, even though he gives so little away in his words or his expressions, she knows they are straying somewhere painful. She doesn't pry.

A track crosses the road, a scattering of stone buildings in the distance. Thursday calls Abel to a stop.

"This here's the farm," he says. "Another bit on up the road to Preston."

They stand facing each other. The silence is, strangely, not uncomfortable. He pushes back his hood, showing all of his face. There is a scar at his temple, half-obscured by the line of his hair.

"Say," he says. "You one of the Jamaicans?"

Cora nods, surprised he knows. But then, being so close to Preston, how could he not?

When he speaks again, there is a small change in his voice. He speaks more slowly. Cora takes it for kindness.

"Must be different. Being here."

The words so inadequate to cover the enormity of everything she has felt in these months of exile that she has to stop herself from laughing.

"Cold," she says.

"So it is."

Cora wonders if she can say more. But she does not feel up to the task of explaining how completely unmoored she feels, how uprooted.

The ox huffs, drawing Thursday's attention away from her. It's time for him to go.

"Well," he says. "Good meeting you, Cora."

She considers him. There has been so much, in these last few months, that is new—the land, the weather, the food. The newness of it shattering, an earthquake. The newness of Thursday feels more like the pull of a changing tide, slow but insistent under the surface. Cora finds herself wondering if they will meet again.

"Oh," he says, before she can turn to go. "Best stay off the woodland paths. All sorts in the forest round here."

A shiver passes through Cora at this. She hides it well.

"Animals?" she asks.

"Some," he says, before he leads Abel away. "Bears and such. But stories of other things, too."

3

Almost dark by the time she reaches Preston. In the half-light, the unfinished huts lie like wooden skeletons on the village outskirts. Winter came on too quick and hard to make enough shelters, so they live here crammed two or three families to a house. Rocky, unforgiving soil, no good for growing. Once a week, they line up to receive provisions. From time to time, some will, like Cora, venture to Halifax for more.

Inside, the smell of woodsmoke and wet clothes draped over chairs to dry. The main room has enough space to walk around a large kitchen table, but not much more. Cora hears voices before she enters—or, more precisely, a single voice, a smooth, self-possessed tone.

She pauses in the doorway. A white man stands inside, dressed in a fine black coat and breeches. The buckles on his shoes gleam when they catch the light cast from the candles and the stove. He is the one talking—about cattle feed and new grain barns. When he catches sight of Cora, he pauses. His smile is slow and uncanny in its uneven stretch.

"Welcome," he says. "Welcome. My sincerest apologies, I shall not trouble you too long. You've been in Halifax, I gather. Very good."

All of this leaving small pauses for answers, but Cora gives none. She edges inside, catches the eye of Leah, who stands by the stove. Sitting at the table's head is Silas. His hands rest on the smooth wood, a soldier's stillness. He gazes at Cora steadily.

"The governor," he says.

Captain Silas Heath is a small man. His slenderness belies his strength. A scarred, expressionless face, but in battle, Cora has seen that face split into something from a nightmare—his mouth a snarling gash, nostrils flared, and his eyes dark pools of hatred.

The governor's smile widens. Cora has never seen him before, up close. But she knows him, of course, as the man who keeps the provisions coming. John Wentworth. He found them this land in Preston, close to his own estate.

A movement in the corner of the room. Cora had not even realized that there was another man there, half-hidden by shadow. Tall, an upright bearing, hands clasped behind his back, the better to show off the lines of his blue woolen military jacket.

Cora bows her head—just as any Maroon would. Colonel Montague James is their leader. They followed him into battle; in surrender, they follow him still.

Montague James does not speak, but the shifting of his weight is enough to draw the governor's attention.

"We should be on our way," Governor Wentworth says.

"The colonel and I"—here inclining his head toward Montague James—"have a few more houses to visit before the evening is out. But we trust, Captain, that you and your people have everything you need?"

Eventually, Silas says, "We do."

"Very good," says the governor. "Snow like this makes for hard traveling. I myself might adjourn to Halifax soon to wait out the worst of the winter. But should things become too difficult for you here, there are always the lodgings on my land just beyond Major Lake. . . ."

A few of the Maroons are quartered there, in barns and laborers' shacks. Put to work by the governor mending storm-blown outbuildings, likely moving to hoeing and planting by next spring.

The slightest curl of Silas's lip. The governor doesn't notice, but Montague James does. The colonel's gaze lingers on Silas before he follows the governor out.

In the silence the men leave behind them, Cora hears a door creak. Then, from the bedroom they all must share, comes little Benjamin. He makes straight for Cora, and she bends and hoists him onto her hip. Her skin warming where he buries himself in her neck. She is thawing slowly, moves closer to the stove for its heat. Leah, who is back to cooking, gives her a glance.

"No flour?"

Cora shakes her head.

Leah sighs. But brushes her fingers lightly against Cora's arm as she passes, heading for the corner and a sack of vegetables, now almost empty—a gesture to say *Thank you* or perhaps *Don't worry*. The touch works; Cora feels a little calmer. The fire in the stove glows bright.

Leah is not Cora's mother but she might as well be. After Cora's mother died in childbirth, Leah took Cora in and raised her, having no children of her own. Cora's father a freeman and a traveler, not one of the Maroons—never seen again, from what Cora can gather, after her mother fell pregnant. The fact that he was an outsider, it has cast a shadow. Sometimes, the Maroons treat her differently. But perhaps this is what binds her most to Leah—Leah who was born not in Trelawny Town but in Africa. Leah who crossed the sea and was a slave on a plantation. Leah is different, too.

Cora doesn't have many stories about her mother. Leah doesn't like to talk about the past. Cora decided a few years ago it must be because Leah misses Cora's mother, and this makes the silences easier to bear. The absence of her mother never felt too strongly, because Leah is enough. A steady presence; short and plump, face kindly, gray hair cut close to her skull. Easily overlooked. But always there when Cora needs her.

All this time, Silas has stayed seated. Finally, he pushes himself to standing, makes a contemptuous noise in his throat. He speaks to no one in particular—

"Putting them folk to work on him land like slaves."

A slight rasp to his voice. He was sick on the boat over, a horrible coughing that settled in his chest and can strike even now, months later, in the middle of the night. But luckier than the dozen who died on the crossing, vomiting and shivering in the ship's holds, their bodies tossed over the side and into the sea.

A hand moves to his throat, tracing a scar. Cora, Benjamin on her hip, watches him cautiously. Leah, peeling potatoes, does not look up.

At home, in Jamaica, in Trelawny Town, their lives were

woven tight together. They all lived close; a trampling cow would ruin your own field as much as your neighbor's. A shared destiny. Now, here in Nova Scotia, Cora thinks there is such a thing as too close and too far at the same time. Living with Silas is like living with a caged animal; she cannot ever quite relax. The others don't have it easier; she hears the fights from their neighbors' huts, late at night. And yet they are also scattered, tiny villages like this one, clustered wooden buildings hidden in the surrounding forests. Some in Governor Wentworth's barns, some camped in tents in Halifax, under the Citadel they are helping to refortify in case of an invading French army.

Little Benjamin tugs the end of one of Cora's braids, a shy smile that might, in time, become a laugh. He, at least, can soothe her unease. She turns away from Silas and makes faces at Benjamin until he giggles. By tapping her ear, he indicates he has something to tell her. She leans close.

"Me see Mama today."

For a moment, Cora cannot speak. Then, swallowing, she manages—

"Where you see Mama?"

Silas's head turns toward them.

"In the trees," Benjamin says. In that tone children use that makes something seem obvious. *Silly Cora. Of course Mama was in the trees.*

Cora is forming the words, as gently as she can, but Silas speaks first.

"Enough."

He is by her side, taking Benjamin into his own arms. His son.

"Remember what me tell you?" he says. Holding the boy up so they see eye to eye. "Mama gone."

Benjamin looks unconcerned. He lives in a world where his mother can be gone, dead in the war, and yet can also appear to him in the trees.

Cora stares at the two of them. The memory comes back to her. Ice and furs, the loping gait—the creature warping until it becomes almost humanlike. Elsy . . . But Cora forces the image away. Goes to help Leah, needing the distraction—the slide of a knife through potatoes, the starchy smell, the sound of the pot bubbling.

She doesn't need to look to know that Silas will still be watching her. That he will blame her for this, somehow. Silas tolerates her because she has become a kind of surrogate mother to his son. But Silas dislikes the way the death doesn't seem to take hold in Benjamin's mind. Sees it as a kind of weakness. Soldiers deal in death; they have to understand it. The fact that Benjamin does not suggests he may not follow in his father's footsteps, may not honor the family legacy—because Benjamin's grandfather was also a warrior, who fought side by side with the great hero Cudjoe in the first war.

It is a heavy weight on little Benjamin's shoulders, all that history. Maybe that is why Cora can help. She has no history. Knows so little about her mother or her father. This and, of course, Elsy—missing her and missing Jamaica all mixed up into one. And Benjamin the last little piece of Elsy left, because Silas certainly doesn't seem to have kept any room in his heart for his late wife.

4

Cora has never believed in ghosts. It's memories that haunt her—that visit at night in restless sleep.

Some memories bittersweet—Elsy and Jamaica evenings, a final flare of brilliance from the sun before it sank below the horizon. Trelawny Town, their home, nestled in the valley at the foot of the mountains. Plentiful meat—chickens and cattle roaming, hunts for wild hogs in the forest, which they roasted over a roaring bonfire. Sturdy houses with provision plots, the bounty of cayenne pepper, trees weighed down with coconuts. Fish from the nearby river. Days of even length, and always warm. The changing of the seasons marked only by the coming and going of the rains. A hundred families living in peace and plenty.

This was Cora and Elsy's childhood, growing up in huts opposite each other. Sneaking away from chores and into the forest, watching tiny hummingbirds hover to drink from brash-colored flowers, glimpsing the black and gold scales of Jamaican boas coiled around the high branches of trees. They would find secret places to sit and talk as overhead, one by one, stars glinted into being in the dark sky.

Elsy's mischievous grin. A fire in her that matched Cora's own; they clashed sometimes, but more often than not, they laughed and talked over each other endlessly. When Silas chose Elsy as his wife, the marriage might have been a rupture; Cora remembers the sense of loss when Elsy told her it was coming. But there was no loss—indeed, their closeness only grew. Silas spent little time at home, preferring the company of his soldiers and long nights on patrol, meaning Elsy and Cora would spend the days cooking together in Elsy's hut. Almost imagining they lived there, just the two of them, three when little Benjamin came.

But there are darker memories, too.

The stench of smoke from gunpowder.

The clammy feel of cave walls against skin; dark hiding places, where they lay in wait.

Rain falling outside with a ferocity that bordered on rage, the weather itself pulled into battle. Water trickling through cracks in stone and falling, cool against their skin. Toward the end of the war, they had to lift their mouths and catch the raindrops. No other ways left to drink.

It is impossible to imagine now, but the war was exciting at first. Because it was war that won the Maroons their land in the first place: runaways, led by Cudjoe, who fought and fought until they forced the British to let them come down from the mountains and settle in one spot. War made them free, and now it was back to the mountains again. Throughout history, so the pendulum swings—war, peace, and back to war again.

They remembered how it was in Africa, war their true heritage, more than gods or language or myths. In Kongo, two kings battling to claim the throne. In Dahomey, armies marching to subdue their surrounding enemies. They did not remember in the sense of having been there. Most of them now the second, third, even fourth generation since those first runaways headed for the mountains. But still, they knew.

What was it all for anyway, this war? Cora can barely remember now. Some idea of disrespect—that the British kept them too tightly controlled, that there was more yet to win, further to climb, to a place where slavery could never touch them again. But they were wrong. Soon, they were scattered across the mountains, weak and hungry, shooting birds from the sky, the meat blackened and stringy when cooked over a fire. Sometimes eaten raw, when they could not risk giving away their position.

There was a promise, at their surrender, that they would be able to stay. Not on the old lands, but somewhere else in Jamaica. Even the thought of that gave Cora pain, but she could grasp it, somehow. Could see the shape of a life on the other side of the island.

The promise was broken. And soon, her island, her Jamaica, was nothing more than a green smudge on the horizon as the ships carried them away.

———

The worst of the hauntings—Cora relives over and over finding Elsy's body. Little Benjamin beside his mother, blank-faced, eyes open. The moment when Cora thinks he, too, is dead. But then he turns his head, fixes her with a stare. She holds out a beseeching hand. Finally, he begins to crawl. As Cora gathers him in her arms she almost chokes—not because he smells of death, but because he does not. He smells of earth and himself, this living smell evidence of the total cleaving of his destiny from that of his mother, who lies unmoving, curled into herself in the mud.

———

Cora jolts awake in darkness. Silence like the very end of an echo—Cora's ears reach for sound but find none, save the steady, even breaths of the others. No one else stirs. Still, Cora cannot shake the thought that something has woken her.

Little Benjamin has moved at some point from his own bed to hers. To sit up, she must gently extract herself from his small hands, clasped to her shirt. She feels her way toward the door and creeps out into the kitchen.

Here, the windows let in the faintest glow of silver moon-light, but it gives everything a sinister cast. A knife swings from a ceiling hook. A dress drying on the stove has one sleeve that sways slightly, though there is no breeze. The fire inside the stove is out. Not even an ember glows.

Cora wraps her arms around her waist against the chill.

She cannot name the feeling that draws her toward the doorway. It can't be fear—because fear pushes rather than pulls. She pauses with her hand on the handle. Then, with a firm shove, she swings the door open and steps into the night.

Bare feet on frozen ground. A gust of wind that lifts her skirt; her eyes screw shut against it, but she forces them open, forces them to see—what? She is searching, half-blind, looking from the outlines of the nearby huts to the distant, indistinct shape of trees.

There is something moving.

Her eyes were looking in the wrong place. Too high to see it—expecting something human. This shadow slinks low. A soft, silent tread.

Cora's mind, still slow from sleep, deals more in feelings than in thoughts. The main feeling being icy dread, as cold as the snow she stands on.

The creature is closer now. Ears, pinned back as it moves, rising as it pauses. It listens. Turns its head toward her. She sees a gleam of yellow eyes and white teeth.

Finally, she screams.

It is as if the change is instant, though later she will think that it must have taken time for people to surround her, torches and candles in hand, banishing the darkness. They have come from huts all around, almost two dozen in all, their voices blending into one hum of concern.

Cora blinks. Flickering light now fills the empty space where there was . . . something.

Leah is at her shoulder.

"What happen?" she asks.

"Wolf," Cora says. "Or . . ." She points with trembling fingers, though she shakes more from cold now than anything else. "There."

Two or three men march out toward the edge of the village. Cora watches, dazed, as they sweep around the huts and then return, shaking their heads.

The crowd is dispersing. Cora hears Silas behind her mutter something about foolish nightmares. Leah is pulling gently on her arm, guiding her back inside. Cora lets herself be led toward the stove—now with a fire smoldering inside it, so why had Cora thought it was out? She stands near it and lets her shivering ease.

Cora has never believed in ghosts. Still, as she goes to the window and looks out, the darkness has a sense of movement, like the slow breaths of a great, sleeping creature. There were stories in Jamaica, of course, that the children would tell one another to induce giggling, hysterical fear—duppies and other restless souls. But spruce trees cast different kinds of shadows; cold nights produce a different kind of chill in the bones. It is easier, here, to imagine the world of the dead. To think of cold, lifeless things that move unseen, just beyond the reach of the light.

5

Maroon Hall lies a few miles to the west, the center around which their leaders orbit. Montague James and his family live nearby. In the hall itself is a white man, General William Quarrell, sent from Jamaica to keep an eye on the Maroons during their resettlement. Since the autumn, the chapel there has held services every Sunday, and each Tuesday morning, the children of Preston can attend lessons, where they learn to read and write by copying verses from the Bible.

For weeks, little Benjamin has wanted to go, but Silas refuses. He, more than most, keeps the old ways—the rites and beliefs that have been passed from generation to generation, preserving the traditions of Africa. It is the morning after the dark night and the creature, real or imagined, that stalked into their village, and Cora—with a certain reckless will to action, a way to shake off the peculiarities of the previous day—decides she will take Benjamin, whether Silas likes it or not.

She drops Benjamin at the chapel, lingering by the window to watch him take a seat in the wooden pews. A white man with thinning hair and spectacles and pale, slender hands stands at the front of the class, waiting for them to settle. Cora notices how small Benjamin looks next to the other children, six years old but not much taller than those a year or two his junior.

On the way back, along the roads, she does not let herself hurry. Proving that she is not afraid. Hums to herself to cut through the quiet. Skeletal birch trees shiver in the corners of her vision. The sunlight hard and white, as if refracted through ice.

Back in Preston, nobody is outside. Smoke curls from the chimneys. Cora's hands and feet ache with cold, but a few paces away from the hut she stops.

"—not gon' wait no more!"

Silas.

Cora hears the murmur of Leah's voice, too quiet to make out anything she says. Except, tantalizingly, a name—*Cora.*

Cora creeps a little closer. Silas says something; Cora catches only the words *wild* and *Benjamin.* Then Leah speaks again, indistinct, but Silas cuts her off.

"If she starting to act like Benjamin her own—"

Now Leah raises her voice, too.

"She still not ready."

Cora's face feels hot. Now she is certain. This is about her.

Crouching, she slips around the side of the house, aiming to reach the window. As she moves, she is better able to hear the end of Silas's reply.

"—that you not gon' let she marry at all."

At these words, a charged silence. Cora brings her head as close as she dares to the base of the window, in case she misses some murmured reply, but Leah says nothing.

"And me think you should not act so," Silas continues. "Seeing what she—"

"Enough," says Leah, at exactly the same moment as movement across the village sends Cora scrambling upright to hide her eavesdropping. One of the neighbors, Dido, has come out of her door with a pail of water. Her eyes rest briefly on Cora, a nod of greeting. Cora, heart beating fast, nods back.

And when Cora turns, hoping to resume her place pressed against the wall, she sees that Silas has come to the window, is looking out. The glass panes warp and twist his features. Behind him, Leah stands in shadow, her face obscured.

When Silas opens the door, he says, "Where you take him?" His gaze sliding over Cora to take in Dido, who has paused her task to watch.

Cora forces herself to straighten.

"Chapel," she says.

Silas's eyes still focused behind her, his face a mask except for the slightest quiver at the corner of his mouth.

"Inside," he says.

———

The hut is so smoky it makes Cora's eyes water. Snowmelt leaks through the window frames and puddles on the floor.

She tries to catch Leah's eye, but Leah is bent over, feeding wood into the stove.

"You take him to all that foolishness?" Silas says.

Cora, not easily cowed, is unsettled by the venom in his eyes.

"Him want to go," she says.

"So you sneak away," he says, "and don't tell him father where you take him? For all me know him was dead in the woods—"

He has moved closer. She smells something on his breath, sour and sweet mixed together. Rum.

Cora steps back. It surprises her—that he is drunk. She has never seen him drink, not in Jamaica with the other soldiers, not in his own hut in Trelawny Town when he came in from patrol to find Elsy and Cora sitting together at his table.

Leah straightens from the stove. Says, quietly but firmly— "Silas."

He snaps to look at her. Then back to Cora—anger simmering close to the surface but not boiling over. The rum fraying the edges of his rage, making it unfocused; usually, he wields it with precision, as a weapon. But he frightens Cora more like this, as he wavers, uncertain where and how to strike. . . .

The door opens, letting in a blast of freezing air. Cora, Leah, and Silas all start; Old Joe, Dido's husband, is framed in the doorway, blowing on his hands.

"The colonel want we for a meeting," he says, not bothering with a greeting. "Captain Smith's house. Them gon' send some letter to England."

Silas takes time to move. It is as if he draws into himself—as if whatever might have been seeping out of him is sucked carefully back in. Looking at him, at the military way he holds himself as he gathers his coat and scarf and follows Old Joe out,

Cora can almost persuade herself that she imagined the rum on his breath.

But when Cora's and Leah's eyes meet, just for a moment, Cora knows she imagined none of it. Not the rum, not the raised voices, the allusions to marriage. Leah looks like she is about to speak. Cora waits. But no words come. And Cora, for once, does not press.

6

Leah and Cora sit in the windowless bedroom, candles lit in all the corners; Cora watches the patterns of light on the walls. It feels timeless doing this—collapses the years, brings them back to Jamaica. The quick movement of Leah's fingers across Cora's scalp, tugging her hair into submission.

Leah, humming, says little. They are always at their most peaceful like this, Leah and Cora. When Cora was growing up, it was not always easy: Cora stubborn and too direct, unafraid to turn her thoughts to spoken words where others would hold their tongue; Leah quiet but reproachful, goading Cora to further anger. But this, the unbraiding and rebraiding of Cora's hair, is where love can flow between them unimpeded.

There was a time when Cora would return the gesture. When Leah would take her turn to sit patiently as Cora's fingers worked. But when the war began Leah shaved her hair, and she has not grown it back since. And so the meaning of the braiding has shifted. No longer a kindness returned. Cora shows her love for Leah now by sitting and allowing Leah to do something for her with no thought of payment. Love, after all, is not about keeping a tally, hoping to bring things done and said, like some kind of bookkeeper, into symmetry. Love is about things left unequal.

Leah finishes a braid. Pauses, fingers hovering where Cora can no longer feel them. She says in a quiet voice—

"Me not always gon' be here to . . ."

Cora waits. Leah doesn't finish.

"Protect me?" Cora prompts.

She turns her head, meeting Leah's gaze with a little defiance. She doesn't think of herself as someone who needs protecting.

Leah looks tired. Despite the long nights, they all sleep fitfully. And Cora remembers Silas's words, those she managed to overhear. Feels her impatience ebb. If Leah is what stands between her and him . . .

"We can't always live just how we want," Leah says eventually.

"Who you mean, 'we'?"

Maroons? Women? Anyone at all?

Leah gives an answer to a different question.

"You gon' have a house of your own one day. That's all."

Not fully satisfied, Cora turns her head again, letting Leah continue. There is a moment when Cora's fingers twitch in recollection of braiding—not Leah's hair, but Elsy's. Cora did hers sometimes, too, before Benjamin was born. After him, Elsy kept it short.

Cora has always lived at the edge of others' unfreedom. Has guessed at but not experienced directly the life Leah had before, on a plantation as a slave. And Elsy; her marriage did not often intrude into their friendship, but sometimes it did. Cora saw the way Elsy made herself smaller when Silas was around. When Cora tries to imagine herself in this position—in any position that would mean losing the way she has always lived, unbound—her mind rebels against it.

An hour passes. Leah starts up humming again, a snatch of song that Cora dimly remembers. It calls back to a time when Leah would really sing, a voice that could carry to every corner of the house, words in a language that comforted in its unfamiliarity. That was when Cora was young, when Quaco was still alive.

Cora's memories of him are faded. He died when she was Benjamin's age. He is little more than a warm, smiling face, a strong pair of hands, lifting her onto his shoulders, letting her see the world from a great height.

After he died, Cora remembers a few months when Leah was quiet and withdrawn, and Cora was too young to know the name for it—*grief*. But then Leah emerged out the other side, defying the expectation to find another Maroon man to marry. Defying also the expectation, less openly expressed, that she might return "home," to the plantation where Quaco had found her. Leah came to the Maroon village at a time when there were not supposed to be runaways. Not anymore. It was the price they paid for peace with the British. But Quaco was respected, maybe even a little feared. He saw Leah and he wanted her and he took her and she let herself be taken, and that was how she became free.

To Cora, Leah is a quietly formidable woman, entirely self-reliant. But as she grew older, she began to understand how much Quaco was Leah's savior and shield. He made and kept her one of the Maroons.

She began to understand, too, how hard it was for Leah when he died. Cora had thought Leah's grief began and ended with those quiet few months, but Leah's pain went further than this, she is sure of it. Each passing year, Leah marked Quaco's death day. Never saying that this was the occasion, but Cora knew why one day a year Leah was more subdued. The kind of long and reaching grief that can only come from deep love.

So although there is much Cora wants to ask, as Leah keeps on braiding, about Elsy and whether the ache of missing her will ease, and about Silas and why he wants Cora, and why Leah can hold him back but not for good—she keeps quiet. For Leah's sake. Because surely, some of it comes back to Quaco. What he gave to Leah while he lived, and what she lost when he died. A little of his power bequeathed to her, but not much. Enough to resist Silas, but not enough to stop him if he truly sets his will.

When the candles have burned low and Leah has finished, Leah says—

"Take care, now."

Not the first time she has said it to Cora, in lieu of love. But it carries a little more weight this time as Cora thinks of Silas, of the rum-tinged anger and the strange unfocused look in his eyes.

7

A storm blows violently through the village overnight. The door of the hut freezes shut—it takes Cora, Leah, and Silas all heaving together to get it open again. Outside, all is blanketed white, silent as a cemetery. Everything living buried deep. Even the journey to Halifax, now, is impossible. Supplies stockpiled in the village must last them through it. Salted meats, tough as leather. Potatoes frozen hard. Nothing green, nothing colorful, nothing like the fruits and vegetables of home.

For a week, Silas barely leaves his seat by the stove, staring into the glowing embers. A strained silence prevails between him and Leah. Cora, he barely seems to notice, but this makes her more, rather than less, uneasy. There is something in the way he holds himself, a slackening of his soldier's posture, that suggests he, too, is changing with the seasons.

Little Benjamin amuses himself by taking stones and twigs and tiny lumps of coal, creating imaginary worlds of mountains and armies and wild creatures—lions and elephants and snakes the size of a man. He mouths to himself the Bible verses from the only day of school he was allowed to attend; Silas will not let him return.

Cora notices that the games follow a circular pattern. Each battalion of twigs must move in the same way. The same fearsome lion comes each time to scatter the troops, who always flee up the same mountain, where they will find buried treasure guarded by a hyena with three faces. Over and over he moves them—perhaps taking some small comfort that the outcome will always be the same, always within his control. Over the game, little Benjamin is master. The rest of them are masters of little else, least of all the snow.

———

Sometimes, Cora stands at the edge of the village. It feels no different from a cliff's edge; the solid ground of the forest floor might as well be water, so total does the divide feel between Preston and the world beyond. She stares out at the glittering wilderness, pristine and undisturbed snow. There is something about the sight of it that tempts her in, calling her to mark it with her footprints. But a man has recently lost a finger to frostbite. The image of it always comes to mind, whenever she is on the cusp of going farther. The black, rotten stiffness of the finger, and now the stump where it once was. She shivers, flexes her own fingers, retreats to the warmth of the hut.

———

Then, one afternoon, their neighbor Sarah passes from door to door, distraught. Has anyone seen her son, Godwin? Not even five years old. She was cooking, thought he was out in the village playing with the other children. But that was hours ago. Now he is nowhere to be found.

Everyone wraps themselves up in coats, dons thick woolen scarves. They gather in the quiet center of the village, boots crunching on snow. Silas moves toward the woodpile, picks up the ax and shoulders it. Everyone else is unarmed. His eyes find Cora's in the crowd; she quickly looks away.

Even Colonel Montague James himself has come down. He organizes the group into search parties. It is an easy task; the discipline of the war, which has seemed so distant over this harsh winter, proves close to the surface in all of them. Cora is paired with Leah and two other women. They are to head east, toward the sea.

They walk apart, close enough to hear one another calling Godwin's name, but far enough that whenever Cora looks around in the silence between the calls, she can see no one.

The pines grow thick. She picks her way slowly through them, careful on the uneven ground, where roots twist up from the frozen soil. The search has a surreal quality—after saying *Godwin* over and over, hearing the syllables echo back to her, the name begins to lose all meaning. . . .

She stills. Listens—the faintest call in the distance, Leah's voice. After that fades, there is only silence, the snow absorbing all sound.

Her breaths come more slowly and deliberately. She can map, precisely, the contours of her body, the range of her senses. Hers is the attention of an animal—hunter or hunted—that is ready for . . . what?

Movement. Cora whips around. A gentle gust of wind like a sigh. A few flakes of snow blown from tree branches.

Nothing.

Nothing?

Look closer.

Cora sees . . . something. A figure slipping between the trees. Pale coat blending with the snow, startling speed.

The name that Cora whispers is—

"Elsy?"

She blinks once, twice. Staggers back a few steps, reeling. The woods are deserted, silent. Her eyes can see clearly now—there is nothing really there.

And yet, as she walks she is unable to shake the slow, creeping certainty of being watched. Of hearing whispers in the trees. Of turning to look, and being sure that something is following, just out of sight.

———

When they return to Preston at nightfall, Cora notices something at the edge of the village. A small snow-covered mound, the lights from the huts giving it a glittering orange glow.

As soon as she sees it, she remembers the movement of the pale figure in the woods: a warning. And she knows what the little mound must be.

8

The men work quickly to get the body out of the snow, in case . . . But he was long dead. Eyes closed in what would be a cruel imitation of sleep, if not for his ashen, bloodless face and the clumps of frost on his eyelashes.

Cora watches as they check the body for signs of an animal attack. The somber silence of the work punctuated by Sarah's guttural howls; the other women have taken her into one of the huts to comfort her. The body is unmarked. But all it might have taken was a childish desire, perhaps for a stick to play at being soldiers, or a rock, the right size to fit snugly in a small palm, drawing him into the forest. One wrong turn, one missed path. Here, the cold kills quicker than you think.

Did he crawl the final stretch to the village, knowing he was close? Or did he fail to see it, nestled among the trees? Did he lie down to die believing he was deep in the woods?

Cora cannot bear to dwell on it. She turns away.

———

It takes all day to dig a grave, the ground under the snow too hard for shovels. But they persist. Men, women, children, all take turns with picks, hacking away at the frozen, rocky soil. Because through everything, they have always buried their dead. Have risked their lives for it in Jamaica, descending from the mountains with the bodies. The sun goes down and they keep digging in the dark, until finally, Godwin is in the ground. Falling snow covers his grave quickly as they gather and sing.

It doesn't take long for the funeral to develop a frenzied edge, bottles of rum passed around. Cora hears snatches of whispered talk. With darkness come the wilder theories about Godwin's death. People speak of duppies that stalk the dark woods. Of avenging spirits. Of shape-shifters that turn to sharp-toothed creatures with a thirst for blood.

Unsettled by the slow unraveling of the evening as a bonfire roars, Cora seeks refuge from the raised voices in the hut. She finds little Benjamin; he has lit a candle and set it on the floor, where he is drawing a shape carefully with the burned edge of a stick. Cora comes to his side. She recognizes it as a letter of some kind, though she herself cannot read. It must be the only one he managed to learn that morning at chapel.

Little Benjamin does not look up. He seems absorbed in his task, tracing and retracing the lines. But then he says—

"Got a secret."

Cora crouches, bringing herself to his height.

"What?" she asks.

"Don't want you to go."

"Go where?"

He still doesn't look up from the floor. The concentration on his face changes his features, makes him more of Silas than of Elsy.

"Away. In the woods."

Cora did not realize he was watching her, all those times she went right up to the edge of the village but no farther. It touches her, that she can be a sort of center for his world, after everything. But the feeling is shot through with guilt; she should be more careful with him. Know when he is looking.

Before Cora can reply, the door springs open, letting in the blaze of the bonfire, the raucous singing. The figure in the doorway, framed in firelight, cannot be made out clearly; it is only when he steps into the room that the candle illuminates Silas's face.

Cora knows, immediately and viscerally, that he is drunk. He is not the only one, judging from the noise outside. But his is a sharp, stealthy kind of intoxication. He is steady on his feet as he advances toward them. Looks down at the charcoal scribbles on the floor.

"What is this?"

Benjamin looks up—not to his father, but to Cora. Perhaps this is what makes Silas snap. With the speed of a snake's strike, he kicks out across the floor. His foot catches the stick in Benjamin's hand and sends it spinning into the corner.

"You bringing that white-man nonsense into my house?"

Cora leaps to her feet, gets between Silas and Benjamin in an instant. Silas does not step back; they stay close enough to touch. Cora has to force herself not to recoil.

Silas's eyes glint as they look at her. And Cora sees something that fills her with horror: sees that, for him, the line between rage and desire has dissolved. Maybe it was there once, but the rum has eaten it away.

She steps back. She cannot find anything to say to him; it is a trap, any possible path ahead leading to only one conclusion.

The door bangs open again. The threshold empty; it was blown by a gust of wind. But the noise breaks a spell. Silas looks over his shoulder, reflected firelight glittering in his dark eyes.

"Benjamin," he says. "Come with me, now."

Benjamin goes to his father's side without complaint. Cora watches him; understands that, whatever mix of awe and respect he feels for his father, there is no fear there. Not yet. Silas takes Benjamin's hand and leads him outside. Neither of them looks back.

A flurry of snowflakes whirl inside, melting quickly on the floor.

The cold rouses her. Cora moves to the door and shuts out the funeral, shuts out the night.

9

Here is what Cora knows: She has seen, felt, heard, the presence of something in the woods that defies explanation.

She spends a restless night trying in vain to make sense of all the fragments. She tries to follow every alternative theory, including that these have been figments of her imagination, her mind addled by cold. Back in Jamaica, even as a young child, she was the one marching off into dark caves and secluded clearings while the others hung back shrieking, warning of supernatural things. But that was before she saw death up close—a body without the light inside it that makes it human. Where does that light go? She finds now that doubt has crept in, because unless that light just winks out of existence like a star at daybreak, it no longer seems so far-fetched that it might leave some trace behind. A shadow.

Her thoughts slip back, again and again, to Elsy. Not as an answer, but more a question—because why would she come? A

benign presence, reflecting her closeness to Cora by appearing
to her alone? Or something more malevolent, a punishment,
Godwin's death part of the evil. Could it be because of what
happened? Cora's share of the blame . . .

She half remembers, half dreams of being hidden in a narrow crack in the rocks on the mountainside, watching a red
Jamaica sunrise. Little Benjamin and Elsy beside her. Silas and
Leah gone for days. Sometimes they heard gunfire in the distance. Mostly, they heard nothing at all.

Their supplies of food had been dwindling. They bore it
stoically, even little Benjamin, but all week Elsy had been tired,
glistening with sweat—they did not know whether it was illness
or exhaustion. That morning Cora was certain of only one
thing: the urgent need to go out and find what she could, to
help keep them all alive.

And Elsy asked her not to go.

Just once—and only quietly. She did not even give Cora
time to say no; she immediately, instinctively, read the look on
Cora's face as a determination that could not be undone. She
quickly said no, Cora should go—and Cora did.

Cora will never know how the hours she was away really
unfolded. Whether Elsy sickened quickly or slowly. Whether
she shivered with fever as she died. Whether she cried or called
out or whether she just slipped silently into sleep. Only Benjamin was there to watch, and he has never and will never speak
of what he saw. All Cora knows is that when she returned with
a meager handful of berries and a calabash full of stagnant
brown water, Elsy was dead.

And Cora cannot stop thinking of her life like a tree, with
branches that split and split again until you reach the highest,

thinnest twigs, with buds only just starting to form. That there is, somewhere, the branch not taken—the world where she stayed with Elsy and managed to keep the sickness at bay. Not through any knowledge of healing, not with any medicines or herbs on hand, but just by being there. Cora has an unshakable belief that if she had just stayed, Elsy would still be living.

———

The road to Thursday's farm is icy and treacherous, but a path has been shoveled through the worst of the snow. Cora sets off early; after the funeral, everyone else in Preston is sleeping. She thought of bringing little Benjamin but knew he would only slow her down. Leah will watch him today, Cora hopes. Keep him safe.

The farm is of a modest size, the fields all snow-covered white. Cora steps over the low stone wall, careless of the boundary. The next field over is fenced, and oxen stand huddled under a pine tree. With them is a figure bundled up in a coat, back turned. Cora makes her way over—but when the figure looks around, it is not Thursday. It is a girl, about her own age, with a thin mouth and piercing eyes.

The girl says nothing as she looks Cora over warily. Cora has opened her mouth to speak, but the words die in her throat. They stare at each other until a sharp whistle cuts through the air.

Thursday is leaning on the fence, a few paces away. Cora goes to him. The other girl stays where she is, still silent and watching.

Thursday frowns, a deep line scored between his brows.

"Thursday," Cora says.

He takes a moment to place her and remember her name.

"Cora. How'd you get in?"

"Over the wall."

He draws a sharp breath through his teeth.

"Lucky Farmer Nash ain't seen you."

"You can talk a moment?" she asks.

"Got work," he says.

"Me can stay."

"Might be trouble."

"Don't mind."

"Trouble for me," he says.

"Oh." She feels a little humbled. She hadn't thought of that.

Thursday looks over his shoulder, toward a stone farmhouse, smoke coming from its chimney.

"Mucking out the barn," he says. "Guess you won't be seen in there."

She ducks under the fence and follows, but she cannot help looking back over her shoulder; the girl she mistook for Thursday is still watching.

"Who's that?" she asks.

He follows her gaze.

"Ruth."

"She work here?"

"A slave."

Cora feels embarrassed—even a little naive. The word *slave* still holding so much power; in Jamaica, it was everything they defined themselves against.

The stench of animals assaults her as they enter the barn. Cora tries to pass her retch off as a cough. Thursday glances at her, amusement in the slight twitch of his mouth at each corner.

"Too much?" he asks.

Cora shakes her head firmly. She doesn't yet trust herself to speak. She marches to the wall and picks up some kind of rake, but Thursday waves her away.

"You'll get in the way," he says.

Secretly relieved, Cora settles herself on an upturned crate in the corner after brushing it free of straw. Watches as Thursday begins to work, forking matted clumps of straw and piling them by the open door.

After a while, the smell has faded—whether because Thursday has made progress cleaning or because Cora is growing used to it.

"When we meet before," Cora says, "you say something about things in the woods."

He pauses. Leans against his rake, considering her.

"Always stories."

"What stories?"

Thursday sighs. A heavy sound, carrying the weight of the past on his shoulders.

"Lots of us living south when we first came," he says. "The ones from America. All round this town named Shelburne. But there was trouble. A big riot. Lots of places burned. Lots of us fled. Some came north to Halifax. But there always been talk about people that went into the woods. Tried to live like Indians. But you ain't living long like that—not here. The cold kills you. Ever since, people been seeing things. A girl."

Cora is silent for a while. Does this make more sense of everything she's seen or less?

"Why just she?" she asks. "If whole families run into the woods and die. Why them not all ghosts, too?"

Thursday shrugs with one shoulder. "Maybe she got African family. When they died, their spirits went home."

"And she spirit?" Cora presses. "Why she not go back home, too? America."

"America ain't home. Not really."

Thursday bends over to carry on with his work.

Part of Cora wants to mention Godwin. Are there others who have died like he has? Is whatever is in the forest some monster that kills? But she does not speak. It is a kind of jealousy that keeps her guarding everything else, her sightings, her suspicions, her confusion, so that she can take it all and figure it out alone.

(And perhaps she is afraid of what he will say if they go further, what theories his words might dispel. She wants to hold on to that sliver of hope, that in the forest she might come face-to-face with Elsy again. That the last words they spoke to each other need not truly be the last.)

The floor is now mostly clear, the dirty straw all scraped away. Thursday walks out of the barn with a pail. Comes back a few minutes later with water and throws it onto the floor. Cora lifts her feet, letting it slosh underneath her, while Thursday takes a brush and begins to scrub. The light from the open doorway does not penetrate far into the gloom of the barn; in most of its corners, he moves in shadow. For a while, the only sound is the harsh scrape of bristles on stone.

When he is finished, he stands close to her crate, leaning on the brush. They watch the water dry, the stone's color moving from dark into light. In some places, where the stones are uneven, little pools of water become ice.

She looks at Thursday, at the way the winter sunlight falls

through the barn door on him, bringing out rust-colored undertones in his hair. She is struck with the urge to know him, to understand him.

"You have family here?" she asks.

He takes his time to answer.

"Ain't got none now."

"What happen to them?" she asks. Gently, in case he wants to refuse.

Thursday says, "It's a long story." But then continues. "They all gone, one way or another."

———

He starts his story in America. Virginia. A plantation. Memories of brutal, punishing labor and fractures—a father sold away, aunts and uncles dying of exhaustion and fever, a sister killed in a beating. These are stories Cora has heard before, though never with such feeling. The Maroons, like Leah, who have lived them, do not speak of them. It is only the ones, like Silas, who can make them like myths, like tales from a distant past, who tell such tales. But Thursday speaks differently. His voice rougher. At one point, it even shakes a little. Cora watches as his hand at his side balls into a fist and then releases.

There is no pride, she realizes. No hidden meaning of the kind Silas would weave into the story—*This is where we came from, and now look at where we are.* Thursday speaks of his broken family as if the distance between past and present collapses in on itself—*This is where I came from, and this is who I am.*

Eventually, he tells her, it was just him and his mother.

"She was called Efe," he says. Then, after a pause: "Is called Efe."

He tells her about the war in America—the white people wanting their freedom. Which made no sense to him, because from where he stood, they had every kind of freedom imaginable. But still, they took up arms, were willing to die, for some invisible kind of freedom that was beyond what he could conceive.

Freedom ran through this war in other ways, too. The British said, if you come and fight for us, we will free you. So he and his mother ran. He was only a child, and she was a woman—their greatest fear was that they would be turned away. Instead, they were put in a camp with all the other runaways.

"It was bad there," Thursday tells Cora. "It was always raining. There was mud. Sickness . . ."

But, he tells her, they were saved. Joined up with the army, they were able to march. Eastward, eastward, farther than he ever thought he would travel in his lifetime. Thrilling and terrifying in equal measure, because the rebel army was on their heels. They realized they were going toward the coast because the British—first their enslavers and now their saviors—were losing. And what then? When they set up camp at night, looking over their shoulders to where fires burned in the distance along the enemy line, Thursday imagined his old master out there in the darkness. Imagined reaching, grasping hands . . . In sleep, he held his mother and dreamed of a safety and comfort that he could never enjoy while awake.

In the end, they were all in New York. Thousands of them, just like Thursday and his mother, cramped together and waiting. He knew a boy, around his age, who went missing. Never came back. The whisper was his old master had slipped into their camp by night and carried him away.

Here he pauses. And Cora realizes how easy it would be for him to fall into the cracks of each memory—to have the past break apart, revealing beneath the surface an ever-increasing array of weeks, days, minutes, each with its own pain, a labyrinth from which he might never escape.

But he continues.

Thursday tells her about coming to Nova Scotia. About the tension that did not unknot until the ships weighed anchor and they were finally free. They were going to a place where those grasping hands could not reach. A promised land. On the ship, some people wept in thanks to God. Thursday's mother wept for another reason—memories of the passage from Africa, held under for many years, now rising to the surface. But soon they were on land. They dried their tears. Here was a new home.

Thursday speaks of rocky, infertile plots of land. Of help promised to build shelter, only for the men and materials to go over to their white neighbors and leave them with nothing but holes in the ground, covered with canvas. Speaks of a hard winter, shadowed by death, then the riot that destroyed what little they had built. The desperate journey north. No food, no money, no wood for a fire.

"We needed work," he says. "Ma came here. Farmer Nash made her a deal. Five years, he said. Five years' work, then big money at the end."

A small shift in his voice again. No tremor in it now, only flint. A coldness.

"Ma don't read," he says. "So she ain't know it ain't say five on the paper. It say twenty."

Cora can't answer at first, stunned.

"But she don't . . . If she can't . . . Him have to let she go after five. That's what them agree."

Thursday shrugs like he has seen many such injustices, and had to bear them.

"That's what she says they agreed. But it ain't what the paper say."

Cora opens her mouth. Closes it again. Exhales. She feels she has no right to any greater rage than what he is showing now, but still she burns on his behalf.

"Freetown," Thursday says. "You know it?"

Cora shakes her head.

"In Africa. Sierra Leone."

There was a man, he says, who came from England to sell them a new promise. The old one had died in the rocky soil, died in the cold winters, died in the hard work on farms, side by side with slaves, died with the men and women who had their papers snatched away, burned, taken for forgeries, who ended up slaves themselves. This new promise was a place across the ocean, and it sounded like home.

This stirs a memory in Cora—she has heard snatches of the other Maroons talking, about all the people who were here and how they went away to Africa. She did not give it much thought, but now she looks at Thursday anew.

"But you stay here?"

He gives her a look that says that he will get there with time.

He tells her how by the time the man came to persuade them all to come to Freetown, his mother was sick. Not a fever, nor the kind of sickness that strikes quick and leaves you either dead or well again by morning. A slow, persistent cough that had her hacking up clear mucus and then, as the months went by, flecks of blood.

They both knew she was dying. Maybe in a month. Maybe in a year. Maybe, if they were very lucky, in five.

Thursday speaks of how he would lie awake at night, paralyzed with grief for a death that had not yet occurred. But the image that plagued him most was not the thought of losing her—not the moment he would find her, one morning, glassy-eyed and cold. Rather, it was the image of lowering her body into this foreign soil. It was the idea of her forever buried in this place that was nothing to them but a broken dream. Virginia had meant suffering and slavery, but at least her husband was buried there. Her daughter. They both knew—they both hoped, at least—that Thursday, one day, would get himself out of this barren place, so there was not even the salve of having his bones one day join her.

Thursday knew what they must do. They must go to Sierra Leone.

"But," he says, "the contract was the contract. No getting out of it. We wasn't the only one. There was folks that wanted to go, just like us. And couldn't."

She waits for him to continue. Through the doorway, watches the oxen in the field, the rising clouds of their breath. Ruth still standing with them.

"Well," Thursday continues. "In the end, she went."

He says this so calmly, so without feeling, that it takes Cora a moment to react. Her gaze snaps to him, aghast that he would finish his story this way.

"What you mean? How? Why she— But you—"

Whenever Thursday almost smiles, little lines appear at the corners of his eyes, betraying the feelings he might otherwise keep hidden. He seems amused by her indignance. But he seems tired, too. She had assumed he was a man of few words; now she sees that he has plenty of words, when he needs them. But he is settling back into reticence.

"I took her place," he says simply. "The contract. I'm working out the other years."

Cora brings a hand to her face. Wants to speak, to impress upon him just how deeply she has felt throughout his story—but makes herself stay quiet. For his sake.

Eventually, Cora says, "You make she go."

"For the best," he says. A hardness in his voice. And Cora must reappraise her first impressions of him—because she is a little afraid of him now. A little awed that he has the capacity to make the choice he did.

She is thinking of Leah. Thinking of a conversation half-finished, during the desperate weeks of the war, when Leah tried to say, *If the time comes, leave me,* and Cora cut across her— *No*—not letting her speak the words . . .

Thursday says, "You best be going. Farmer Nash'll come out soon."

Cora's feelings are almost too muddled for her to answer. But she pulls herself back to the present.

"Me gon' see you again?" she says, half a promise, half a question.

Thursday taps her once, lightly, on the shoulder.

"Watch yourself, now, on your way home."

10

On the road, Cora stops walking. She is listening even before the sound—but then it comes, something between a bark and a howl. She shivers. Animal? Or human?

She peers into the trees. Perhaps it is the sunlight that keeps her fear at bay, the forest a glittering world that feels dreamlike. And, as in a dream, she feels as if she can come to no harm. So she moves toward the sound, does not heed Thursday's warning, slips and scrambles her way onto the woodland paths, heart beating fast, grasping at tree trunks, moving toward the final answer—the truth.

She does not see it until she falls over it; falls into the snow, knocking the breath from her. Turns over quickly, lying on her back, and then is given such a fright she starts to scrabble away. The hulking animal that lies on the snow is three or four times her size. Her eyes dart over its dark shape, taking in the spread of its antlers. . . . A moose. Finally, she sees the blood spreading across the snow.

Dead.

She stands. Moves cautiously toward the carcass. Pauses for a moment, arrested by the black, empty gaze of its still open eye.

Her frozen mind starts to thaw. She is thinking . . . Whatever blow killed this creature, there is no sign of it. The blood, she discovers, is coming from a wound in its side, a strip of skin sliced and pulled back. Someone, or something, has started the process of skinning. Surely human—a bear or a pack of hungry wolves would not have been so patient. The wound is steaming— still warm.

Cora feels half animal herself. Turns one way, then the other, almost sniffing the air. Knowing that she is close now. That this mystery is ready to unravel itself before her.

She looks down at the red stains around her feet.

And here is the thing about snow. So often, it keeps secrets— it melts away, or fresh flakes fall to bury whatever lies beneath. But sometimes . . .

Tracks. Not quite footprints, more like lines, something with weight dragging itself over the ground without lifting its feet.

Cora's pulse does not quicken. It slows, as calm certainty descends. Head down, she begins to follow.

Stop."

The voice seems to come from the trees itself.

Cora stops. She starts to turn her head, looking for the source of the sound. But the voice comes again. A woman's. Quiet, though it carries through the air without trouble.

"I'll shoot."

Cora raises her hands slowly, a gesture of surrender.

She tries to catch sight of the speaker in the corners of her vision. Sees a dark shadow that might be a person. Strangely, she does not feel afraid, but her body coils tight, ready to fight or flee.

She has so many questions that her mouth cannot form them. *Who are you? What are you? Why did you hide from me?*

She hears something stir. Come closer to her. She hears its breath.

She cannot bear it any longer. She turns.

There is one moment—joyous and sickening in equal measure—when Cora thinks it really is Elsy. This small, slender, dark-skinned girl. But no. She takes in the angles of the cheekbones, the shape of the mouth, the rounded chin. And the eyes like darkness itself, absorbing light and letting none back out again. The girl has a hood, but it is pushed back, revealing close-shorn hair; her temples a small hollow on each side, as if, when the bone was still soft, two thumbs were pressed into her skull.

A stranger.

And then Cora sees the bow and arrow, pulled taut, and feels immediately that she has misjudged. Raises her hands again. The girl's expression is hard and unreadable. Her aim does not waver; the tip of the arrow does not even shake, directed straight at Cora's heart.

"Why'd you come?" she asks.

Cora shakes her head, fumbling for the right words.

"Anybody else know you're here?"

"Me—"

Before Cora can answer, there is a low noise—a growl. Cora looks down; at the level of her waist, she sees gray fur, bared teeth, yellow eyes.

She steps quickly backward, startled, as this wolfish animal lets out another growl. Her feet catch something on the uneven ground, and she falls, ending with her head level with the approaching animal's jaws. . . .

A sharp whistle. Immediately, the nightmare creature looks away, back toward the girl with the arrow. Cora catches her breath with a gasp. As the animal slinks to the girl's side, it seems to grow smaller, less threatening. Its fur is slate gray, but its ears are not nearly so large nor its snout so pointed as Cora first thought. A dog?

The girl watches Cora get to her feet, a wariness to her. And for the first time, Cora realizes she might be afraid, this girl. That she is no forest monster. That it is she, and not Cora, who might be in danger.

Behind the girl, Cora can just make out, through the trees, a clearing. A dozen more paces and she would reach it. There is, in the middle of it, a hut of some kind. A conical shape, the color of tree bark. Smoke drifts up, curling silver, from the ashes of a fire hastily put out.

"You live out here?" Cora asks.

The girl shifts her head sideways, a move that reminds Cora somewhat of a snake—sleek and watchful.

"What's your name?" Cora tries.

This earns her a tight-lipped look.

"My name is Cora."

The corners of the girl's mouth waver, as if she is fighting back the words. But still, nothing. She remains nameless. She does, however, lower her bow.

"Dark soon," she says. The way she speaks is light—not

quite musical, but more like the natural music of the forest, like the sound of rustling leaves, the call of an owl.

Cora sees it is true; the sun is low on the horizon, and it is the time of year when darkness comes on quick. Cora wonders how far she is from Preston. An hour? Maybe more. She has no real sense of the way she came to get here.

She should go, and yet she lingers. Aware she is staring at this stranger and yet not able to look away. Feeling the delicate thread of a connection, inexplicable but undeniable. She has been drawn here—followed the tracks, yes, but it was more than just this. Despite the girl's brittleness, despite the almost attack of the dog, Cora feels as if the world has structured itself to bring her here, to this moment and this clearing.

"You should go," the girl says. The softness of her voice makes it hard to say whether she means to be harsh or kind.

"Me don't know the way," Cora says.

The girl points upward, toward the distant crest of a hill.

"Keep the hill in front. You'll get to the road."

"The road to Preston?"

"Yes."

More questions at this—how does this girl know where Cora is going? Every time this winter that Cora has felt a presence behind her, eyes somewhere among the trees, watching, has that been because there really has been someone there?

(And Godwin. The little body in the snow. What might this girl know? What might she have seen of all the dark things that pass through the forest?)

But Cora holds the questions back.

Girl and dog are as still as wood carvings. Waiting for Cora

Eleanor Shearer

to go. Overhead, the moon is out already, briefly sharing the sky with the weak afternoon sun; a pale crescent, surrounded by blue.

Cora walks, sure she can feel the girl's gaze on her all the way. She glances over her shoulder only once, when she has walked a few dozen paces. The girl is gone, but the dog still sits where it was sitting before—its silhouette a little more menacing now Cora is farther away—watching carefully, as if to be sure Cora will not turn back.

———

It is night by the time Cora reaches Preston. She stops at the edge of the village, prolonging her time in the darkness; the fires blazing in the huts, casting light through the windows, lack their usual brilliance. Instead, it is the night that holds more wonder—that seems to be more than just the absence of light, but rather has color of its own, a deep navy blue, flecked silver where moonbeams touch the snow.

She exhales slowly. Feels—what, exactly? She cannot name it. But the world seems more saturated. A richer place than it was when she went out walking this morning.

When she reaches the hut, Silas is standing in the doorway.

"Late," he says.

Cora says nothing.

"Where you go?"

"Just walking," she says, without hesitation. All the way back, she has been certain—she will keep her secret.

The hidden girl in the forest is hers alone.

The Trial

January 1798

Ruth is a thief and what she steals is time. She takes her inspiration from the oxen, Cain and Abel, who are slow and ponderous—obedient, but moving at their own pace. She stays just the right side of a beating; Farmer Nash thinks she is stupid, maybe soft in the head, but how else can she exert some small control over the rhythm of her life?

She steals moments like this one—standing at her window to watch as Thursday walks up the road, a flurry of snow swirling around him.

A heaviness to the way he walks. He wouldn't tell her where he was going. But she knows, has overheard. He had to ask Farmer Nash for the time off, exchanged it for an extra six months of service.

He is going to the courthouse.

She remembers the girl. The time she came—the way she hopped the fence and walked across the fields without fear. She watched her, wanting to commit her to memory, and in watching, Ruth recalled a story from long ago, one she had almost forgotten. It was one of those half-true tales, passed on until it concerns someone so distant—a friend of a cousin of a husband of a sister—that it is impossible to verify. There was a woman who fled her plantation in Georgia and tried to hide herself in Savannah, to disappear among the crowds of people. But as soon as she got to the city, she was arrested, because a white man saw her and he knew, just from the way she walked, that she wasn't free, that the papers she carried were forgeries and the name written on them was a lie.

Ruth thought of that story when she saw the girl here on the farm, because she felt, for the first time, that it must be true. There was a way the girl moved that Ruth could study for a hundred days and never be able to imitate. Light on her feet, the swing of her arms smooth and easy. She was, in effect, the opposite of the heavy, plodding oxen—she was a creature that had never been yoked to a plow.

———

Once upon a time, in a different country, Ruth was quick. She darted in between the cabins on the plantation in Virginia, too young for the fields. She ran down to the stream and danced in the fast-moving water, imagining that she, too, was a current, that her life would surely flow to its intended destination.

By rights, she thinks when she meanders across frost-stricken fields, it should be the other way around, shouldn't it? Slow and steady in the summer heat of the Deep South, dashing around in the Nova Scotian winter, where people will do anything to keep warm. But the cold here dulls her and turns time to sludge—freezes it, like the layer of ice that covers the well that she must break through every morning to draw water.

She was almost free. That is the cruelest thing. But there is no such thing as almost free—only free and not free, as far apart as darkness and light. She ran, just as others on plantations across the South ran, but when she came to the British camp and gave her name, they would not take her. Her master still loyal to the Crown and thus still entitled to his property.

Perhaps, if she reflects on it now, that was the moment that the slowness set in. Because a little piece of her shattered to realize the truth—that what made her unfree was not the whips and the guns and the stocks and the prisons, the noses and ears and hands and feet cut off for running, the gallows that would hang her in the end if she resisted too much. It was not the fences around the cotton fields, it was not the swamps and the sea that bounded her in on each side and made escape impossible. In the end, her freedom turned on the most intangible and capricious thing—the heart of her master, and whether it beat for the rebels or the Crown. That was all that separated her from the people the British freed. The only difference between her and Thursday, who performs the same work each day but knows that there will be an end. That one day his contract will be done and he will be his own man again. Where is her contract? Where is it written that she will know no other life but this one?

Besides Thursday and Farmer Nash, she speaks to no one. Goes nowhere—Thursday is the one entrusted with going to Halifax for supplies or taking their produce to market. She might, at nighttime, slip out to the surrounding farms, see if there are people like her there. But she does not. She does not steal distance, does not steal love or friendship, or any of the other things that enslaved people have, throughout the centuries, taken for themselves to try to keep alive the belief that they are human after all. She steals only time: standing in the middle of a field, leaning on a hoe, and lifting her face to the sky to feel the snowflakes on her skin.

Sometimes, Ruth dreams of her old quickness, feels it warming her stiff, cold limbs. And in the dream she is able to make her body move the way the girl did, a little taste of freedom that grows bitter when she wakes and it all fades too quickly and she is herself again. Nothing but unfreedom and her meager treasure, small moments looted over the course of a lifetime.

SPRING
1797

11

There are now some rare days when, with the sun at its highest, its rays carry a teasing hint of warmth. But the weather is fickle: sometimes snowing, sometimes raining, often misty, usually damp. Mornings and evenings still have a winter chill, even if the light is creeping to take back more and more of the night.

Cora battles with two impulses so strong that they keep each other in balance, keep her trapped in Preston. On the one hand, she is desperate to see the girl in the forest again. Dreams of Jamaica have started to shade into something else—tropical forests are suddenly blanketed with snow, darkness descends, and there she is, in this strange in-between place that is both Jamaica and not, Nova Scotia and not, searching blindly through the trees because she is sure the girl is there somewhere, out of sight. On the other hand, she feels a sense of caution. Silas has kept close watch on her, and Leah, too. A brief thaw melts the snow and clears the roads that connect the scattered Maroon settlements in and around Preston, and Cora's absence would be noticed in all the gatherings that take place, as people begin to look impatiently to the year ahead. It feels urgent that she avoid prying questions about where she goes.

Weeks pass. Little way to stave off boredom; more and more of the men turning to rum, to bring them what comfort it can, a twisted nostalgia for their old island. They start up cockfighting; Cora goes only to the first one. Silas has arranged it all, stands right on the edge of the ring as the frightened birds are goaded into turning on each other, talons scraping feathers, piercing skin. Cora turns away, the little droplets of blood falling on the soil somehow unbearable, though this is not the first time she has seen blood spilled. She resolves, then, that she will not come again; listens to the other nights from her bed, the screams of the dying cocks mixing with the laughs of drunken men.

———

A chance comes in March. Old Joe, their neighbor, falls sick; Leah goes round for the day to help his wife tend to him. Silas heads for Maroon Hall, for a meeting with Colonel Montague James. And little Benjamin goes to lessons at the chapel—since the night of the funeral, Silas has let him go. A concession, perhaps, that his anger went too far.

Cora is alone for the day. The forest calls to her. Slipping into it feels like unfurling stiff wings.

It has rained that morning, but little patches of snow still dot the ground. The way to the clearing where the girl had her shelter is hazy in Cora's memory. It is only when she stumbles on the bones of the moose, now picked clean, that she has faith the whole thing was not just a dream. She presses onward. There are no tracks this time. She has to move slowly, deliberately. Never quite certain which path is the right one.

She understands, as she goes on, that in all her previous walks, she was moving too quickly. Stamping the ground, sending the creatures of the forest scattering. If she stands still for a moment, considering her next path, that's when she sees what secrets the woods have kept. A fox, its fur a shock of red against the brown and silver bark of the trees. A muskrat, a long-tailed rodent that scuttles along the edge of a half-frozen lake. And even a hare, its fur as white as the snow, almost invisible until it leaps, fleet-footed among the rocks and tree roots, its little body stretched in each bound.

Dark rain clouds are visible in the distance, and Cora is just losing hope when between the trees, something stirs. Wolf-shaped, pulled into a cautious position, ready to run.

Cora stands still.

"Is me," she says, in as gentle a voice as she can. "You remember?"

The dog slowly stands upright. Its soft ears rise. It doesn't come closer, but Cora risks taking a few steps forward.

"Where is she?" Cora asks. The dog stares back at her. Not a blank stare; there is a sharpness there, a sense of understanding. But the dog does not move.

Cora looks around her. The forest is gloomy and silent, the air heavy with the anticipation of approaching rain. She feels frustration growing—to be so close, and to have the trail end cold . . .

But then her eyes see it. The distant clearing. She is sure it is the one, though there is no sign of the little dwelling there now. Cora strikes for it. The dog hangs back a moment and then follows with loping strides.

When Cora comes to the gap in the trees, she stands at its center, where the thing that was almost a hut and almost a tent once was. Has the girl gone?

At the corner of the clearing, a large rock breaks the tree line, its surface craggy and dark, glistening wet from the snow-melt. Cora notices a cedar, uprooted and fallen against the rock in a tangle of branches. She looks closer. What seems accidental is not—the tree is not one piece of wood but many, stacked together to form a shelter. Cruder than the carefully constructed tent from before, but still a shelter.

This is the place.

The dog walks past Cora and sniffs around the little camp— Cora now sees, a few feet from the lean-to shelter, a circle of stones around some ash, the remnants of a fire. Settles itself in the shadow of the rock, resting its head on its paws and curling its tail around its body.

Cora looks around. Nothing. But not the kind of nothing-ness she has felt before, the sense of something slipping away, just out of sight. Cora is sure the girl, wherever she is, has been away from here for some time, maybe hours. Not hiding, but going about the normal rhythms of her life. So—no choice but to wait. The air is crisp and chilly, but, out of the wind, with her back against the soft moss of the rock, it is not too bitterly cold.

She must doze. On the edge of sleep, the colors of the forest shift, light and shade dancing in hypnotic patterns. When she jerks back to full consciousness, the girl is there standing over her. Watching.

"You came back," she says.

She sounds neither pleased nor displeased.

Cora gets to her feet. They are almost the same height; the girl is a fraction taller. Her eyes look down at Cora like black holes in the ice—at first glance, dark and empty, but in fact there is movement and life in the depths.

Cora wants to try to explain the way she has felt in the weeks since they met for the first time. Something that has sat in her chest, halfway between hunger and ache. But not an unpleasant feeling; rather, something that fills her with energy, that has carried her out of Preston to here.

"Me did think you leave," Cora says.

The girl has a face that is constantly moving. Cora watches the muscles work under the skin; watches the way her eyes flick from one place to another, and the way the corners of her mouth twitch. She takes time to answer, and in her face Cora can see written the steps she takes to get there. Her hesitation, worn down until it recedes, replaced by a nervous but firm expression.

"Thought about it." She gestures to the makeshift shelter. "Took the wikuom down."

The girl's expression shows some further conflict. When she finally speaks again, she says—

"Cora?"

Cora's name, spoken in that soft voice with the long vowels— it stirs something in her.

"Yes."

The girl lays a hand on her own chest.

"Agnes."

The dog has come over to Agnes's side. It makes its presence known, pushing its head into her hand.

"And Patience."

The sound of the name sets the dog's tail wagging gently. It trots toward Cora and sniffs around her in a relaxed, friendly way.

"She likes you," says Agnes. Patience looks back and meets Agnes's gaze, the fondness between the two of them clear.

They hear the rain before they feel it—a few light drops that patter against the muddy earth. Cora and Agnes lift their heads together, looking up at the gray sky, feeling the water on their faces.

"You're cold," Agnes notices. Cora is shivering.

"Just a little."

Agnes glances at the shelter, the branches leaning on the side of the rock. Cora watches as Agnes thinks, and then decides.

She tilts her head, an invitation. Cora crawls inside; the effect is rather like going into the trunk of a tree itself, dark, with a mossy, earthy smell. But it is at least dry.

When Cora's eyes adjust, Agnes is sitting on the other side of the shelter—close, given the whole thing is only a few feet across. Agnes has her knees drawn up to her chest, and it is the first time that Cora realizes she is wearing trousers rather than a skirt—made of animal hide, a brown so dark that it almost fades into the shadows. Cora finds herself staring at Agnes's knees. Everything Agnes wears is bulky, but there is something about the fact that the material splits, encasing each leg, that gives Cora a stronger impression than ever of the lines of Agnes's body.

Patience is still outside. They hear the sound of her paws as she retreats into the forest.

"She don't mind the rain?" Cora asks.

Agnes shrugs.

"She can find someplace dry."

They sit in silence. In the gloom, the whites of Agnes's eyes are more pronounced; the gentle sound of her breath.

Finally, Cora says, "How long—"

Just as Agnes says, "Where'd you—"

An awkward pause. Cora says, "You first."

"Your accent. Where'd you . . . ?"

"Jamaica."

"Why'd you leave?"

"No choice. Them make we go."

Agnes nods slowly.

Cora, hoping she can trade one question for another, says, "How long you live out here?"

"This clearing? A few months."

It's not what Cora was asking, and Agnes knows it. Cora makes a small huffing noise, registering her displeasure.

Finally, Agnes says, "I don't know."

"You don't know?"

"A while."

"Alone?" Cora asks.

"Not always."

Agnes speaks slowly and deliberately. Her tone not exactly suggesting, *Do not pry*, but more like, *Do not pry yet*.

"You tell anyone?" Agnes asks.

"Tell them what?"

"That you saw me."

"No."

"Don't tell," says Agnes softly. There is something in her

voice that reminds Cora of water, in all its forms. Sometimes like the patter of rain. Sometimes like the sound of waves on the shore.

The shelter warms gradually with the heat of their bodies. Cora can no longer see her own breath when she exhales. It feels like their own world: quiet, only a little light filtering in. A place to keep secrets.

The rain eases. Agnes turns her head, peering through the branches. The energy in the shelter shifts; a restlessness descends. Before, Cora had Agnes's full, undivided attention, and now, quite suddenly, she does not.

Cora knows she must go. Can guess only a little at the ways of the forest but understands that Agnes will need the daylight to find food. Cora would stay inside with her until nightfall if she could, but it would be selfish.

"Two more questions," Cora says.

Agnes starts, as if she has forgotten Cora is there. Her hands rest against the tops of her knees; she has slipped off the mittens that were on them, revealing long fingers, crisscrossed with scars, calluses dotted across the palms.

She does not speak. Cora takes this as permission.

"Me can come again?"

Agnes looks at her, assessing.

"Why?"

Cora makes a gesture with her hands, trying and failing to capture an answer from the air. In the end, she cannot come up with a reason; at least, not one that she can put into words.

"Well," says Agnes.

"That mean yes?" Cora presses.

A little half smile, gone before it has a chance to fully form.

"Don't give up easy, do you?"

Cora shakes her head. Smiling herself.

"Well," says Agnes. "Yes."

Cora sits up a little straighter. Pleased.

"The other question?"

"What?" asks Cora. Forgetting there was a second, distracted by the idea of more moments like this, tucked away in some hidden place.

"You say you got two more questions," says Agnes. "What's the other one?"

"Me don' see you before."

Agnes holds her gaze.

"That a question?"

"All them times," Cora persists. "On the ice. Or just beyond the road. Me always did think . . . somebody there."

Cora can tell Agnes is close to not saying anything at all. But then she sees the idea that Agnes might admit it all seed itself, sees the spark in Agnes's eyes.

"It was me," Agnes says softly.

Cora wants to ask—

So you follow me?

But maybe it was she who followed Agnes. Or perhaps somewhere in between, neither statement quite the truth.

And Godwin comes to Cora. . . . She suppresses the memory of the child as best she can. It makes her uneasy to think of him, when she feels this new warmth toward Agnes. She doesn't want to dwell on darker things. Selfish, perhaps, not to ask. But she is growing surer of the pull here, to Agnes and the forest, surer that she will return. There will be time yet to bring up Godwin, to understand what Agnes knows.

Suddenly, a fat spider drops from the branches above, square into Cora's lap. Her reaction is instant—an undignified squeak, scrabbling backward. The spider seems equally startled, scuttling quickly away, soon hidden in the walls of the shelter.

Cora's racing heart slows, and she starts to laugh—at herself, at how silly it is to be frightened by something so small. Agnes has been watching carefully, seems to take this as permission to be amused, too. A small smile at first, that becomes a giggle that grows. When Agnes laughs, she brings a hand up to cover her mouth, and there is barely any light in the shelter, but what little there is seems drawn to her, seems to settle in her eyes until they shine with it, until the light is not around them but inside her. This lasts just for a moment, before the light is gone, back out in the world where it should be.

———

A few weeks ago, Cora was helping Leah with some mending. They had a ball of yarn that was tangled; Cora's task was to untangle it. Painstaking work, tugging and teasing at all its knots. It seemed like the untangling would never end, until, quite suddenly, Cora pushed a handful of it through a loop she had prized apart, and everything unknotted in an instant.

She remembers that sensation now, of everything falling into place—the small *oh* that she spoke aloud when it happened.

She remembers as she watches Agnes laugh, and thinks again—

Oh.

12

A few days of rain leave behind a softness that heralds the coming of spring—in the ground, which after the frosts feels yielding underfoot, and in the air, which for the first time lacks the hard chill of winter. And there is a softness, too, in the strange porosity between light and dark at the edges of the day, long, lingering dawns and dusks.

Leah goes to Halifax, taking Cora with her, in search of seeds and grains. Cora wanders down to the harbor. Sees a familiar broad-shouldered shape, sitting quietly on a bench; is surprised how pleased she is to see him.

"Thursday."

When he looks up at her, she is unable to keep from noting the differences between him and Agnes. Cora considers his face, the slowness with which it moves. How much he keeps hidden underneath the set of his mouth and brow. Whereas Agnes can move through a dozen expressions in only a moment, her face constantly in motion—brows dancing, mouth quivering, eyes reflecting patterns of shadow and light.

"Good to see you," he says.

"How's Abel?"

"Working now," Thursday says. "Steady with the plow."

They lapse into silence. She still standing, he sitting, watching as, over the horizon, a ship glides through the mist, heading for the harbor.

Thursday says unexpectedly, "That's what I want."

"What?"

"The ship," he says. "That's how I'll get out one day."

"Well," says Cora. "Yes. A ship the only way out."

Smiles slowly so he knows she is teasing.

"I mean work," he says. Smiling, too.

Cora thinks of the skinny, ragged boys in the crew on the ship from Jamaica. Ship work is hard. Perhaps as hard as the farm.

"Work," she repeats. "You ever dream about bigger things?"

"Sure," he says. "But dreaming ain't the same as doing. What I can do is work. What a ship can do is take me."

He pushes himself to his feet, stretches. The bustle of the harbor around them means this is not a place that lends itself to waiting for long. They part wordlessly but with a shared look of fondness, the small buds of early friendship.

———

Silas resents what Leah and Cora bring back from Halifax. He sees any planting as a concession that they will remain in Nova Scotia, but Leah will not be deterred. Over at the governor's farm, they have started to prepare the soil for spring. Leah is determined it will be the same here, too.

They spend a long afternoon weeding and clearing. The rocks make it slow progress; they shovel the earth to loosen it, but the metal of their spades strikes often against hard stone, sending tremors through their bones. Soon, Cora is sweating— and she almost cannot believe her body is warm. It feels as if she, as much as the world, is waking up again after a long winter.

The little garden becomes Leah's obsession. For a while, Cora works alongside her, and her attention is briefly diverted from dreams of the woods. There are little glimpses of Leah's old life, something always kept hidden, in the way she insists on arranging the furrows, or the way she alternates the rows of seeds. Nothing said explicitly, of course, but Cora realizes Leah has done this before. In Jamaica, Leah was the keeper of a herd of sheep and goats, leaving other women to do the planting. So Cora did not know Leah possessed this drive to make things grow. She wonders if it comes from the plantation, or from far-ther back, from somewhere across the sea. And she wonders, too, if things learned in warmer lands will still work here, where the winds of spring can blow almost as bitter as those of winter.

But by absorbing Leah's focus, the garden is a gift. It gives Cora the chance to get away.

———

There is a day when it doesn't rain but it mists—tiny droplets, barely felt, but over time they settle, soaking through clothes, cold against the skin. When Cora steps away from Preston and off the well-worn paths, it is into a world of shrouded, half-formed shapes—at once eerie and exhilarating.

The way to Agnes's clearing is stored more in her body than her mind. She navigates by instincts she didn't know she possessed—sensitive to the sound of running water that takes her to a stream, or to the smell of fallen pine needles that leads her to a clutch of trees that lean slightly northward, pointing her along her way. Moss and bark glisten, damp and shimmering, as the sun begins to lift some of the mist. Cora feels light—always finding sure footing, even among the twisted roots. Her eyes drawn upward toward glimpses of the sky through the dense thicket of branches.

But when she reaches the clearing, it is empty. Even the lean-to shelter is gone. Her heart stumbles; the good mood that has buoyed her all the way here falters. It did not even occur to her that Agnes would be gone.

She turns a slow circle at the clearing's center. But the woods, which moments ago seemed so clear to her, now keep their secrets. She is lost, with no sense of where she might go. . . .

Then, emerging from the trees is Agnes. She comes forward with a note of caution, but then—slowly and shyly—she smiles.

Patience is with her. She looks at Cora, sniffs the air, and then seems satisfied, sitting back on her haunches and letting her pink tongue loll out.

"Heading for spring camp," Agnes says. Almost as if they are old friends and have no need of greetings.

Cora feels a little twinge between her ribs.

"You leaving?"

"A little way south."

The woods all around them seem to go on forever, and Cora

feels like for Agnes, *a little way* could mean anything from an hour to three days' walk. Perhaps this worry shows in her face, because Agnes says—

"Want to come?"

Cora relaxes.

"Yes."

They fall into easy step beside each other. Cora is surprised that Agnes walks slowly, realizes that she thought of Agnes as fleet-footed, darting between the trees. But in fact, she seems in no hurry; it is Patience that runs off ahead, disappearing for long stretches, the gray of her fur blending in perfectly with the shadows of the forest. They are silent, until Agnes comes to a stop—holding up a hand, a command to *listen*.

Cora listens. It takes her a moment to pick out a single sound from the noise of the forest. But there it is—birdsong. A high, trilling sound, the vibration of a plucked string. And Cora watches as joy comes over Agnes's face like rays of sunshine piercing through the mist.

"A warbler," she says. "First one of the year."

Cora closes her eyes, the better to tune in to the song. It sounds like so many other birds she has heard before, it is hard for her, at first, to imagine she would be able to name it the way Agnes has done. But. She listens harder. Finds the distinctive melody. And it touches something unexpected in her heart.

She opens her eyes. Agnes is turned away, her face tilted toward the treetops, rapt attention on her face. She is lean, the cheekbones stark under her skin. Everything about her frame is meager—a sense of the barest elements of a body, preserved. She is built for survival. For lasting the long winters, the heavy rains. And yet, in this moment, she looks profoundly happy.

She has found space, in between the work of survival, for de-light.

They walk on, and Agnes does this again—pauses to draw Cora's attention to something in the forest. Under a clutch of spruce trees is a crop of golden mushrooms, a faint glow in the shadowed gloom. Agnes picks one and holds it up for Cora; the smell takes her by surprise. She was expecting something musty, but they smell almost like fruit.

"Have to be careful with mushrooms," Agnes says, "but these are safe."

They walk on. Cora speaks little. She is, in truth, a little awed, but a little comforted, too, by the easiness of the rhythm they have slipped into. Of the demands it places on her atten-tion, keeping her anchored to the physical, the present.

Eventually, she says—

"You know so much."

A pause. An enigmatic smile—as if Agnes acknowledges and gently refuses this attempt to bring history back into things.

"Had to learn quick," is all she says.

Cora has little sense of where they are in the forest, or where they are going, but she is struck, once again, by her growing sensitivity to what, just a few months ago, would have looked like identical paths and identical patches of trees. The woods are as varied as a crowd of human faces. They pass from fir trees huddled together, green and covered in needles, blocking out the light, through stretches of mostly birch and maple, still bare branched, unable to hide the sky.

They climb gently upward until, at the crest of a hill, the landscape opens up underneath them. This time, it is Cora who stops.

The sea. Gray mists still hang low along the shoreline, so that the water's black edge soon fades away into mystery, like the very edge of the earth.

It is, at once, otherworldly and yet also a harsh reminder of the fact of life—of the existence of others. Because along the coast, Cora can see smoking chimneys, can see wooden wharves that reach out across the water, fishing boats moored along them.

Patience has reappeared; she comes and sits between the two women, and Agnes's fingers run automatically through the fur on her head. Agnes scans the horizon, and when she spots something in the distance, the relief is clear. She points.

"See the rocks there?"

Cora follows Agnes's finger to a smattering of jagged gray shapes that sit in the ocean, close to the coast. The shoreline they defend looks like little more than cliffs; there are no chimneys there and no boats.

"Made camp there before," Agnes says. "Can't always come back to the same place. If there's people."

They are skirting close to Cora's most burning question— why is Agnes hiding? And with a strange sense of detachment, Cora is able to watch herself, to see herself keeping quiet and leaving the question unasked, and it is strange because she so rarely shies from saying things when others might leave silence. But there is something about Agnes that holds her back. A fragility that is at odds with the hard realities of her life out here, alone, that Cora feels she is only at the very beginning of being able to comprehend. And perhaps, too, Cora intuits that for Agnes to open up, she will have to be patient. An intuition that is rewarded when Agnes says—

"It was different before. Mi'kmaq camps all over the coast by summer. Now . . ." She trails off, with a touch of melancholy.

"Mi'kmaq?" Cora asks.

"Indians."

"You was with them?"

"I never saw those days," Agnes says. "Just heard about them." Which is an answer, of sorts, just to a different question. She flashes Cora another one of those enigmatic smiles, a sign that she will say nothing more.

The sun is mostly obscured by cloud, but Cora guesses it is afternoon.

"Need to get back," she says. "Before dark."

She has no sense of how far they are from Preston. But Agnes points along the coast, toward a little clutch of settlements.

"That town there has a road. It takes you back to Lake Echo. You know the way from there."

Cora nods slowly. Impressed anew by the way Agnes's knowledge spans both worlds—the natural and the human. But Godwin breaks through: the memory of his little frozen body. The fact that Agnes knows her way to where the Maroons are—it becomes impossible to imagine she might not know something of what happened. Cora finally has to ask.

"In the winter, a little boy, him get lost. . . ." she starts. Gets her answer. Agnes's face twists in pain; she has to turn away to compose herself. Speaks still facing the ocean.

"Found him frozen," she says softly. "Out in the woods. But I thought . . . I knew. He had family, they'd want the body. Left it where it'd be found."

Cora thinks of Elsy. Of the preciousness of something left to bury. So inadequate—the person gone from it, only cold flesh left behind. And yet, so unimaginable—the idea of saying goodbye without it.

"We always bury we dead," Cora says. "It important for we."

She reaches out, because it feels like the right thing to do—to join their bodies, momentarily, Cora's hand on Agnes's shoulder, able, even through her coat, to feel the warmth of the skin underneath, until her fingers are almost too hot and something about the touch feels strange and Cora lets her arm drop back to her side.

———

On the way home she follows the roads, human cut through the woodland, tracks of mud and horse hoofprints and long gouges where carts have trundled over the soft ground. Only once does she stray back into the forest, on a whim. Searching—stumbling as best she can toward what she wants. She feels like a newborn. Or, more precisely, she feels like she has had to wipe herself clean of years of useless knowledge—of cultivation, of one hut and one home, immovable. This is no good to her now.

After just one day with Agnes, she is hardly expert. It takes her time. But she finds them again—a crop of mushrooms sprouting from the hollow trunk of a fallen tree, pushed over long ago by some storm and now covered in moss. She carries them home in her skirts. Presents them to Leah. It is a story—she was out foraging. It is an offering, to keep the peace between them, even though she has stayed out later than she should. And it is an alternative—food that cannot be found, yet, in the frost-shriveled shoots of their little garden. Leah puts the mushrooms in a broth, and their meal is all the richer for them.

13

In June, the governor hosts a dance at his home near Preston, an attempt to throw off the cobwebs of winter. Colonel Montague James himself—sharply dressed in his uniform, as quietly imposing as ever—comes to deliver the invitation, making it impossible for Silas to refuse. And so Leah and Cora both must dig in the trunk that they keep in the corner of the dingy bedroom, which has gathered dust since they came from Jamaica.

How strange it is, to pull out silk dresses and petticoats that now smell damp and unused, their colors dull but not entirely faded. Purples, indigos, reds, and greens. Patterns of flowers or fruits. Lace trims on the sleeves. Cora lays out a dress she has not worn in almost two years and stares at it. A reminder of the strange fickleness of wealth. Not that she has ever had wealth of the governor's sort, nor of the sort that the planters of Jamaica had—no white houses with columns and porches and grand pianos inside. But the poverty of this winter has belied the fact that most of them, in chests just like this one, have possessions the likes of which Leah, in her old life on a plantation, could barely have imagined. Cora touches the fabric of the dress, bringing back memories of dances gone by—of bright days, sticky with heat.

The governor's house is on a hill, elevated above the farmland that surrounds it. The path takes them down an avenue of trees, carefully cultivated, their lower boughs cut back to give them a similar shape. The uniformity is uncanny; Cora finds herself longing for the true forests, for the wildness of the trees there.

The house itself is uniform, too, recently built, the angles of it clean and unambiguous; the whole thing devoid of mystery. Soft music already drifts from inside, the windows ablaze with light.

The ballroom is filled with people. Most of the Maroon families are here, and white people, too, mostly strangers. This early in the evening, small groups stand apart from one another, awkward and reserved, but the governor's pretty wife glides deftly around the room, drawing them little by little closer together.

Once the party is in full swing, the effect is bewildering—the music, the talking, the elegant sweep of bodies across the room in polkas and minuets. Cora loses sight of Leah but stays on the edges, drinking first one glass of Madeira and then another, so quickly that she soon feels woozy and unsteady. Her body is here but her mind is elsewhere—is in the forest, gathering mushrooms; is tucked inside Agnes's wikuom, warmed by a fire. She has now spent maybe half a dozen mornings or afternoons with Agnes, hours snatched here and there. Always carrying some foraged food home.

Agnes's world has rhythms, has music, of a different kind from that played here, which seems so small, so confined, the relentlessness of the underpinning beat and the sameness of the dance steps. Cora aches for the rhythm of waves breaking on the shore, where each sound contains a vastness, a swell.

Partners fill the floor each dance. A sense of time bending in on itself as the couples start to move, their steps set in advance, the metronomic beat of their shoes on the hard wooden floor. Outside, night has fallen, the windows offering no view except that of darkness and, reflected in the panes, a shimmering picture of the scene within.

———

They are halfway home when Silas stumbles. Slips in the mud, goes down to his knees. Cora is closest to him, but she hesitates a fraction too long. It is another man, Captain Smith, who goes to his side. Silas brushes his help off, gets to his feet. Still unsteady, he sways, his eyes sweeping around until they find Cora.

She does not look away. His eyes narrow. In the ballroom, he stood for hours in the corner, speaking to no one, drinking steadily whenever servants brought over a glass. Cora herself is a little flushed with wine. And to be out here in the forest, away from the hut that feels increasingly his—it feels like more favorable terrain.

Silas looks her up and down—his expression dancing on a knife-edge between resentful and possessive. She hates it, feels the heat rising in her cheeks.

"What?" she snaps.

Leah touches Cora's arm. Cora shrugs her off.

"Someday," says Silas, voice thick with contempt, "some-body gon' teach you how a woman behave."

Leah steps between the two of them.

"Silas," she says.

He is undeterred, leaning a little so he can look around Leah at Cora.

"Somebody have to teach you," he continues. Then casts a withering glance at Leah. "Because she don't—"

Leah being caught in the crosshairs stirs Cora into life, anger hitting her so forcefully she starts to shake.

"It not your business," she spits.

She is trying to goad him into finally saying what has stayed unsaid so long. But she also believes that it is impossible for him to say that he has some claim to her, wants her as his own. Be-cause why would he want her if he so despises her, so craves to see her break?

Silas doesn't answer. Not directly. Instead, he says—

"Always sneak off like me don't see you go. Headstrong."

"Me can go where me like," Cora says. "Why you care?"

Leah's hand on her chest, trying to guide her backward, be-cause she and Silas are coming together in anger, circling, and Leah is caught in the middle, but Cora cannot think of any-thing beyond the oppressive weight of the unspoken expecta-tion, the future that has been decided for her somewhere, somehow, without her consent.

"Me never gon' marry you," Cora says. "Never."

"Cora."

That is Leah. A sharp tone; Cora has gone too far.

Cora watches as Silas decides how he will react. Readies

herself for a physical blow, would almost welcome it, the way her heart is pounding . . .

"Elsy warn me about you."

His words are so impossible that they take time to sink in. They numb more than they hurt her. She steps back; he might as well have hit her.

"She say you was selfish," Silas says. "That you—"

She will not hear it. She cannot hear it.

"You not fit to speak her name. You kill her. You and your war, you kill her and she never mean nothing to you and—"

Cora is falling backward, off-balance, before she even realizes what has happened. Silas's hand still raised, Cora's cheek stinging, his eyes wild with grief, and she cannot understand it because she has never seen this part of him before, the part that misses Elsy.

Silas lunges forward again, but Captain Smith and some of the others are back, drawn by the raised voices; Smith seizes Silas and holds him firm.

"Easy," he says, as Silas snarls at him.

Cora scrambles to her feet, her wild mind unable to settle on any thought but *Run*.

She turns and flees. Into the darkness, into the trees. Leah calling after her, but Cora hardly hears. She lets the woods swallow her, twisting, hidden paths that the others cannot hope to follow.

14

Cora moves quickly through the night. The trees make menacing shapes in the corners of her vision. At one point she is sure she sees Patience, feels relief, but this creature is mangier, thinner. It slinks past her and away. Now she knows Agnes, Cora is back to not believing in ghosts, but she still quickens her pace. This is not the kind of night to be out alone.

She reaches the wikuom, exhausted and shivering, to find Agnes sitting outside by the embers of a fire.

Patience trots to Cora and noses her hand, but Agnes is wary, taking in Cora's fine dress, the hem now dark with mud.

"Me can stay?" Cora asks. No point dancing around it.

Agnes says nothing.

"Just one night," Cora says.

Agnes's expression gives little away, not because it shows no emotion but because it shows too much. Shows the whole of the struggle, as she thinks through the reasons to send Cora away and the reasons to relent.

"Please?"

Agnes sighs.

"One night."

Agnes has a blanket around her shoulders, some kind of fur. She tosses it to Cora. Then, kneeling, Agnes stokes the fire, coaxing back a small flame. Cora pulls the fur tight and waits for the fire to warm her. Agnes sits, her back against a rock, and looks up, to where the stars overhead seem remote, dimmer than usual.

Cora fiddles compulsively with the edge of the blanket, twisting strands of fur between her fingers. Out here, in the black night, with the distant sound of waves washing against the shore, her anger seems so pointless. She feels it ebb away, leaving only cold and exhaustion.

"They gonna be worrying where you are?"

Cora snaps out of her reverie.

"Who?"

"Your people."

"Oh. No."

It's a lie. Agnes must know it's a lie; her lips purse. She still might send Cora away.

"No parents," Cora says. "Both gone."

A pause. Then Agnes says, "Mine, too."

Cora chooses her next words carefully, not wanting to jeopardize this small glimpse Agnes has offered of herself.

"Me never know my father," she says. "My mother dead when she did birth me. You?"

Agnes gives a tight half smile but says nothing. Cora sighs, sitting back. Thinking she will get nothing more today. Until—

"Me and my father," Agnes says. "We was together. Out

here. Mi'kmaq people helped us. Taught us things. And we survived. We was . . . happy."

Agnes pauses. Still not meeting Cora's eye. Tilting her face up, just a little, as if the memories are written in the sky.

"He died," she says. "Then it was just me."

Finality to her tone. She will say no more.

In the ensuing silence, Cora's attention is caught by something in the trees. A flicker of light, like the brief flare of a candle. Then another. A glowing chorus, a ripple of luminescence. Her breath catches as she stares.

Agnes follows Cora's gaze. A softening of her face that memory had hardened.

"Fireflies."

Cora has seen them before. They bring back the lush warmth of home—twinkling in the forests around Trelawny Town. She never thought she would see them here.

"The cold . . ." she says. Thinking of winter, the long absences of the sun. Surely these, too, are creatures that need heat; how else would they glow?

Agnes takes a moment to understand.

"Born in summer," she says. "Little worms that can't fly yet. In winter they go underground. Sleep. Come out with wings in spring."

The lights continue, winking in and out, calling to one another in the dark. Spiraling in flight, the way dust motes swirl when lit by the sun. The forest after dark a different place, holding different wonders that, stumbling here, Cora never thought to slow and see.

Agnes gets to her feet, the movement taking Cora's focus from the fireflies.

"You should sleep," she says. She sounds tired. Nods toward the wikuom. Then walks away, into the darkness, Patience loping after her.

"Where you gon' go?" Cora calls. Gets no reply. Sits a moment, as the fire dims, feeling strangely hollow, wondering if she has done something wrong. But eventually, the call of sleep is too strong. Alone, Cora crawls inside the wikuom, which is warm and smells familiar—smells like moss, dirt, dog, and Agnes. Curls up, swaddled in furs, and sleeps. Despite everything, she sleeps peacefully and dreams of nothing at all.

———

Cora wakes before the sun, head aching and mouth dry, and knows she will not return to sleep. She is too restless, needs open air.

The darkness has a soft quality to it, the promise of a coming dawn. A little moonlight falls on the surrounding forest, turning it silver. The effect might be almost ghostly, if everything did not seem so solid. Cora breathes in a sense of age, of something ancient and unchanged. This might be any time, or any place. She, indeed, might be the ghost, incorporeal witness to something that was here long before and will survive long after she is gone—tree and rock and, in the distance, sea.

Two dark shapes curled against a nearby stone. Agnes and Patience. At some point in the night, they returned, Cora realizes, but Agnes chose to sleep out here rather than come into her own wikuom. As her eyes adjust to the darkness, Cora can better see how Agnes seems smaller in sleep. Vulnerable, almost.

Agnes shifts, rolling from her side onto her back. Her lips

are slightly parted; she releases a breath that comes out as a kind of sigh. Then she is back in a deep sleep, unmoving, the expression on her face not blank exactly, but caught somewhere between an easy innocence and something darker and more painful: the hint of a frown or of suffering that disturbs her dreams.

Cora looks away. Puts a hand to her chest, where something feels tight and constricted. Feels her own heartbeat under her clothes.

She wonders if she should leave. Is still considering it as the first rays of sun peep over the tops of the trees. Has not by the time Agnes wakes, stands, stretches, and looks at Cora, her face soft but unsmiling.

"Let me show you something," she says.

15

Down by the sea, a mist blankets everything. Dew, not frost, on the ground. Cora is struck by the signs of new life—small shoots springing from the soil, buds unfurling. Somewhere in the forest will be moose calves and bear cubs stumbling after their mothers. The seasons as a cycle of death and rebirth. Cora thinks she understands more now about the people she has met here. Thursday and Agnes. Now that she has lived through winter, spring, into summer, she sees why, for all their differences, they are alike. They have a watchfulness to them. A patience. It must come from waiting for this thawing time. Waiting for warmth again.

Agnes takes Cora to a small rocky cove. The path down from the clifftop is invisible, indistinguishable from the rock face itself. Agnes and Patience descend quickly, surefooted; Cora follows slowly. Bobbing on the water, almost hidden among the rocks that protrude all around it, is a wooden boat—small, sleek, and made from birchbark.

Cora pauses.

"Oh," she says.

Agnes looks back.

"We ain't going far."

Cora looks out. Sees only mist. An eerie quiet, except for the hushed lapping of the waves on the cliffs. The sea is as calm as she has ever seen it. Where is the harm?

It is Patience who jumps first, landing in the boat with a thud. Its sides sway, already low in the water. Her ears are pricked, alert and ready. Agnes settles herself in the stern; Cora perches at the bow, where the tip of the boat curves upright, pointing to the sky, Patience in between them. Agnes pulls out an oar from the bottom of the boat.

"Ready?" she asks, with a glance at Cora.

Cora nods. She is ready.

Agnes uses the oar to push them off the rocks, and then they are out to sea. There is movement to the water, even on this windless day; the boat pitches gently, but Cora does not feel afraid. Or, rather, she has passed beyond fear and into a strange kind of acceptance—the knowledge that she is so fragile out here on the ocean, so vulnerable, that her fear will make no difference either way.

Soon they are swallowed in mist. Since they are robbed of sight, this is a world of taste—salty ocean spray—and of motion, the ceaseless roll of the sea. They move swiftly, Agnes pulling the oar with strong, practiced strokes. Cora, for a moment, closes her eyes, feels the slightest of breezes that dances through her braids.

They stop. Cora opens her eyes. The mist surrounds them;

she hardly dares breathe, for fear of disturbing the absolute quiet. Not even the gulls are calling. She has no sense of how far they have come; land, in any direction, is invisible. A few hundred feet ahead, the fog looks impenetrable as ice. It is only close to the boat, where its tendrils curl on the surface of the black water like wisps of smoke, that the solidity is revealed as an illusion.

Agnes has a dreamy look on her face as she stares out into the empty nothingness.

"What now?" Cora asks. She has only just realized that they have brought no fishing equipment.

Agnes exhales, head tilted back toward the sky.

"They'll come today. Or maybe not. But I think they will."

"Who?"

Agnes does not reply.

Patience sniffs the air, contented. Cora sits back, resting her weight on her hands, and watches a dark shape move out of the fog and settle on the water—a solitary seabird. Minutes, or hours, pass. There is no telling which.

Then—a sound like bellows on a blacksmith's fire. Agnes, who has been still and rapt in the canoe's stern, seizes the oar and starts to paddle furiously. Cora, startled by the sudden rocking of the boat as it charges through the water, grips the sides, not sure if she should be excited or afraid.

Agnes is a woman possessed, beads of sweat on her brow, tilted forward, eyes darting around in search of—

"There!"

She points, and the urgency of her tone has Cora spinning wildly to face the water—just in time to see, through the haze of fog, something as sleek and black as wet stone break the surface, shooting spray into the air. That sound again, a huff or sigh. And then it is gone, slipping out of sight.

Cora says, "What—"

But she is cut off by the roar of a whale breaking the surface.

It does not seem possible, the path it cuts through the air. Scattering spray, stark against the misted sky. The moment it hangs at the top of its arc, elegant. The curve of its fins like a dance. Breathless, Cora watches it fall, close enough to see the barnacles on its skin. Green trails of seaweed.

The whale hits the water's surface like a cannon's boom. The boat rocking underneath them. Agnes makes a noise, somewhere between a laugh and a shout. Patience answers with a bark—she is on her feet, body quivering with excitement.

Cora gasps for air. She feels tiny, smaller than a drop of water, a speck on the ocean's surface.

When Cora can breathe again, she looks at Agnes, who has spread her arms wide in exultation, her skin gleaming, wet from the spray.

Cora realizes how much she thinks of Agnes as a shadow, something creeping through the woods, wound tight and ready to pounce. Out here, she is open, bright.

They lock eyes. Agnes grins.

"I knew they'd come," she says.

They hear the noise of the blow again, a whale coming up somewhere ahead. Agnes grabs the paddle and heads in the direction of the sound, Cora leaning forward, almost over the side of the boat, desperate for another glimpse. . . .

And almost before she realizes it, they are among them. Agnes stops paddling. The boat drifts and then stills. Cora looks around. Counts five, maybe six whales. Hard to tell—their backs slide above and then below the water.

Silence except for the occasional spout from the whales, the gentle noise of the sea lapping against the side of the birchbark boat.

Cora is awestruck again, but this time in a quieter way. The whales do not leap. One turns on the surface, offering a brief view of its fin, but otherwise they remain mostly below the water—and it is these tiny glimpses, in a world already shrouded by mist, that take Cora's breath away all over again.

One by one, the whales start to dive. Cora and Agnes fix their eyes on the back of a whale that curves more sharply than before, starting off the slow descent, until finally, its tail lifts out of the water—Cora's imagination runs wild, picturing the creature underneath the surface, its face angled down, into the black depths of the ocean. Slowly, slowly, the tail sinks down out of sight. And they are alone.

The eerie sense of stillness breaks. Patience still on her feet, still excited, barks, and in one bound is on Agnes, licking her face. The sound of Agnes's laughter spreads across the water in all directions. Soon, Cora is laughing, too. The boat drifts gently across the ocean; out of sight, the whales move together, singing to one another as they go.

"They come every year," Agnes says. Eyes bright. "Just for summer. A few months, then they be gone."

"Where?" Cora asks.

"Not sure."

"Someplace warm."

"Maybe. But they always come back."

"Home," Cora says.

Agnes shakes her head. "The whole sea's their home. If they're swimming and they're together—they're home."

Agnes reaches for the oar. Her fingers brush against Cora's wrist, a ghost of a touch, barely there at all, and yet it leaves a mark. A memory. And all the way home, Cora can feel it as a kind of heat. Runs her own fingers over the point where Agnes touched her, again and again, and feels her pulse fluttering underneath the skin.

———

There are other times when Agnes has touched Cora. A hand on her shoulder as they walk. Pressing berries into her palm, encouraging her to eat what the forest can give them. Or sitting close enough to her that sometimes they brush against each other, knees and elbows.

Cora could tell you the story of every touch. She could point to each place on her body that felt it—each place holding with it the image of where they were, and the way Agnes smiled, or the small light that glinted within her eyes.

Compare this to the evening, about a month ago, when Cora was lining up to get provisions and was surprised to see Thursday there with the crates. The governor had asked Farmer Nash to send over food to the Maroons that week. Thursday offered to take it. Cora was one of the last to arrive, so it wasn't long before she and Thursday could spend a little time sitting together. It was dark already, and they sat outside and watched the stars appear in a cloudless sky.

Thursday pointed to one that shone a little brighter than the others.

"The North Star," he said.

"Studying for the ship?" Cora asked, smiling.

He shook his head. "That one I knew already. We all did."

The moon, a thin crescent of silver light. Cora grew tired. She was sitting close enough to Thursday to rest her head on his shoulder. When she did she felt . . . It was not an empty touch. It was not a touch without meaning. It was peaceful, reminding her of Leah or little Benjamin. But her skin did not burn with it.

It is only Agnes's touches that get into her dreams, mingling strangely with other memories. With Jamaica itself. She dreams of walking through hot, humid, tropical forests. Of tendrils that drape from trees, that brush her face, but then those tendrils become Agnes, and Cora feels the cool press of fingers on her cheeks.

———

On the way back to shore, Agnes's grin is still infectious, keeping Cora from thinking ahead to what must happen when she returns, the truce that must be brokered to keep the peace between Silas, Leah, and herself.

"You don' see them before," Cora says, teasing Agnes for how happy she seems.

Agnes takes this more seriously than Cora intends it, tilting her head. "But," she says eventually, "you never know if you gonna see them again."

"What you mean?"

"We only see them when they want to be seen." Agnes looks back, toward the way they have come, toward where the whales might be still, deep underwater. "Some days I come out and fish. Glimpse one once, and then it's gone. But other days, they come up to the boat. Stay with me. They're happy for me to look. So every time, it's a blessing to see them."

When they are almost back to shore, Agnes says, "The Mi'kmaq, they said there were more whales before. All over the oceans. But they're hunted. Not so many now."

She speaks without much emotion, but Cora immediately feels sick at the thought of it. Is surprised by the strength of her reaction; she has learned, with Agnes, to be less sentimental. Not to grieve animal death. Agnes does not hesitate when she draws her bow to kill a creature that might otherwise spend many years in the forest. But the whales—the whales are different. They seem too giant to be killed. And despite their scale, despite their strange anatomy, honed to a life in water rather than on land, they seem closer to humans than do the moose or deer or marmots Agnes hunts. It feels an injustice, the idea of men killing them.

Something of this anger must show in her face, because Agnes gives her an appraising look.

"What's wrong?"

Cora is piecing together all the little fragments and does not like the picture they make.

"You say before, the forest quiet once. Now too much people. And the oceans was full of whales. Now they all gone. It— not right." She wishes she had stronger words for it but fails to grasp anything more than this, the simple fact that it seems a deep unfairness to her, the way people here have wrought destruction on the world.

Agnes's smile takes a while to form—a private sign of some inner dialogue.

"What?" Cora asks.

"Just . . ." Agnes says. "The way you see things. It's different."

Cora feels self-conscious, despite Agnes's gentle, almost affectionate tone.

"Different how?"

"You care about right and wrong."

"You care, too."

"Once, I did."

They have landed. Agnes pauses to tie the boat to the rock. Only when they have climbed up almost to the edge of the trees does Agnes pick up the thread of this conversation.

"Now," she says, "things like the whales just make me sad. So I don't think of them. But you—you get angry. You can only get angry when you think something can change."

Agnes says no more. Skirting, as ever, around her history.

Once, at the beginning of spring, Cora said, "Walk back with me? To Preston?"

And Agnes said, "No. I can't."

The past like a shadow; or like the whales, as they pass underneath the boat, dark shapes deep in the water.

The Trial

January 1798

Colonel Montague James's horse steps uneasily over the snow-slicked streets of Halifax. There is a reason Nova Scotia is ox country: It rewards the plodding, the steady, those with thick hides to last the winter, when frost freezes slippery over rock and soil.

Miserable place, he thinks, casting a bored eye over the houses choked with woodsmoke, the relentless gray stone, the weather-beaten, drink-swollen faces of the passersby. A line comes to mind, one of his captains, quipping in the depths of that first, bleak winter—

The Jamaican cannot flourish where the pineapple does not.

He, Montague James, is no ox. Takes no yoke, looks down on those who do. The son and grandson of Maroons, untouched by enslavement. His scars are battle-won, not painted by any whip. But as his horse shudders beneath him—slender legs, breakable, one snap of bone, then rendered useless—he reflects that he is no horse either. During the war, before their banishment, he climbed a tree to get a better look at the British encampment; the branch gave way beneath him, a bad fall, left arm broken, shard of bone piercing the skin. He bit down on the leather of his musket strap as he realigned the arm himself, binding a stick to it to keep it straight, straining to keep silent so as not to give their position away.

Beside him rides the governor; Montague James is long used to tuning out the inane stream of his patter on everything from the weather to the state of the farms around Preston and the governor's plans for elegant new arboreal plantings on his various estates. They are on their way to the Citadel, the new fortifications finally finished with help from Montague James's men. The governor has grand plans now for integrating a Maroon platoon into the militia, commissioning new uniforms in their honor, blue wool with a gleaming silver button, carved with the emblem of a crocodile.

A crocodile, Montague James thinks with a small, private smile as they pick their way through the thickening crowds on George Street. A patient predator, able to drift out of sight just below the line of the water, camouflaged perfectly in muddy depths. Now, there is a creature with which he has some affinity.

The governor slows his horse from a trot to a walk as they pass the county courthouse, his eyes falling on a carriage stopped out front.

"That must be . . . Ah, yes. Matthews!" he calls out across the road.

The man who has just emerged from the carriage gives a shallow bow of greeting to the governor. His dress and bearing work to create opposite impressions: the somber robes of a judge combined with the bulk and ruddy complexion of a farmer. This man, Matthews, looks up at Montague James, and it is clear from the slight drawing together of his brows that he is surprised to see a Black man on horseback. Not the first such glance Montague James has attracted here, where most of the people pitched up from American plantations. But this man, at least, has the decency to hide his surprise quickly with a smile.

Montague James and the governor dismount. Brief introductions are made, the governor smooth and quick with social pleasantries. It is the one skill in him Montague James acknowledges, the root of his authority: the soft power of clasped hands in dining rooms at dusk and agreements made in a haze of cigar smoke. It is not Montague James's way of governing his own people, but it works for Wentworth. Matthews leans congenially toward the governor as the two men trade a few bits of gossip, dinners attended, notable men embroiled in scandal or exalted in triumph. Montague James listens in silence. His is the authority of sparing words, a straight-backed stance, calloused hands that fit easily around the barrel of a musket.

Uninterested in the governor and judge's exchange, Montague James's mind wanders, as it often does, back to Jamaica. Being in front of the courthouse stirs the memory of a meeting, all the captains gathered together in Trelawny Town, the practical business of arranging a deputation to Kingston dealt with, such that the conversation could move to more philosophical matters. At this time, the war that would force them off their land and back into the mountains was many years in the future.

The issue they discussed that night, as the sun set and the darkness outside filled with the chatter of cicadas, was where their freedom came from. Montague James recalls how two men were arguing over the issue of the death penalty—in those days, the Maroons administered all aspects of justice themselves, save for executions. It was different in the old days, in the days before the treaty with the British, when Cudjoe, their leader, could kill any man who stepped out of line. And so, one captain said, as the talk grew heated, this proved that their present freedom was an illusion, built on sand. They were not truly free for as long as they lacked the old privileges, the old mastery over death.

The other man disagreed. No, he said, freedom was not an illusion. Their freedom was built on swords and guns. Look, he said, at the slaves. They wear no military uniforms, and they carry no weapons. Yet the Maroons do. And that is how we are free. We share in the military might of Jamaica, and in the military might of King George.

The colonel's recollections are interrupted by Wentworth and Matthews's conversation drawing to a close.

"Must be getting on for the morning session," Matthews says.

"Can't leave the thieves and drunkards waiting," the governor quips. "Which unfortunate gentleman will you be sending to the jail today?"

Matthews is already off, long strides across the street, but he glances back to throw a reply over his shoulder.

"Young lady, in fact. Negro."

His eyes falling on Montague James on the last word.

Montague James lets his gaze linger on the judge's retreating back, long enough that Governor Wentworth takes notice.

"One of yours in there, Colonel?"

Montague James shakes his head. A Maroon in court?

Impossible. He would know. It would be his business to know. But there was something in that last glance. . . .

He blinks, the spell breaks, and he turns away, ready to remount. Perhaps he is still unused to being seen by some as one and the same as the other Negroes of this place, by ignorant people who can't read the caliber of his warrior's lineage in his bearing.

His horse follows the governor's. They continue on past the jailhouse, and the colonel returns to that old conversation on the nature of freedom.

Montague James did not speak at the time, as this debate unfolded between his captains. He was then, as now, a man of few words. But if he had been called on to speak, he would have said something like: This was an argument built on a false premise—the distinction between free and unfree. It is the greatest swindle of history that the white man ever convinced us that we were not free. We have always been so, even when we were in chains. There is a core of us that will never be taken or subdued. The Maroons are simply the ones who realized the truth of this. The enslaved, the unenlightened, are those who still live inside the lie.

Power. That is the heart of it all. That, to him, is the more interesting question. Freedom is an abstraction, beside the point. In the end, they are all free. It is power that is differentially distributed. Power is something one can hold—that has a texture, almost a taste. The governor has it. The king, somewhere across the ocean, has even more of it. Montague James has spent his life cultivating it, as lovingly as he would a garden. And now, among his men, his orders are followed without exception. Now, when he sets his mind to something—such as leaving this place and finding somewhere warmer—he feels he cannot lose. Give him power over freedom, any day. That is the way to make your mark on the world.

———

When the governor and Montague James reach the top of the street, the colonel does not look back. If he had, he might have checked his horse. Might have ridden back toward the courthouse, suddenly interested in what was going on within its walls. Because, despite his certainty that there could be nothing there of his concern—there is a woman, *one of his*, waiting outside, looking as if she is working up the courage to go in.

SUMMER

1797

16

Cora arrives one afternoon to find Agnes weaving a basket. She realizes she has never seen Agnes make something that is not functional before—stone tools, bone awls, snowshoes for winter. Cora thinks that everything Agnes makes is beautiful, in its way, a sparse beauty that comes from being no more and no less than it needs to be, an object perfectly molded to its purpose. But this basket has beauty of a different order, the rushes woven into a complex pattern of swirls that look like flowers.

Agnes glances up and sees Cora. She almost smiles—a brightening of her eyes, though her mouth remains still. The usually sharp angles of her face softened by the sun.

The year has thrown itself full-throatedly into summer. The world is green—leaves covering the birches, the maples, and the beech trees, coloring the light. Back in Preston, the night that Cora spent out in the woods has never been spoken of since. One wrong exchanged for another, she supposes. Each of them—she and Leah and Silas—carrying their private hurts.

It pushes Cora more and more back out here with Agnes, as if she is daring Silas to challenge her again. She does not know how long their fragile truce will hold.

Cora is surprised how easy it is to forget the cold. Yes, there is still a chill at night—a chill brought in by winds off the sea. But she cannot remember how it felt to be really freezing. To stand barefoot in snow. To lose all sensation in her fingers. To feel robbed of breath by the cold. To understand how easy it would be to die—that was the cold that was with them all winter, and now she cannot recapture it.

She sits opposite Agnes. Patience, who has been circling the wikuom, nose to the ground, lopes over to say hello.

Three things happen so close together that they seem instantaneous. Agnes opens her mouth to speak. The thought arrives in Cora's mind, fully formed, that this will be the moment that Agnes really reveals something of herself, the secret of her past. And Patience, who is still pressed against Cora, gratefully receiving a scratch behind the ears, suddenly stiffens.

Whatever Agnes was going to say, it is cut off by Patience barking. One soft bark at first, a warning. Then, louder and more insistent.

Agnes is on her feet. Terror in her face. Cora, too, scrambles up, heart pounding.

Patience's barking trails off into a growl as she keeps herself between Agnes and whatever it is she has seen in the forest.

Then, from the shadows, over the sound of Patience, a soft, uncertain voice.

"Cora?"

Cora recognizes it, with a gasp.

"Benjamin?"

Her fear shifting abruptly—fear for Agnes becoming fear for the lonely little form she can make out a few feet away, almost hidden by branches.

"Benjamin!"

Cora runs to him, gathers him in her arms. She turns, still holding him close, and sees Agnes, standing frozen, trembling. Patience still growling, a low, mean sound. Through the thin cotton of her shirt, Cora can feel the fluttering of little Benjamin's heart.

Cora starts and fails to finish three sentences in quick succession, unsure of whom she should address first.

"He— You— Me—"

Cora senses more than sees some tensing of Agnes's limbs, preparation for flight.

"Wait!" she cries.

Releases Benjamin, straightens up, but keeps a hand on his head, her fingers nestled among his dark curls.

"Agnes," she says. In the slow, placating voice used with a frightened animal. "Please."

Agnes turns but does not go. In hiding her face it is as if she hides her whole self—Cora does not know, cannot know, what Agnes is thinking.

From beside Cora, little Benjamin speaks, barely a whisper.

"Me see you go," he says. A tremor in his voice, though his eyes are dry and fixed on Agnes. "Me see you go be with Mama."

Cora's heart does not quite break, but it does crack—she feels the pain of it in her chest. She picks him up, his familiar weight, balances him on her hip. She walks toward Agnes—as if she might be able to bring them together. She can rescue this, keep the fissure in her heart from yawning open, breaking her in two.

"Agnes," she says again.

Patience still stands between them. Watchful but no longer growling. Cora pauses, not wanting to come closer. Something in both of them—Patience and Agnes—and the way they are holding themselves keeps her back.

Finally, Agnes looks back at Cora. Fear and hurt and anger chase one another across her face before she pulls it into a blank mask.

"Agnes," says Cora. "This is Benjamin."

"Not Mama?" Benjamin asks. Cora feels the warmth of his breath on her cheek. It is a marvel that he is so calm—that he speaks with genuine curiosity, and without a trace of fear. The tremor in his voice is gone.

Agnes looks from Cora to Benjamin. Something softens in her face.

"No," she says. "Not your mama."

Cora releases a breath.

"This is my friend," she says to Benjamin.

Patience has taken a step forward, sniffing the air.

"And this," she says, "is her dog."

Benjamin seems more unsure of Patience than he does of Agnes. He huddles into Cora, keeping himself away from the dog's nose as she tries to investigate. On Agnes's face, there is something close to a smile as she watches little Benjamin, the quick brave face he tries to make as Patience pushes against his foot, and the nervous laugh he makes when Patience licks the bare skin of his ankle.

Cora catches Agnes's eye. They communicate briefly and

wordlessly, and Cora is flooded with relief. Agnes will not flee. The wikuom will still be here tomorrow, and the day after, Cora is sure of it. There is something tethering Agnes now—not a tight binding but a loose thread that will keep her where Cora can find her. There is too much between them. Afternoons on the water, chasing the whales. Evenings in the forest spreading out the bounty of a day's foraging—mushrooms, elderberries, glasswort gathered from the shore. Whole days of wandering with Patience by their side, saying little, no need for words, sharing the sights, sounds, and smells of this place—noticing how they change with the seasons as frost melts and spring buds cover the trees and then summer brings heat and an abundance of sunlight. Too much to give up, if Agnes hides again.

"Come, we gon' get you home," Cora says to little Benjamin, speaking softly.

He looks back at her, wide-eyed. Over the winter, his face has lost a little of its childish roundness. It is narrower now, with clear cheekbones and a sharper chin. Elsy's face, Cora realizes with a pang—the grief buried deeper these days, but it will never truly leave her.

She keeps him on her hip and they start to walk away, back in the direction of Preston. Cora does not say anything more to Agnes. She knows she doesn't have to. Instead, as little Benjamin rests his head on her shoulder, she whispers to him.

"The others, them don't know," she says. "About my friend. Me keep her secret because she . . ." She pauses, not wanting to lie to him, but not having any real truth that she can share. "Because she shy. One day she gon' meet them. But we can't tell them 'til she ready."

They walk on. The shadows lengthen; on the edge of twilight, the forest is quiet and strangely still.

———

Cora returns to Agnes with a strange fear. Strange because she is so certain that Agnes will be there, as she always is. That she will crest the little hill, round the three large, jagged rocks that stand like sentinels, guarding the clearing in which Agnes has built her summer wikuom, and there Agnes will be. Whittling or carving or sewing—doing something with her hands, fingers that look too slender to be as strong as they are. But the fear comes from this certainty, because if she was unsure, if she held in her mind an image of Agnes both there and not there, it would be easier to round the corner and take whatever she saw. The impossibility of Agnes vanishing, slipping off to some remote corner of the province, never to be found, is so great that it will shatter Cora's world if it proves to have happened after all.

She rounds the corner. Agnes is there—but she is still. Unoccupied. Staring out, face angled upward. Patience sits by her side.

Cora goes to stand beside Agnes. Looks up, too, sharing what Agnes sees. The sky, streaked with white, the treetops that reach upward, as though brushing up against the clouds is their goal. The forest in full green; like the cold, it is easy to forget the way the branches look when barren, when only the pines and firs show signs of life. When the birches stand forlorn, frost covered, waiting for spring.

"Me can explain?" Cora asks. Agnes does not seem angry or afraid. But Cora knows how fragile it all was, the way they existed with no intruders these past few months. Worries more has been broken than just their solitude.

Agnes says nothing. Cora continues—

"Him name Benjamin. Me did know his mama. . . ."

A moment of silence.

"She gone?" Agnes asks.

"Yes."

And little by little, she explains. She does not say Silas's name, focuses instead on Elsy. Finds there are tears in her eyes as she struggles to name it—the way she felt about her. That they were close as sisters. That loving Benjamin started as loving the last thing of Elsy that was left. But that it has grown because Benjamin is his own person, an extraordinary entire being, and it was only when Cora was able to understand this that she was able, not to let the grief go, but to grow around it, like the memory of Elsy has become a piece of lung or heart—living, fed with her own blood, the scar where it was conjoined to the rest of her fading with time.

Cora talks and talks. She keeps her face to the sky, where the clouds arrange themselves into new shapes, into impressions of her memory. The silhouette of Elsy in profile, or the shape of the village in Jamaica, as if seen from above. At one point, Cora is certain that the clouds become a staircase or a ladder—they give some sense of a pathway to a world beyond. Cora has no idea of where we go when we die, but in that moment she is certain that Elsy is there, just behind the curtain of the sky—that she might reach up and pull back the blue that hangs over the heavens like soft silk and there Elsy will be, unchanged.

When Cora finishes speaking—when her words trail off to

nothing and her stories are spent—she glances at Agnes. Expecting that she, too, will all this time have been looking upward. But Agnes is watching Cora intently, face so open and unguarded that Cora has, for a moment, to turn away.

Like the ebbing of a tide, Cora feels her stronger emotions fade. Grief, passion, and a tight nausea caused by something unnameable but felt just as strongly all the same. These all leave her, little by little, until she is left with only the aftermath of them, a sort of echo; the vibration of them within her as a bowstring, drawn back and then released, will continue to thrum quietly long after the arrow is gone.

Instead, she feels at peace. Without looking, she can sense Agnes beside her, and the proximity gives her comfort. This is the wonder of Agnes—that she can cause, in Cora, such turbulence, such strength of feeling. But these are only passing storms; underneath, there is calm. There is an ease that Cora has not known for a long time.

Agnes touches Cora: fingertip against her wrist. Then draws away. It is enough. Cora turns, smiles. Agnes looks serious. Has a way of drawing her lower lip inward when she is thinking, thinning out her mouth.

"Bring him by," Agnes says.

17

Cora waits a few days. She has to be sure of little Benjamin's silence. It is not a question of trust—he has neither guile nor malice in him. But he is so young. He might, even without meaning to, give away the secret of Agnes.

Observing him around the village of Preston, Cora is re-minded of how quiet he is. How solitary. When she is busy with work in the garden or in the house, he keeps to himself. Can sit for hours, moving sticks around in complicated patterns on the ground, creating an imaginary world known only to himself. He has few friends his own age. And though, when Silas is home, Benjamin does stray close to his father from time to time, the two do not speak. Silas will absently place a hand on Benjamin's shoulder, as Benjamin stands next to him like a shadow, a copy of Silas made in miniature, until he moves, and from a new angle it is all Elsy in the shape of his mournful eyes. Silas shows no interest in asking about Benjamin's day, or how he has spent his time. Benjamin does not volunteer to say. And so, by the time Cora takes Benjamin off to meet Agnes again, she trusts the secret will be safe.

They make a game, on their walk, of naming the trees. Agnes has taught Cora, and now she is filled with a sense that this is knowledge she should pass on. She points for little Benjamin, teaches him the unfamiliar words. Ash, beech, maple, spruce. She reaches up and pulls leaves from the lowest branches so that he can compare their shapes, holding them up to the light. Cora's favorite is the oak leaf, formed like some animal has taken soft bites from each side. Benjamin likes the beech leaf—at first glance, a simple, rounded shape, but look closer and you see the tiny points, like little spikes, that surround it.

When they reach the clearing and the wikuom, Benjamin comes over a little shyly. Agnes seems shy, too. Both hang back, leaving Cora hovering between them, until little Benjamin comes forward and, unclasping his hand, shows Agnes his beech leaf.

Agnes takes the proffered gift.

"Thank you," she says. Strangely solemn. Cora cannot help but laugh—and when Agnes catches her eye, she laughs, too. Little Benjamin joins them, not because he understands but simply because he can, and together their laughter fills the forest. Cora is glad that Agnes does not flinch—no shadow crosses her face—at the idea that the noise will carry. Cora likes to think that, little by little, Agnes has become less guarded, less fearful of discovery.

Agnes takes them to the shore, not to the cove with the boat, but a little farther along, to a sandy beach. It is a sunny, blue-skied day. Some of the grains of sand seem to be made of silver; when they catch the light, the whole beach shimmers.

Cora races little Benjamin to the sea. Head down, arms pumping furiously, he is determined, and she lets him think he will win until, with a final burst of speed, she catches him. Lifting him up, laughing, she holds him tight and throws herself forward, sending them both into the water. When they emerge, spluttering, rubbing salt from their eyes, they find that Patience has bounded in after them, paddling around happily with her tongue lolling from her mouth. Only Agnes stays on land, watching, shielding her eyes from the sun.

The day moves toward noon. Benjamin is full of joy, dancing in and out of the waves with Patience at his heels. Cora sits on the beach with Agnes, letting the sun dry out her wet clothes. She watches him, feeling easy and content. Wriggles her toes, burrowing them deeper into the sand. Sees, for the first time, a path to the future—a narrow shaft of light, like a sunbeam, shining on where she will go. A future that is not made of memories, not Jamaica, which every day becomes more an idea than a place she can see, smell, feel. A future here. In this land.

But then again, maybe it's the summer talking. Everything seems brighter when the days are long and the ground underfoot is soft and warm.

"Sometimes," Cora says to Agnes, "is like me can remember my mother. It not possible. But still, me can."

Agnes's arms are bare, dark skin gleaming in the sunshine all the way up to the curve of her shoulders. Thin, sinewy arms; but Cora knows they are strong.

"I must remember Ma," Agnes says slowly. "I mean, I do. She ain't so long gone. But sometimes . . . it's like I don't remember."

Farther along the beach, little Benjamin has made a game of jumping through the waves. He waits until one reaches its highest point, when the upright water grows translucent, then dives through to the other side. Sometimes, he waits too long, and the wave crashes over his head, and he emerges a few moments later from the white foam, giggling.

"What she was like? Your ma?" Cora asks.

Agnes takes her time to answer. Tracing patterns in the sand with one finger, then, abruptly, bringing her hand across the surface with force, erasing what she has drawn.

"Strong," says Agnes. "Kind."

Agitation flickers across her face. It must have been the wrong question to ask.

"There ain't the words," Agnes says. "For all she was."

They fall silent. Listening to the sound of little Benjamin's laughter, Patience's answering bark. Despite Agnes's reticence, Cora feels loose, talkative. The barrier between her thoughts and her spoken words worn thin. So, as she watches Benjamin and Patience in the water, Cora speaks again.

"You gon' have children one day?"

Agnes looks at her.

"No," she says. "You?"

"Maybe."

"With who?"

A prickliness to Agnes's question.

"Don't know."

Agnes moves suddenly, turning onto her stomach, spreading herself over the sand. Mercurial as ever, her face shifts; mouth twitches upward. Her eyes are bright.

"Sweet boy," Agnes says. Even though she is facing away from Benjamin, toward the forest.

"Yes," says Cora.

"You care 'bout him." Looking at Cora as if it's a question, though her intonation does not make it one.

Benjamin is back on land. He has, after some cajoling, made Patience lie down, and is now digging with his hands, flinging sand over her legs and tail to bury her. The sand is wet; when Patience moves, as she does often, it cracks like parched earth in drought, chunks of it falling away, but this doesn't seem to bother Benjamin. Round and round he goes, piling the sand up again, the futility of it oddly touching.

"Yes," Cora says.

"And his ma. You cared 'bout her, too."

They lock eyes, Cora and Agnes. The sunlight brings out different colors in Agnes's—flecks of gold and green.

"Yes," says Cora.

They do not look away from each other for what seems a long time. Agnes shifts her position, pushing herself up onto her knees. Stretching her arms up to the sky—the movement, like so many of her movements, both loose and fluid and intensely controlled. Agnes moves like someone who is aware of and can manipulate every individual muscle in her body at will.

"Cora," Agnes says suddenly. The syllables sound strange. Cora realizes how little they say each other's names. When it is just the two of them, there is no need—they just speak and know the other is listening.

"I don't say it," Agnes says. "I don't know . . . I don't always know how. But I'm glad. That you found me."

The sun is shining behind Agnes, so she is framed entirely by light. And Cora feels as though everything they have said to each other has had a double meaning that remains just out of reach.

"Me glad, too," Cora says.

On the sand, little Benjamin has quietly finished burying Patience. He steps back to survey his work, pleased. Patience, for a moment, holds very still. Then she rises, shaking off the sand, and makes a loping dash for the waves.

18

They are walking back from the beach. Usually, Agnes would peel away to her clearing, leaving Cora to make the journey alone. Today, Agnes comes with her. Every step closer to Preston is a step closer to whatever horror Agnes must imagine will befall her if she gets too near to the village, but under this warm summer sun, past secrets and present dangers seem so far away.

Benjamin and Patience run ahead. They have taken to each other; Cora is pleased. Thinks there is a wonderful symmetry here, child and dog playing together, full of energy and life, while she and Agnes walk behind. They pass through a patch of light, a gap in the trees—their shadows stretch out in front of them, long-limbed, seemingly holding hands.

They come to a forked path. Agnes pauses, and Cora knows without needing to be told that this is as far as Agnes will go.

Cora waits. For what, exactly, she cannot say. They do not usually say goodbye. Often do not even plan their next meeting.

But now Agnes seems on the verge of speech. The moment is charged with possibility; crickets chirping produce a background hum that seems more vibration than noise, moving the very air itself.

Cora finds her eyes drawn to strange, small details, as if she is unable to fit all of Agnes in her mind. She notices the size and shape of Agnes's wrists. Notices her eyelashes, her fingernails, a tiny strip of skin that has been peeled away from her lip, revealing something raw underneath.

It strikes Cora, quite suddenly, that Agnes is beautiful, though hers is not the beauty of a painting or a sculpture or the kind of women Cora has seen that hold themselves with poise and grace, wanting to be looked at. It is beauty in motion, beauty that shimmers in and out of focus, that is breathtaking one moment and humble and ordinary the next.

Cora feels something gentle brush her cheek. Sees, in the corner of her vision, a tiny whirring of yellow and black.

"Oh," says Agnes. "A butterfly."

Her voice is soft—so soft it might threaten to melt away into the forest around them. But Cora hears: hears Agnes and hears the noise of her own heartbeat.

Agnes leans toward her. Only inches now separate their faces. She brings her finger slowly to Cora's cheek. Pulls it away, and on her finger is the butterfly. Such a small, delicate thing, its wings quivering in the breeze.

Agnes's eyes flick up from the butterfly to find Cora's. Their faces are still so close. Cora finds she is calm and exhilarated all at once—like standing on the verge of a great height, the moment before the fall. She has never been so aware of distance, of her own body. Of the way she would need to move, the muscles she would need to call on, to close the gap between them . . .

A scream. Cora jerks back. Agnes spins around—quick, practiced ears turn her to the source of the sound.

"Benjamin!" Cora cries out into the forest.

No reply. Then they hear Patience, close enough but hidden somewhere in the trees. An awful, haunting howl.

Agnes runs. Cora, rooted to the spot, does not move straightaway. It is only when Agnes is almost out of sight that she finally snaps out of her frozen horror, begins to stumble after her. Arm raised in front of her face to shield herself from the branches, but unable to stop them from tearing at her skin.

Cora sees Patience first. Standing at the foot of an old oak tree, the kind so wide it must be hundreds of years old. Feels sick—feels a bottomless pit of dread opening beneath her. Benjamin nowhere to be seen.

When Agnes drops to her knees, Cora doesn't understand. It's only when Agnes says—

"Still breathing."

Then Cora can grasp it. Her mind can finally resolve the crumpled shape on the ground, the dark heap.

Suddenly Cora is all action. Indecision has gone. She runs to Benjamin's side. Stares up, through the leaves of the tree; notices where a branch has broken, a little way up. He must have been climbing.

She puts a finger to his forehead, to a gash oozing blood. So much blood. Her hands shake. She tries to wipe the blood away as best she can, but it's no good. It keeps coming.

His eyes are closed.

His chest rises and falls. The breaths shallow—too shallow. Agnes's hand still resting there. Bent over the body, Agnes and Cora do not see the approaching figure or hear its footsteps, until the snap of a twig sounds so close that Cora thinks she has broken it herself. But Agnes whips around immediately—a movement Cora has seen in deer, at the moment they hear Agnes's arrow loosed from her bow.

"Cora?"

Cora turns, too.

Thursday. Cora's dull shock immediately gives way to relief.

"I heard the scream from the road."

Behind him, through the trees, are the marks of the human world—a road, beyond it a fence. They have strayed closer to Preston than Cora, and probably Agnes, realized.

Thursday looks down at little Benjamin. "Is he . . . ?"

"We need to get him home," says Cora. "Now." Her voice firm and clear, as if by sheer force of will she can keep Benjamin from . . . She does not even let her mind form the idea. Will not even glimpse the barest outlines of it. Impossible.

Thursday moves immediately, gathering little Benjamin in his arms. Gentle, in spite of his strength. One hand held underneath Benjamin's head, almost the same size as his skull, preventing it from lolling backward.

Then Thursday looks—beyond Cora.

Cora had almost forgotten. She turns in time to see the stunned expression on Agnes's face—Agnes, who has been backing slowly into the trees, hands outstretched as if in supplication or self-defense.

For a moment, all three stand suspended in time, unmoving—

Thursday, holding Benjamin; Cora, hands wet with blood; and Agnes, face filled with horror.

Agnes turns and flees. Patience at her side—both little more than a streak in the shadows, disappearing sooner than seems possible.

The sight causes Cora no pain and no indecision. She is moving, too—in the opposite direction, toward Preston. And Thursday is there, by her side. Half running; both of them soon breathing hard, not speaking, Cora trying to build a map in her head of the path in front of them. Imagining the distance. How many miles? The forest takes on a horrible sameness—she does not lose their direction, knows they must head toward the setting sun, but she does lose any sense of where they are on the journey.

They might have been walking for minutes or hours, Cora does not know. There is nothing except the path, half-hidden by the undergrowth, and the tiny, quivering movements of little Benjamin's chest.

————

Cora thinks

Let me die. If that is what it take. Please.

Thinks

Is this because of Agnes? Because me lean close to her like me want to . . . ?

Thinks

Elsy. Me make you a promise to take care of him, and now it break.

Her mind cycles through these three thoughts until they become one incoherent mess of transgression and punishment, with Elsy sitting as some kind of divine force in judgment over it all.

Cora does not speak or cry until they reach the edge of the village.

Then she sobs. She falls to her knees, overcome, unable to continue—but Thursday, with one arm, pulls her to her feet again, and she must stumble on, one hand clutching his shirt, blinded by tears and hardly able to breathe.

The only person home is Silas. He is at the table in the center of the room. He stands when they enter—Cora first, then Thursday. Looks between them and then, comprehension dawning, looks at the body of his son in Thursday's arms.

Under different circumstances, Cora would be afraid of him. Would be afraid that the shock on his face would surely, at any moment, give way to rage. But now she just says—

"Doctor. Him need a doctor."

And it must be the soldier in Silas that responds to her voice, responds to the urgency. Because without another word, he turns and runs out into the twilight—toward Maroon Hall, to where the white doctor lives, the one the governor has provided them.

There are a few plates and cups on the table. Cora sweeps them off, not caring when they fall, not hearing the sound of them cracking. Thursday lays Benjamin down on the wooden surface—but pauses, his hand still underneath Benjamin's head. Looks to Cora.

"Something soft," Thursday murmurs.

Cora runs to the bedroom, to her own bed, and takes the

blanket. She folds it over until it is thick enough to spare Benjamin's little head the hardness of the table.

When they have rested him down, Thursday takes a step back, but Cora stays close. The wound on Benjamin's forehead is still seeping, blood trickling down into the corners of his eyes. Cora takes the edge of her own skirt and starts to gently wipe it away.

The desperate prayer that accompanied them all the way home has become just a single word—

Please.

"Dark," she says suddenly. It's true—the light has faded, leaving the hut dim and colorless. "Too dark. The doctor—him gon' need—"

She is up and moving, cannot bear to stay still. She gathers all the candles she can find and lays them on the table, encircling little Benjamin with them. She lights them with shaking hands, fierce concentration on her face. When it is done, she steps back. A moment of silence, the candles casting dancing shadows across the room.

"No, no, no," she says—her voice coming out as a low moan. Then, louder—"No."

It looks like something you would do for the dead. She has a dim memory of Quaco, Leah's husband—of sitting up at night, the body lit by candles.

In an angry swipe, Cora knocks all the candles she can reach off the table. Some extinguish as they fall, but a couple land still lit on the mud floor. Thursday, who has watched her in silence, leaps forward, jumping on the tiny flames before they can catch.

"Cora," he says. "Stop."

And he is holding her now, strong arms keeping her still—but keeping still means facing what has happened, and that is more than she can bear. She struggles to free herself, springs back, and stares at him with wild eyes. His hands, briefly, stay raised, holding on to the memory of her. Then they fall to his sides. He looks away.

Silas comes with the doctor. There are others, too, waiting outside—Cora hears the murmur of their voices, but she doesn't care.

The doctor is an old and stooped white man with a straggly, graying beard. As Cora watches him bend over Benjamin, she feels a mix of desperate gratitude and burning hatred so intense she fears she might faint. He is at once their deliverance and an outsider, one whose very presence she is suddenly convinced will bring death. . . .

The air in the room feels too thick to breathe. They wait for his judgment.

"A nasty cut," the doctor says, "but no lasting damage, I think. When he wakes up, you'll see for certain. But to my mind, the boy will be fine."

A sob catches in Cora's throat. Thursday moves to her side, hand under her elbow to keep her upright as she sways but does not fall.

Silas gives a tight nod.

"Thank you, Doctor," he says.

The doctor leaves. Silas turns his gaze on Cora, face etched with fury.

"You—" he begins, his voice low and deadly. But gets no further. Leah comes rushing in.

"Me was fetching water," she says. "Me hear— Me see the doctor."

For a moment, the room's insidious stillness—the calm before the storm—is shattered. Leah all activity, rushing to Benjamin's side. But then she slows. Must feel a little of what has been and what is to come—looks from Silas to Cora.

When Silas finally speaks, it is to Leah, not Cora.

"Me was always against it," he says. There is a strange flatness to his voice in anger, but that only makes it all the more terrifying. Cora still leans heavily on Thursday's arm.

"Silas—" Leah says. Cora barely sees Leah, all her attention focused on Silas. If she had looked, she would have seen a growing fear on her adoptive mother's face.

"It was wrong," Silas continues. His voice increasing a little in volume. You can hear in it the undertone of command; it carries a sense of battle, of leading soldiers into the charge. "It was always wrong we keep she."

Finally, he glances at Cora—a glance full of pure hatred that sends Cora reeling.

"She don't belong."

He takes a step toward the table, toward little Benjamin. He looks at his son, and the love that comes into his expression does not temper the hatred, but seems to enhance it, his face twisting into something appalling, something monstrous.

"Look what she do."

Cora finally finds her voice.

"The doctor say he gon'—"

Silas turns with frightening speed. Something within him has snapped. Nothing holding him back now. No restraint.

"After we protect you," he says. Still not raising his voice to a shout—but every word precise. Tonight, he must be sober, or clearheaded enough to lay aside the effects of the rum. His anger is sharp as a bayonet.

"We take you in—*she* take you in." Here he points to Leah.

"Silas," Leah says. "Enough."

Her words have no effect.

"She take you in and it was wrong and it bring us nothing but pain. Your mother—"

"Silas."

Leah has grabbed Silas's arm, finally silencing him. They stand opposite one another, the four of them, as if before a mirror—Cora still leaning against Thursday, and now Leah keeping a tight hold of Silas.

"Enough," Leah says again.

Cora looks from one to the other. Feeling cold—the mention of her mother bringing a sense of dread, of absence. Of a hole at the heart of things, something that cannot be looked at head-on, like a spirit whose eyes will curse you if you look into them.

"My mother?" she says.

Silas tugs himself free of Leah's grasp. He moves forward, his eyes now flicking to Thursday.

"We should have known," Silas says. "Out there, running around with her own kind, and *my son*—" He breaks off abruptly, looks off to one side. Pain and love and fear and grief rolled into one formless mass in him, too strong to be contained.

Beside her, Cora feels Thursday draw up a little taller, though he is already several inches above Silas, his head almost brushing the low ceiling of their hut.

"I'm free, sir," he says. "Same as you."

"What about my mother?" Cora says. Her face feels hot and her heart is racing and in the corners of her vision there is something dark lurking, gathering storm clouds, and she cannot bear the waiting any longer.

Silas gives a low, mirthless laugh.

"You should have tell her," he says to Leah. He has yet to address a word to Cora directly, and this only makes her more furious.

Cora drops Thursday's arm. Able to support herself now, her anger holding her upright.

"Don't talk about my mother," she says. Hands balling into fists.

Silas laughs again, the same chilling sound. "But, Cora," he says, "you don't want to *know*? You don't want to know what Leah—"

Leah has been standing frozen to the spot, her expression like that of a trapped animal. Finally, she seems to come to life again. She moves quickly—but Silas is quicker, grabbing her wrist as her hand swings through the air, catching it inches from his own face, before the blow lands. Leah wrenches her arm free and Cora finds herself between them, snarling, "Don't you touch her."

The room is still. Candle flames dancing. No one sees—no one thinks to look—but little Benjamin has opened his eyes. Quiet, he watches them—his father breathing hard, one hand at his waist where his musket would be, grasping for the weapon that is not there. Cora, made bigger by rage. Behind her, Leah—who has her own anger, too, but it is less visible; it has been kept buried deep so long her body has been shaped around it, keeping it out of sight. And Thursday, who has backed close to the wall, caught between fighting and fleeing, his eyes on Cora.

It is Silas who speaks first.

"If you not gon' tell her . . ." he says. Looking over Cora's shoulder.

Cora is ready to explode, feels a roaring in her ears. It takes every shred of resolve to grind out, through gritted teeth—

"Tell me what."

Silas does not so much smile as pull his lips back to reveal his teeth.

"That all this time, she lie to you. About your mother."

There are not many things Silas could have said that would have made Cora turn away from him, but this is one of them. Cora looks at Leah—needs to see on her face that Silas is lying, is mad. . . .

The face that looks back at Cora is like Leah's but not—a cruel imitation. It has Leah's nose, eyes, lips. But it is cold and set hard, and the mouth curves upward, as if on the verge of a smile.

"What . . . ?" says Cora.

The woman who looks like Leah but cannot be Leah takes a breath.

"Well," she says. No tremor to her voice. No hesitation. "Perhaps it is time you know."

The room falls away, leaving only the two of them. And there is one wild moment when Cora believes the lie is this: that all along Leah has been her mother.

"Leah?" she says softly.

When Leah speaks, it is clipped and precise.

"Your mother was not a Maroon. She was a runaway."

Cora frowns, then almost smiles. Feels something close to relief. This is all? The big lie? It changes nothing. If anything, it gives everything an easier symmetry. Her mother was like Leah—born a slave. No wonder Leah stepped up to take in her daughter, when the time came.

The relief must show in Cora's face, the fact that this does not hurt as much as expected—and if it does not hurt she does not truly understand. For the first time, Leah wavers. A vulnerability in her face. Then, quickly, the steel returns.

"Not a Maroon," Leah says again. "She never . . . She never live in Trelawny Town."

Cora blinks. Gathers her memories—not memories really, but the things she has imagined—about her mother. A woman, kneeling, alone in the forest. Crying, in pain. She is giving birth and she is afraid. But then, there, in the shadows, is Leah—emerging cautiously, but seeing immediately what is wrong. Going down in the dirt beside Cora's mother, a hand on her shoulder . . .

"You mean she die," Cora says. No question in her voice. The picture in her mind sharpens, growing so clear it cannot be anything but the truth. "She die before you get her to the village."

This time, Leah shows no uncertainty.

"No," she says. "She was a runaway. She never come to the village."

The picture—of Cora's mother and Leah, together in the forest—shimmers, as if it has been submerged in water, but does not disappear. Not yet.

"Me don't understand," Cora says slowly.

From behind her—from empty darkness, because the hut does not exist, not really—Silas makes a scoffing noise. He sounds distant, almost too far away for Cora to care.

"Yes," he says. To Cora's ears, his voice is no louder than a murmur. "You do. You know."

Cora is shaking her head. The smile of relief is still fixed to her face; it cannot be dislodged.

"She die before you take her to the village," Cora repeats, as if these words can keep the truth where it is. "She die, but you take me."

She dimly hears Silas again. "She was a runaway. Leah take her back where she belong."

Cora turns slowly. As if seeing through fog, but the outline of Silas is there and anger has her in its grip again because this is a lie.

"No," Cora snaps.

Silas's features break through the fog, his look of utter contempt.

"Should have take you, too."

Cora looks to Leah. Almost pleading. But the woman before her is a stranger. Where has the love gone? Years of it.

"No," Cora says. More of a whisper. Then, a little louder—with a hint of venom. "You can't do that. Not back to the plantation. Not when you know—"

"You was always free," Leah says. The only sign of emotion a trembling in her hands. "You don't understand what it take."

Cora takes a step back. Feels dizzy all over again, but this time Thursday does not come to her aid. She is alone, reeling; she almost reaches for Leah to steady her, but at the last moment, her hands fall back to her sides.

A new picture is emerging. A woman in chains. A back bloody with open whip wounds. In the forest again, but now the shadows take new forms. They are dangerous. And the shadow that is Leah, musket in hand, out on patrol, is the most dangerous of all.

There is a gap between this image and the pain of it hitting Cora, almost knocking her to the ground. And in the gap is a dreadful understanding—because Cora knew, didn't she? The Maroons took runaways sometimes—took Leah, when Quaco saw her and wanted her as a wife. Took them during the war, for a time, before the loyalty of slaves proved too fragile and too fickle. But otherwise . . . There was something there that Cora never dwelt on for too long. There was talk of patrols. There were men who went out hunting and returned empty-handed but seemed as satisfied as if they had been carrying the carcass of a wild boar.

Trelawny Town was founded in the space between slave and free. Life existed for them outside the plantations only for as long as the plantations themselves survived. Cora both knew and did not know this; she chose, like so many others, not to know.

This woman in her mind, a woman in chains, is dragged screaming back to bondage. Her mother. The horror is not in the act itself, but in the fact that Cora did not feel the cruelty of it until she was bound to it by blood.

The Maroons captured runaways and returned them to their masters, to be beaten and tortured and killed for daring to flee.

"Me take you," Leah says. Her voice a little quieter, almost thoughtful. "She beg me to. Me tell them you die in the woods."

This was her kindness. She offers it to Cora as a salve; as evidence that, from the beginning, Leah has fought for Cora. Has protected her.

"She die?" Cora asks. A strange calm to her tone.

Leah does not flinch.

"Me don't know."

Cora's chest feels tight, the bones of her ribs pulling inward and trapping her lungs like a cage.

"You don't try to save her," she says. Half question, half accusation.

Again, Leah seems unmoved. Seems at ease with what has been done. Looks on Cora with hardened eyes.

"No," she says.

"But Quaco save you."

Only now does Leah recoil. And Cora will think—later, much later, when thinking returns to a mind now made blank with pain—that if Leah had not reacted, it might have been different. Faced with that unrelenting stare, perhaps Cora would have unraveled. Begun to doubt. But Leah's quivering lip, the little flicker of hurt behind the eyes—it hits Cora like the scent of blood, like the first wound in battle. Doubt cannot make its home in a mind filled with anger; and with the moral clarity of an avenging god, Cora begins to vibrate with rage.

"You don't try to save she," she says again. No question now. "You let she die."

The world splits in two. Down one road is contrition—and who knows where that road might have led, had Leah taken it. But down the other is unrepentance, and a sense of right and wrong on each side that refuses to yield.

Leah rearranges her face back into its cold, alien mask.

"Me have to do it," she says. "To stay free."

When Cora goes to the door, she does not run. She moves slowly and deliberately. Around her, all is silent. At the threshold, she turns for one last look at the room behind her. The others have remained in place—Leah, Silas, and Thursday, all standing in their corners—although the candles cast a slanting light that gives the impression of movement. The impression, in particular, of moving faces—of expressions that shift and grow distorted, almost demonic in their strangeness.

And little Benjamin. Cora notices, for the first time, that he is awake, is watching. The light from the candles falls across his face just so, and it becomes Elsy's. But even this cannot weaken her resolve.

She steps out into the night.

19

Cora comes to Agnes's camp in the dark, the night thick around her, moonless and starless, all light blotted out by clouds. She is shaking, though it is not cold.

It is only when she looks around for the familiar shape of Agnes's wikuom and sees it is gone that she starts to feel anything other than the hollowness that has accompanied her on her journey from Preston. She feels despair.

The woods are still. Quiet in the way nature is quiet—a dimming but not an absence of noise, the ever-present whine of midges and the occasional mournful owl's call. There is some evidence of a hurried departure, a fire hastily put out, some embers still smoking. It makes sense, of course. The memories of the afternoon have fractured, the largest and most coherent pieces those concerning Benjamin and the all-consuming fear that he would die. But now, sifting through the wreckage of the day, Cora recalls the moment Thursday saw Agnes. Of course Agnes would have fled.

Cora sinks to the ground and begins to weep.

"Cora?"

She lifts her head. In the darkness, she cannot find the source of the sound. She feels the familiar wet touch of Patience's nose against her hand, and she understands that this is not an invention of her desperate mind.

"Agnes," she says, the name almost a sigh.

Finally, she sees Agnes emerging from behind the rocks at the clearing's edge.

"I packed up," Agnes says. "Ready to go at dawn."

Silence. Cora runs through everything that could be said in this moment. She could apologize for endangering Agnes's peace out here in the woods. She could explain what has happened, the way the past has tonight been rewritten forever. She could ask whether, in the morning, she can come with Agnes, to wherever is next. But she finds each choice inadequate, somehow—the thought of fixing words to this moment is too much. So she stays quiet, and so does Agnes.

Agnes comes close, as if to help Cora to her feet. Close enough that, out of the darkness, her features appear, hard to discern clearly, but still the unmistakable shape of eyes and nose and mouth. But she does not hold out her hand; she waits, still and silent, as Cora pushes herself up to standing. Cora follows Agnes to where a rug of moosehide is spread between two rocks, well hidden.

"Lay down," Agnes says.

"Where you gon' . . . ?"

"I slept plenty."

Cora catches Agnes's wrist as she turns to go.

"No," she says. "There's room. Look."

Slipping into the gap in the rock, she presses herself tightly into the corner. It is too dark to read whatever comes over Agnes's face as she hovers, uncertain.

"Please," Cora says.

Agnes relents. Crawls in beside Cora. They lie curled away from each other like butterfly wings.

Sleep comes slowly, despite Cora's tiredness. Her mind trying hard to hold back memories, real and imagined: a faceless mother, beaten and alone; Leah, the hardness that set her face. The knowledge that, underneath love, there is a need for survival. And little Benjamin, the glimpse of him just before leaving. The echo of Elsy in his face.

Agnes's breathing has slowed. She shifts slightly; now they are touching. And when Cora finally sleeps, her dreams are filled with strange and fleeting images of bear cubs holding each other in slumber and of trees that grow together until their branches intertwine.

In the morning, Agnes does Cora another kindness. She does not ask. Not even about Benjamin, the fall, whether he is badly hurt or worse, though Cora suspects Agnes can see whatever drove Cora out of Preston was grief of a different kind.

Cora, who had always been the one waiting, tiptoeing around Agnes's past, collecting hints and fragments to try to understand her—who had always been ready to share her own story if it came to it—now finds she understands Agnes's silences better. Cora is not naturally reticent; has found, over the course of her life, that giving voice to problems gives them an easier shape than letting them stew in your mind, all in a tangle. This time is different. She wakes with the sun, a little stiff, cold despite the warmth of the morning because Agnes is already up and waiting, leaning against the rocks and watching the dawn break—and she, Cora, knows that what happened last night is too big to share all at once. For now, they will both keep their secrets.

It is never said aloud that Cora will stay. Agnes merely starts walking, and lets Cora follow.

———

The days are still long and warm, but Agnes says they will have to live like it is winter. Away from water and into the interior, to rocky outcrops and sparse forests, where they will make small camps and move often.

They go first to the coast; Agnes must take her boat and hide it in the woods, hoping it will still be there when she returns next summer. Cora stands high on the rocks as Agnes descends. She closes her eyes, lets a breeze off the sea hit her face. Numbness giving way, little by little, to an ache that she does not understand, because it is hard to tell if she misses most what she always knew—Leah—or what she never really knew until now—her mother. And the pain is too fresh for Cora to understand, but later she will think that the root of it, perhaps, is that, for the first time, she has to pull these two women apart. In her mind they had always been inseparable, Leah filling her mother's role, her mother watching from somewhere beyond death, glad to see a fellow Maroon raising her daughter when she could not. How can Cora explain, now, what Leah did? How can she take all the love given over the years and square it with the image of a slave rechained by Leah?

And how can she, Cora, explain herself?

She thinks of seeds, carried far from where they first fell. Do they not grow into the same trees, no matter the soil?

But then she thinks of the parakeet in Trelawny Town, its egg discovered by a stubborn child who wanted to keep the bird alive. Who reared it alongside the chickens. The parakeet moved like a chicken, clucked like a chicken. It never even flew, not beyond a few flaps of its wings.

This discovery, then, of who her mother was. It might mean nothing, the greatest part of herself being formed by the Maroons and growing up among them. Or it might mean everything. How is she to know?

Agnes waves to catch her attention. Cora is forced back to the present, looks down to see Agnes standing in the little canoe with Patience. Cora tilts her head, confused.

"One more time," Agnes says. Nodding to the distance, the open sea. "To say goodbye."

———

They sit for what must be more than two hours on the water. A stiff breeze roughing the sea, the boat moving up and down with the waves. Cora, still feeling low, keeps looking to Agnes, wondering when they will give up waiting. But there is always something in Agnes's face that stops her speaking aloud: an openness, a hope. So, they stay.

"You ever miss a place?" Cora asks. A way to fill the silence between them.

Agnes looks at her, surprised she has spoken. Pauses the movement of her fingers, gently scratching Patience's head.

"After you leave it," Cora says. "You miss it?"

"Well," says Agnes, after some thought. "There is a place where . . . where Pa is buried. Don't go back much. I miss it there."

Cora thinks of Elsy's burial place in Jamaica—thinks of the fear of scrambling down from the mountains, closer to the British lines, just to find some earth to bury her. Not caring that they risked their lives, because it had to be done—was done for all their dead, who could not be left to rot out in the open.

Then, although she is trying so hard to repress it, Cora thinks of her mother. There was a burial place in Trelawny Town; the graves were not marked, as it was not a place where you sought out someone specific, but rather sat and considered all of the dead together. Cora had gone there with flowers, with offerings. Had believed that her mother . . .

Now she will never know where her mother is buried. And her father—always an insubstantial figure in her mind, a wanderer and a stranger; now even those bare bones of his biography have been snatched away. She will never even know the smallest part of the truth of him. Whether he was slave, free. Whether he loved her mother or was indifferent to her or hated her enough to hurt her as he put Cora inside her. She will never know whether her mother or father lives on, somehow, in the shape of her eyes or hands, her laughter, the way her lips curve into a smile. These two strangers are utterly lost to her, and thus lost to history itself, with no one left to mark who they were, to light a candle on a dark night and remember them.

A few tears fall; Cora lets them. Counts the passing of time by her shaky breaths. Then, very deliberately, wipes her face and stops crying. Puts the thoughts from her mind. They are no use to her now. They will bring her only pain.

Patience, with an animal sense for distress, moves toward Cora. The dog cocks her head; the movement causes her ears to flop to one side. This coaxes a small smile out of Cora.

"Cora," says Agnes. With a tenderness that is too much, that threatens to undo the work of stemming the tears.

"What?"

"Your people," Agnes says. "They gonna miss you. . . ."

Cora turns to Agnes, eyes flashing, quick to anger.

"You don't want me here?" she says. "That so? You want me to leave."

Agnes is taken aback. Does not answer right away.

"I want . . ." she says, but does not finish.

They are interrupted by a sound—that great exhale of a whale breaking the surface. They spin together, searching. . . .

Not far from the boat, another whale's back appears, sleek and black, then dives below the surface again. And everything leaves Cora's body—pain, anger, it all drains away. Replaced only by a total presence, a being-in-the-world.

Then, close enough that Cora can see the trails of seaweed caught on the barnacled skin, a humpback raises its nose out of the water. An eye, winking black and the size of her fist, finds the boat. Cora gasps. To be seen—to be not the watcher but the watched—is unlike anything she has ever known. Tears spring in her eyes, but not like the tears before, which came from some small, human place. These new tears draw from the well of the entire world.

The whale sinks below the waves. They wait. But the whales do not appear again. It is as Agnes once said—they can only be seen when they want to be.

Agnes picks up her paddle but does not use it yet, perhaps

to preserve this moment for as long as she can. They will not see the coast again this winter.

"What I mean," she says suddenly. Not looking at Cora. "Is you can still go back."

Cora doesn't answer. Agnes reads into the silence, heads for shore.

———

That night, at camp, as Cora and Agnes sit in darkness, Agnes points up at the sky.

"The North Star," she murmurs.

It stirs a memory of Thursday that makes Cora feel heavy, even more tired than before, her mind soon full of all the people of Preston, everything she has left behind.

She starts to doubt. It seems a dream, to think of a life with Agnes. Them and Patience, walking the woods, summer turning to winter and then back to spring. The magic of the forest is that it shortens the future to an hour, a day. Where will they find water? What will the next hunt bring? Beyond that, the path is shrouded in mystery. The other possible futures shine brighter; they brim with people, with everyday tasks, with family and friendship and marriage and expectation.

Then Agnes turns her head. Her skin shines with moonlight. Her eyes reflect the stars. Fireflies, flitting through the night, bright bodies calling out to one another through the dark, pass over her head, hover a moment—a kind of halo.

Agnes is here, now, with Cora. And she is the brightest thing of all.

20

Cora has, in the months since meeting Agnes, spent so much time with her out in the woods that she believed she knew the rhythms of Agnes's life. But Cora realizes now that she was merely a guest in the forest. That home, easy meals, ready access to the market at Halifax, kept her insulated from the harsh reality of the wilderness. So much work, just to survive. Time spent gathering wood, fetching water, fashioning arrows, mending torn clothes.

They live quietly, leaving few footprints. Do not farm, build nothing meant to last more than a few months. Instead, the land changes them; Cora feels the way it shapes her body, the muscle that forms under skin. Her hands grow tougher and more calloused. Her braids grow out; she decides she will cut them off, but Agnes stops her. Says—

"Here. Let me."

And Cora spends an evening sitting cross-legged while Agnes bends over her, fashioning braids that are messier than

Leah's, but Cora doesn't mind. It is one little piece of her old self she is able to keep, her hair.

One day, Cora slips and grazes her knee. A small cut, without much blood, and at first she cannot understand why Agnes is so fixated on cleaning and dressing it, insisting Cora keep the makeshift bandage over it until it is healed. Then she remembers—no doctors here. No medicine apart from the salves and pastes Agnes mixes herself. The smallest wound, left to fester, could mean death.

The nature of Agnes's lessons subtly shifts. Where once she pointed out the forest's wonders, now she makes Cora see the danger. Teaches her the shape of bear tracks and which berries and leaves are poisonous. Cautions her against getting between a mother moose and her calf. Over a week, Agnes spends hours making Cora her own knife, sharpening the stone blade. A tool with many uses—carving, cutting, shaping—but as Agnes hands it over, Cora understands that it is also a weapon, should she ever need it to be.

———

Cora and Agnes sit opposite each other, a fire between them. It is dark, and they have moved camp today—a long walk east, almost to the coast, but Agnes is afraid to get too near in case of unknown fishing villages scattered along the shore. These are always long and exhausting days, packing up, finding new ground. Building the wikuom—Cora lays the birchbark and Agnes, with more nimble fingers, stitches the pieces together with spruce root, overlapping like the shingles of a roof, starting at the bottom and moving in a spiral until they reach the top. And yet, these are always the days they stay up latest, sometimes until the softening of the sky just before dawn. It is as if they need to know the night in a new place, staving off sleep until they are sure that the darkness here cannot harm them.

Patience has settled next to Cora, her head on Cora's lap. A rare thing; she usually stays close to Agnes. It is a sign, perhaps, that they are truly becoming three—because Cora never thinks, anymore, of just herself and Agnes. Cannot ignore Patience now she knows her, loves the easy devotion she shows.

Cora runs her fingers gently across Patience's head, feeling the ridges of bone just under her soft fur.

"How you get her?" she asks. Agnes is leaning back against a boulder, her eyes drifting closed—though not dozing, Cora knows, because of the way Agnes's face always has an alertness to it that only fades when she truly sleeps.

"Patience?" Agnes asks. At the sound of her name, Patience raises her head. Looks between the two of them. Cora scratches her under the chin, smiling.

"Yes."

Cora waits. She knows there is no guarantee of an answer. Agnes still keeps the past guarded, even after all these weeks spent together, and the promise of many more. There are times when Cora asks, "Where you learn that?" or "You come here before?" and Agnes will say something evasive like "Somewhere, don't remember" or "Maybe, don't know."

Agnes looks at Cora across the fire, the flames high enough that sometimes the orange light moves across Agnes's face, obscuring her eyes.

"Many Mi'kmaq have dogs," she says. "For hunting."

It's not an answer really, but Agnes's voice does not have

that usual strained quality that it takes on when Cora gets too close to a subject Agnes would rather not discuss. So Cora risks a question.

"You get her from the Mi'kmaq, then?"

"Yes."

The short answer, and Agnes half turning her face away from the light, do not fully dissuade Cora. But do encourage caution—a sideways approach.

"The Mi'kmaq all gone now?"

Agnes shakes her head.

"Not so many. But they are still here."

"You never . . ." Cora trails off. As soon as she starts to speak, the question becomes ridiculous. *Never tried to join them?* As if it was that easy, to enter and leave communities at will. Thinks, briefly, of her mother—but quashes the thought before it can hurt her.

"They teach you," Cora says. "Me remember you say that. Teach you how to survive."

"Yes," says Agnes. "Me and Pa. When we first came out here."

"That's when them give you Patience?"

Cora runs her hand over the dog's head once again, across the soft, fine hair that covers the ears.

"Well," says Agnes. "No."

Cora waits. The fire crackles, shooting sparks up toward the sky—they look, briefly, as if they might join the stars, but they fade to ash too quickly, burning out to nothing. Gray flakes fall outside the circle of firelight, settling somewhere in the darkness, unseen.

"After Pa died," Agnes says softly, "I met a Mi'kmaq family. They had a dog, just given birth. They let me take a puppy."

Patience, as if sensing Agnes's mood—the pain creeping into her voice—gets to her feet and pads around the fire. Noses against the side of Agnes's face.

"She came to me when I had no one," Agnes says. "Not to replace Pa. But . . . it helped."

They bring their heads together for a moment, Agnes and Patience. A gesture of profound connection, soft and gentle and filled with love.

Cora has so many questions.

How did your father die?

What about your mother?

Why did you stay out here so long?

Why are you always moving, afraid to be seen?

But before any single one can come to the forefront of her mind, Agnes speaks again. Quietly—almost a whisper.

"Cora," she says. "Why did you run?"

Cora lets out a slow breath. It is time—she knows it is time.

"My mother die birthing me," she says. Not sure where else to begin, figuring this is as good a place as any. "That's what them always tell me. . . ."

From here, she tells the story of Leah's betrayal. It doesn't take long; she keeps the details sparse. She is expecting it to hurt, preparing for tears, but as she goes, the overwhelming feeling is anger, her rage building and building until she is burning hot with the injustice of it, of her mother left unfree.

"Now me know," Cora says. "Me can never forgive her."

"For giving you up?" Agnes asks softly. Cora blinks at her, confused.

"Not my mother," says Cora. "Leah. For what she do."

After her words, there is silence, filled by the sound of the fire—the crackle of the burning wood and the hiss of smoke.

Agnes looks down at her feet. Cora, anger still lodged inside her, hard to dispel, waits for a reaction—some sign that Agnes shares her righteous fury. But Agnes just looks thoughtful and melancholy.

"What she do was wrong," Cora says, her voice rising. Agnes does not look up but gives the ground a forlorn little half smile.

"Perhaps," Agnes says.

Cora's face feels hot. She gets to her feet, ready to—what? Run again?

"You gon' defend her?"

Finally, Agnes looks up. Her eyes filled with reflected firelight that shimmers like unspilled tears.

"There ain't no perfect choices," she says. Gentle but firm. And somehow, the timbre of her voice, the expression on her face—they are enough. The anger diffuses—fades to an ache. Cora sits again. Rests her head on her knees, sapped of all energy and strength.

The moon rises higher in the sky as the flames of the fire sink. Nearby, in the trees, a bird calls out into the night—no melody in the sound, but a kind of pure vibration. Cora wonders what species it is. Agnes would know.

Cora hears a soft sigh, and Agnes shifting her weight. She must be ready to sleep. Keeping her head down, Cora asks the question that has been lurking just below the surface of her conscious mind ever since she fled to the forest, when she saw Agnes emerge from her hiding place in the old clearing.

"What was it like? On your plantation?"

A moment of quiet.

Agnes says, "Cora."

Still, Cora does not look up. Speaks to the earth—

"Please. Me have to . . ."

"It was hard," Agnes says. "Very hard."

Cora wraps her arms around her shins, drawing her legs closer to her chest.

"Hard," she echoes.

"Cora," Agnes says again.

"No," says Cora. "Tell me. What else?"

"There was . . ." Agnes pauses. Cora can almost feel the way she reaches for the memories. In some dim, silenced part of her mind, Cora knows this is hurting Agnes, perhaps as much as it is hurting her. But this is the cleaning of the wound, the point of greatest pain, without which there can be no healing.

"So much loss," Agnes says finally. "Death. People sold. We were lucky—me and Ma and Pa. To stay together. Others, not so lucky."

Cora waits. Knows there is more.

"The work," says Agnes. "It ached. There are hard days out here. But not like that. Never like that."

Cora finally lifts her head. Finds that Agnes is staring right at her.

"Do you know," Agnes says softly, "how it feels? To be—"

She breaks off, frustration crossing her face. There is a gulf between them, and Agnes is searching for the words to cross it.

"Pa was a slave," Agnes says finally. "His pa was a slave. And then his pa was, too. It was this . . ." Her hands reach out, grasping at the night. "This *weight*. It was heavy. All the people born and died knowing just that life, not owning nothing. Beaten and broken and crushed and killed. That was my life. Some days I thought it couldn't be no different. Too much history to be any way else."

Agnes's face is alive with memory. With pain. But then, something shutters, hardens.

"You have to keep on living," she says. "Keep finding ways to hide. When you're a slave. Keep a little part of you back."

Cora does not know what to say. Had she hoped Agnes's memories might bring her closer to her mother? Help her understand? Instead, the person who comes to mind is Leah. A slave, too. A master of survival. She made it out. So did Agnes. Cora's mother tried and failed. Maybe she was different; maybe she didn't know how to hide.

Cora gets to her feet and moves silently around the fire. She sits next to Agnes, close enough that they touch—bare arms pressing against each other from elbow to shoulder. Maybe there are no words that can close the gap between them, but there is this. There is skin against skin. There is Agnes, until now bolt upright, made stiff with hurting, letting her body sag, her head resting against Cora.

They sit unmoving. Moments pass; time, unmarked and unmeasured, will still march on, but it lacks a regular rhythm. It is only humans who force time into even parts. Out here, in the forest, as Cora and Agnes think only of each other—of hitched breaths and shivers on their skin, of closeness and shared warmth—time slips past unnoticed, uneven in the way it lingers and then hurries, making hours minutes and minutes hours until the time it takes for Cora to watch a single leaf, come loose from a nearby tree, drift down to earth is the same time it takes for the sky to lighten, promising sunrise.

The half-light makes the world feel eerie; it suggests possibility, that there might be things that can be done only now, in the brief moment between night and day.

Cora feels Agnes shift slightly. Feels her turn her head. Knows with cold clarity that if she, Cora, turns her head, too, it will bring their faces—their lips—close. . . .

There is a future ahead of them, a thin thread, as delicate as spiders' silk, glistening with dew in the dawn. . . . And then, just as suddenly, it is gone. Cora has hesitated too long. Agnes sits upright. Stands. She is heading for the wikuom, to snatch a few hours of sleep before they must finish setting up this new camp. Cora is left alone to watch the colors of the sky, feeling as if the grief inside her changes with the light, flitting between the dark blue of something strong and certain—the loss of her mother—and something pale and strange and nameless that has to do with Agnes and the lingering sensation of their arms touching.

The Trial

January 1798

Leah was in love once, but it was a love she grew herself, not one she found.

She was sure her heart was barren after the ship from home. A home where she had tended a garden and looked after the land, was known for her skill at it. On the plantation, one of the sharpest cruelties was how they took something so good, so life-giving—the work of nurturing plants and soil—and turned it into a prison. The fields were what killed you, one way or another. The exhaustion, the heat, the whip wound turned infected: All of it came back to the merciless cane.

She felt nothing when Quaco first came. He and his men were called in by the master of a neighboring plantation to plan the capture of a runaway. Quaco saw Leah in the fields. She was beautiful in a striking, muscular way. He was bored of the Trelawny Town women; she represented something new and—more alluringly—a boundary to be transgressed. He might have been called to any plantation on the northeast of the island. He might have seen any beautiful woman and had the same glint of desire. Leah has always been clear-eyed about this. She was as interchangeable to him as she was to her master when working down a cane row, where any other slave might pick up her machete and keep cutting.

So when, after dark, Quaco approached her in secret, pulling her from the village and walking with her around the plantation paths, it stirred in her no emotions. She stayed quiet and let him speak. He came across the way she later discovered he truly was—a straightforward man, not unkind, with a clear will to bend the world to his liking. In time, these would be qualities she would learn to appreciate. But that night they left no mark.

What he offered was a way out, a gentler one than poison, drowning, cutting your own throat. She would have been a fool not to take it.

———

She cannot say what made her decide to start loving Quaco. It was a choice, of that she is certain. It did, perhaps, make her position in Trelawny Town more secure—because Quaco might, at any point, have decided to return her. But she would not have been the first woman to don the costume of love, nor would Quaco have been the first man to mistake her performance for sincerity.

Maybe, without her knowing it, the seeds were already planted by his surprising gentleness, by the fact that he treated her well, even after the novelty of her faded. Maybe, in slowly softening toward him, she discovered that she was wrong about her barren heart, and in knowing she was wrong, felt the urge to push and see how much love could truly take root there. Or maybe she was simply in search of a way to exercise her new-found but still precarious freedom—and she set herself to the task of love because it represented, for her, the culmination of her escape. A life in three acts—with love, without it, and now with it again.

Whatever the reason, she worked at the love until it flourished, until it was sturdy as an old tree and bore sweet fruit.

———

The woman in the forest. The woman who begged and pleaded. There was never any doubt in Leah's mind what she would do. Slaves back to the plantations: Those were the rules. She, more than anyone, was in no position to bend them. What did it matter that she, Leah, was once in bondage, too? Leah remembers from the passage over—thrown overboard, it's the ones you're shackled to who will drag you down.

But the baby . . .

Tiny wrists, unbound, a body not yet marked by cruelty.

The mother must sink, but need the baby go with her? Might Leah take her, this small thing (a thing she cannot create herself though she and Quaco have tried), and stay on the surface, still breathing?

Leah took the baby into her arms and the love arrived fully formed. A love that never needed tending to grow.

Now Leah stands outside the courthouse, gathering strength to enter.

This was what she hadn't bargained for. That the love itself is the binding, the unfreedom. The love has come, all these years later, to drown her.

AUTUMN
1797

21

Summer slides into autumn. Slowly at first: the slightest change in the hue of the leaves. The fading of the light as evenings shorten and the sun waits a little longer to rise.

The pain and shock of what happened with Leah fades, too, with time. Life in the forest has a numbing effect, leaving no space to ruminate. They still move often, packing up and then reestablishing camp in some other part of the forest. Still so much to learn, about the best barks for kindling, the sweetest berries, the shapes of the mushrooms that are edible and the ones that are not. Cora throws herself hard into all of it, because her greatest fear is that she will become a burden to Agnes. Agnes would never say so directly, but Cora is sure she must have thought of it, when Cora first arrived in the middle of the night with nothing but herself. Cora wants to show her that life might be easier with two instead of one. Wikuoms built faster, heavier logs that can be carried between them and then split for the fire.

Little Benjamin is the hardest to forget. The thought of him catches Cora off guard sometimes, a painful mix of small details, like the sound of his laugh, that are still as clear as if he were there in front of her, and the other memories—the smell of him, the feel of her hand on his cheek—that are now harder to recall. It hurts to think of the way he will be growing in her absence. He is the innocent victim of a larger tragedy, but she holds firm to her resolve. She cannot go back for him.

And then there is her mother. She cannot forget what she has never known, so her mother is more like an idea that diffuses through everything. Cora looks at her own hands, hard at work whittling or gathering, and wonders how much of these hands are her mother's. She falls asleep to the sounds of the forest and thinks that perhaps this is the only way she will ever be close to her mother. By existing in this strange world, outside of time. Living in the wilderness, the place her mother ran to. Did she dream of a life like this one?

———

Agnes and Cora find an equilibrium about the past, somewhere between silence and speech. Mostly, they deal with the routine, discussing the day's foraging or the bear tracks that might mean they have to move on earlier than planned. But sometimes, they will let a memory break through. Agnes will share a little something about her father—about the way he cooked meat, liking it charred enough your jaw ached from chewing it. Or the way he would carve patterns into the shafts of arrows; he could not read or write, but he made shapes he thought might be letters, symbols that kept their secret meaning from him, that held a kind of power he once feared but then wanted to harness for his own.

Cora accepts these offerings and gives a little of herself in return, talking of life in Jamaica—small, everyday things like taking the laundry down to the stream with Elsy.

Leah, Cora does not speak of at all.

Something also has changed between them in the manner of touch, since that night when Agnes leaned her head on Cora's shoulder. Now Agnes keeps her distance. She is never cold, never awkward. But Agnes is less ready to brush a hand on Cora's arm, or nudge her to get her attention, than she was before. Each night, they sleep apart.

———

It grows colder. Some trees stand evergreen—pines and firs and spruces. Others begin to change, their leaves flaring out in a riot of color.

As Cora adjusts to the rhythm of this new life, and its demands upon her body, her mind frees itself up to think of other things, straying further and further from the everyday.

There is no sudden moment of clarity—no shaft of sunlight that pierces the clouds. But as gradually as a slow autumn sunset, Cora realizes that there is something about Agnes. Something that draws Cora in. That makes her feel, as a constant ache, the absence of Agnes's easy, thoughtless touches. Agnes has become her whole world, but this alone cannot explain the intensity with which Cora's mind turns to Agnes on first waking or on the cusp of sleep.

There is an uneasiness as Cora considers these things—a

discomfort that seems to fit the season, as the days darken and the trees shiver in the wind. It often rains, turning the reds and oranges into a relentless gray. All the while, Cora worries at the question.

What is Agnes to her?

This is not the first time language has failed her, that she has been caught in the space between words. Leah, after all, was both mother and not mother. And after Elsy died, Benjamin became, in all but name, her son. Agnes is friend and she is sister and she is sometimes self—almost a part of Cora's mind stored in another body. And yet she is . . . something else.

One night, Cora lies awake, listening to the sound of rain on the birchbark of the new wikuom—their winter camp now established, a little hollow in a rocky, inhospitable part of the southern woodland. As she waits for sleep, Cora thinks of all the stories she has ever heard about creation. Of gods who make the world and everything in it. She has a few scraps of them, here and there—from Leah, from other Maroons, and dim memories of the white priest at Preston reading from the Bible.

In these stories, sometimes, the gods themselves are double—a god of land and a god of water, a god of earth and a god of sky, a god of the sun and a god of the moon. Sometimes, the gods make doubleness, fashioning people from clay or from moonbeams or each other's flesh. Always two. A world always in balance, as she and Agnes are. There are days when Cora is short-tempered and sour, and Agnes will patiently draw her out of herself, bringing her back into the world through complex tasks like fashioning a new awl from bone or skinning a small rabbit without tearing the soft pelt. And then there are days

when Agnes is morose and withdrawn, and Cora will do whatever it takes to make her cheerful again—pointing out increasingly absurd shapes in the clouds or speculating on the kind of
voice Patience would have if she could speak, pretending to be
the dog and inventing accents more and more ridiculous until
finally, Agnes's hand flies to her mouth to hide her laugh.

But the problem that keeps Cora awake is this. These gods,
these early people, they are always a man and a woman. The
natural pair; the opposites that keep the world in balance. How
can it be any other way?

———

In the end, the word Cora settles on is *love.*

A small word with so many meanings. It is a blanket over
every kind of fondness. It defies precision. And yet, it feels right
to say it to herself—to use it, falteringly at first, then growing
more confident each time she holds the idea in her mind.

What she feels for Agnes is love.

22

Toward the end of October, the leaves fall from the trees in earnest, but the sun still shines, and it is almost warm—the very last of summer hanging in the air.

Cora can tell Agnes is thinking of what is to come. There is a wariness to her, an alertness for signs of winter. A growing tension settles over both of them; for the first time, there are days when they both stay quiet, when happiness slips away and neither of them has the strength to chase it.

"Winter's hard," Agnes says one night. Looking sideways at Cora, and somehow the words grate.

"Me know that," Cora says. Trying to make the meaning clear—that she is not weak, will not need Agnes's protection.

And yet, how can Cora not be nervous? Each morning, as she wakes, shivers, feels the growing bite in the air, rubs feeling back into stiffening fingers and toes, she is reminded of it. The promise of winter is all around them.

———

One afternoon, Cora and Agnes walk deep into the forest to check their traps—deadfalls and snares scattered in the miles around their camp. The dying leaves give the morning a reddish tinge, reminiscent of firelight.

The first snare is sprung but empty. Cora watches as Agnes kneels beside it and then sighs.

"Tripped by something too big, most likely," she says. "Needs resetting."

She has brought spare cattails and sets to work, fingers quick and nimble. Cora tries to follow the movements, but it is of little use. Agnes has tried to teach her many times, the way the mechanisms on these snares are set, and how to arrange the deadfalls, too, but Cora has not taken naturally to it. So now they have to check the traps together, rather than being able to split and halve the time it will take to cover them all. Cora can only watch Agnes for so long, a reminder of her own inadequacy. She walks a few feet away and stares into the distance. The trees grow thickly here; under the soil, roots twist together. It is only above that the forest gives the impression of being formed of separate things—below, it is one living organism.

Perhaps this mass of trees is the reason that Cora feels they are not entirely alone.

Agnes works on. Cora, from the corner of her eye, sees Patience raise her head from where she has been sniffing the undergrowth, and the sight makes her uneasy. She and Patience wait together—seeing, smelling, listening for danger.

But there is only quiet. A soft rustle of leaves as the wind blows. Patience goes back to investigating the ground. Agnes stands and wipes her hands on her moosehide trousers, satisfied. And Cora turns away from the empty point in the forest that had somehow drawn her attention, dismissing her superstitions. Turns away—and so does not see, as she and Agnes and Patience walk onward, the hulking shadow that follows.

———

The second trap is empty and unsprung. The next has been completely destroyed—Agnes curses under her breath when she sees it. It happens, from time to time, that a moose will trample one, and means hours of work to build another.

They reach the fourth trap, and finally luck has come their way. Inside is a large snowshoe hare, still with its brown summer coat. Cora is becoming immune to death out here, but sometimes—as now—she feels a slight pang, to see something so beautiful snuffed out. As Agnes unwraps the snare from the body, Cora moves away, following Patience—who, whenever they stop, will move in circles of increasing size, disappearing in and out of bushes and weaving between the trees. Cora likes to wander like this sometimes when they are out in the woods. Never too far from Agnes, and not with any particular purpose in mind. Like a muscle, this new freedom of hers simply needs to be flexed—she is struck anew by the fact that she is far from the place she once called home, far from all the people she used to know. Her life has its rhythms and chores, it's true. But at present, nothing is required of her except to look up at the canopy, take a deep breath, and live.

Through the leaves, Cora sees a patch of lilac sky. The air feels charged and damp.

Storm, she thinks, wondering if this has been the cause of the tension she has felt ever since that first trap.

A twig snaps.

Cora turns quickly. But it is just Patience. The dog stands a dozen yards from Cora—close to where Agnes has gutted the hare, preparing to carry it home.

A low growl. Cora sees, now, that Patience is quivering. Eyes fixed on formless shadows, shifting beneath the trees.

Agnes, too, lifts her head.

Says, "Patience?"

Time fractures. Cora experiences things not as a continuous stream, but as a series of images. Each one a frozen horror—something captured in motion, in transition, but Cora's mind can only grasp it as a single picture.

First—the shadow in the trees. A mass of dark fur.

Second—Patience, mouth open in a snarl. Rearing over the dog, a bear, up on its hind legs, raising a paw for the strike.

Third—Patience gone. Now nothing between the bear and Agnes—Agnes, who is still crouched, holding the body of the hare, unmoving not because time has broken but because she really is rooted to the spot, neither running nor reaching for the bow slung over her shoulder . . .

Cora bursts into motion. Her feet barely touch the ground as she runs. Her breathing is not fast but slow—steady, each exhale timed to one of her strides. The bear is rising again, and of one thing Cora is certain. If she does not go faster—stretch her limbs farther—the bear's paw will come down on Agnes and it will kill her.

The noise that rings in Cora's ears is her own screaming—a

primal sound, of a pitch with the bear, which lets out its own answering roar. . . .

Cora's mind catches up with her body at exactly the point where her momentum carries her those last few feet, right toward the bear. She smells blood and something fetid, rotting—as if there are dead things nesting in the bear's open jaws.

Her outstretched hands meet a wall of fur. With the last of the air in her lungs she yells something that might be

Go

or might be a wordless battle cry.

And for a moment, darkness descends, her vision temporarily overwhelmed by the reality of touching this predator, this killing thing. The darkness could be death. But then it is gone, and Cora is standing, panting, opposite the bear—which, she registers with shock, has drawn back slightly. Now on all fours, about level with Cora's waist, it leans forward, as if to charge, and there is some distant part of Cora's mind that tells her to run. But at the point she and the bear made contact, she mastered her fear. Cora stands her ground. Yells again, and this time it is a word—

"No!"

This is enough. The bear steps back again. Considers her one more time—she cannot see its eyes, only the hollows of them, two dark shadows in its face. Then, lowering its head, the bear slinks away.

A hand on her arm and Cora screams again, the sound now emptied of all its power—fear finally let loose from the place where she had buried it. She might fall—but it is Agnes, of course, who has touched her, and who now rushes to hold Cora up, bringing their bodies together, letting Cora cling to her.

Cora starts to tremble, all the terror she did not feel before hitting her at once; she feels a phantom claw across her back, bone-crushing teeth closing over her skull. She gasps, "Patience." Remembering how the dog was there and then not there—brought down, surely, by the bear's lethal swipe. Cora tries to pull away, but Agnes holds her fast and says,

"Alive. Scratched. But alive."

They have all survived it.

Cora and Agnes stand, holding each other, for a long time.

Little by little, Cora's mind escapes the past. No longer relives the horror of the attack. Instead, comes into the present.

Feels things like Agnes's breath on her cheek.

Agnes's heartbeat against her chest.

When they kiss, it is soft. At first, the touching of lips to lips feels like any other touch—just skin against skin. Then a slight press, Cora leaning her weight into Agnes, Agnes's mouth parting.

One of Agnes's hands moves to the back of Cora's neck. The ghost of a touch, enough to make Cora shiver. Her own arms, still around Agnes's waist, tighten their hold. Once again, the pressure of the kiss increases. They move through the stages of desire in increments, and Cora has started to ache, but knows they cannot rush. They must stretch out this exact moment. The simplicity and the depth. Just a kiss, and yet so much more.

When they break apart at a small whimpering sound, their heads turn together and they see Patience, blood staining her fur, nursing a wounded paw. Her eyes are at once full of pain and also somehow reproachful, as if she has been waiting for them to understand what they truly are to each other all along.

Cora starts to laugh. She can't help it. It is relief, it is exhilaration; it is the thrill of survival and the inexpressible joy of the world finally falling into place. It is as it has been all along—Cora loves Agnes. A word chosen for its ambiguity, for the way it can hide secret feelings. But now Cora understands the full breadth and depth of it. She loves Agnes in all the ways it is possible to love.

So Cora laughs. Despite her injuries, the noise seems to make Patience perk up. Her tail starts to wag. And Agnes is laughing, too, arms still around Cora so her hand cannot cover her mouth as it usually does—she simply throws back her head and allows the sound to come out unimpeded. The forest fills with it, but they don't think of danger. They do not think of who or what might hear. The brush with death has made them bolder, rather than more afraid.

This is how they stay a long time. Clinging tightly to each other, catching each other's eye, and falling back into laughter again and again until tears stream down their faces. Hysterical joy, made all the sweeter because Cora knows that, although this moment will pass, when everything seems heightened, every sensation intense—what will come after is the easy peace, the simple comfort, that Agnes always brings.

In the distance, the rumble of thunder. The darkening sky threatens rain, and the storm is nearly upon them. They need shelter. But they linger a moment longer. Agnes rests a hand gently against Cora's cheek. This thing still beyond words: It exists only in smiles and gestures, and is richer for it.

Agnes's cool fingers on Cora's skin say,

Home?

Cora's answer, tilting her head further into the touch, dark eyes catching the light, reflecting back the world—

Home.

23

About halfway back, it starts to rain—real, pounding rain that reminds Cora of Jamaica. She shrieks at the sensation of drops trickling down the back of her neck, sharing a look of equal parts horror and delight with Agnes. Because of course there is a storm—of course the heavens have opened and the world has become gray water and thunder roars and lightning in the distance splits apart the trunks of trees that have stood, undisturbed, for hundreds of years. The world reflects back the power of all that has passed between them.

They make it back to the wikuom, soaked through, Patience limping on her injured leg but looking better now that the rain has washed away the dried blood from her coat. On the threshold, Cora hesitates. Ever since the bear, things have moved at an unstoppable pace; this is the first moment she realizes she is not caught by some inevitable current, but rather is shaping a future from every choice she makes. And now she is uncertain. She does not know what comes next—after the kiss. She has no path for this, has heard no stories. Can rely only on instinct, an instinct that pushes her inside and into Agnes's arms.

That night, they speak without words. They kiss and they part to gaze at each other. They exchange gentle touches. It is not shyness—more like reverence, like a need to hold this moment carefully or it will break. It feels so much like a dream that the exact boundary between waking and sleeping is not clear. It is only when morning sunlight creeps through the gaps in the cloth hung over the wikuom's door that Cora realizes the night is over.

They are a few inches apart now—too used to the nights when they kept space between them. Agnes is curled on her side, facing toward Cora, sleeping. Cora takes time to study that face. The way the lips are shaped; the roundness of each nostril. Thin lines, small scars, and yet also all the places where the skin is perfectly smooth. Cora is able, through a certain trick of unfocusing her gaze, to consider the features in turn, as if detached from the whole—but then Agnes stirs slightly, and her face in its entirety comes rushing back, enough to take Cora's breath away.

Cora reaches over the space between them.

Their morning touches are firmer than before. They grow in confidence; they are an exploration. Cora marvels at this body that is like hers in some small ways, and yet totally unfamiliar. Agnes wears an undershirt and her moosehide trousers. Cora experiments with texture, running a hand from Agnes's clothed shoulder, over to her bare collarbone, and back again.

There are so many questions Cora wants to ask in this moment. She settles for—

"How long you . . . ?"

Agnes traces a finger along Cora's wrist, feeling the tendons under the skin. A sensitive place. Cora shivers.

"When I saw you, I knew," Agnes says. "The first time. Through the trees. It was snowing. You looked . . . beautiful."

She is able to speak simply and plainly, even as Cora feels hot with embarrassment and a lingering sense of confusion—some parts of her still trying to catch up with where they are now.

"But how long you know about yourself?" Cora asks. "That you . . ."

"Ah."

Agnes sighs.

"A long time."

Cora props herself up on one elbow.

"How long?"

Agnes makes a small humming noise that might be dismissal or might be an indication that she is thinking, finding the words. Cora waits. Still making a study of Agnes—enjoying, as ever, the quick play of different emotions across her face.

"Well," says Agnes. "I was young. Not in the fields yet. I had all these thoughts—about love. But it was hard on the plantation. Not a lot of love around. This when Pa was gone. Hired out to another place. So love was just something missing—it was Ma missing him every day."

She closes her eyes for a moment, in pain. Cora touches Agnes's cheek, wanting to take the pain into her fingertips, but it fades from Agnes's expression as quickly as it came, and when Agnes speaks again, her voice does not even waver.

"I tried to figure it out. I knew about . . . things. Between men and women. And I knew I looked at some women and thought they were beautiful and I looked at men and I ain't feel nothing. Maybe even a little scared. But the thing was, whatever happened between men and women—lots of times it did make people scared."

Agnes's voice still steady. But she pauses, swallows. It's work, Cora knows, to tell all this.

"You don't have to," Cora says quietly.

Agnes shakes her head. "I want to."

A brief silence. Agnes collects herself. Continues—

"On the plantation, bad things happened. Overseers taking women out into the fields who come back crying. Or making a man lie there with a woman while they hold the whip. They made Ma—"

She stops abruptly. Looks at Cora—wide-eyed. She cannot say it, but she does not need to. Cora understands.

Agnes exhales slowly.

"So I was thinking maybe everyone felt the way I did," she says. "All scared. I never saw wanting. I never saw love."

Cora can hear Patience outside the tent, starting to amble around. She can hear wind through the trees, shaking the dying leaves. But she can also hear other things—sounds from long ago, carried across time. Sighs and groans and quiet sobs. Agnes has summoned them here. Cora feels as though, were she to close her eyes, she would even see what Agnes saw. But she dares not try it. She is afraid of what would be lurking there, in the dark behind her eyelids.

"Then Pa came back," Agnes says. "He came home and it was different because he . . . he . . ."

She swallows again.

"He loved Ma so much," she says. Voice a little thick with

grief. But she is smiling. Her eyes, still raised to where the sky would be if they stepped out of this wikuom and into the world, are gazing far away. She collapses time, and she is there, with them—her parents.

"Almost happy, those years," Agnes says. "All together. A family. But there was this—shadow. The way they were together. If I imagined getting what they got, I . . . I knew it ain't gonna be with a man."

Agnes turns her head toward Cora. And suddenly, she is not very far away, but very close—inches from Cora's face, gazing at her with an intensity that registers as a physical presence on Cora's skin—a heat.

The look means something like—

Do you understand?

And Cora nods. She understands.

"You tell them?" Cora asks.

"Not for a long time."

"But . . . ?"

"I told Ma. Before she got sick, before she—"

Another hard stop in Agnes's story. She gathers herself. Cora still only has fragments of what happened to Agnes's mother. Part of her hoped that this moment might be an opening that might let her into all of Agnes's past. But it is not. They are chasing a single thread through the years, the thread of love and the way Agnes feels it, and Agnes clearly does not wish to get off course.

"I was tired of secrets," Agnes says. And seems like she might not say more.

"And?" Cora prompts. "What she say?"

Agnes takes time to answer. This is not time taken to find

the words, or time taken to sift through something and decide what must be hidden and what can be laid bare. In that silence, Cora feels the presence of memory—Agnes is lost in it. The present has fallen away completely, and Agnes is gone, back to her mother, and all Cora can do is wait.

When Agnes speaks again, there is roughness in her voice. But there is gratitude, too. Almost a smile.

"She said her grandmother came from Africa. And she had these stories."

Sudden movement. Agnes sits up. Her face above Cora's now, rather than below.

"People have always been like this," Agnes says. With a firmness that suggests an oft-repeated mantra, something fragile at first but now unbreakable; and in that moment, Agnes looks so beautiful, so aflame, that it makes Cora's breath stop. "Ma said in Africa there was men who marry men. Women who marry women. Not all the time, but sometimes. Sometimes people let them. Lots got lost on the way from Africa. Maybe that got lost, too. Those other kinds of love."

Agnes turns the blaze of her eyes on Cora. They stare at each other, the fierce defiance in Agnes's gaze aimed not at Cora but at the world—a daring invitation to judgment. It is a glimpse of the same hard, unafraid thing that has let Agnes live out here all these years. It is pure survival, but also it is more than just this—it is a deep self-knowledge, honed from years of being alone. But perhaps never really lonely, Cora thinks, as she watches Agnes, waiting for her to speak again. No human company, but Agnes has known other comforts—like the comfort of history, of knowing there were others who loved as she did. And maybe there is comfort of that kind, too, in the winter forests, some instinct that others must also subsist and survive in the cold and the ice, and even the most fleeting and imagined communion with these people scattered through time and place is enough to sustain her.

"So," says Agnes, finally. "Ma knew."

"And your pa?"

Agnes turns her face away, toward the wall.

"Ma said he . . . wouldn't understand."

A pause. A shaky breath.

"Maybe he guessed it. Over the years, a few girls I . . ." She trails off. "But I never told him. Ma made me promise."

Cora notes, with surprise, that the mention of others causes no wrenching sensation inside her. Agnes is a tapestry, each stitch a part of her life lived—some sewn by her own hand, and some by others. She has let Cora see, this morning, a part embroidered by her mother, precious lines that mark out acceptance and understanding, in spite of fierce odds against it. It does not occur to Cora to mind that there are other places where the stitches are from women Agnes has loved before— what matters is that they are part of Agnes now.

Still sitting upright, Agnes draws her knees into her chest. The loose shirt she wears comes untucked from her trousers, and there, at her hip, is a strip of bare skin. Cora reaches for it. Her fingers find it, and they trace a small circle.

Agnes's face softens.

"Cora," she says—so tenderly that Cora has to shut her eyes for a moment, because she cannot possibly see, hear, smell, and touch at once; it is too much.

She feels the featherlight brush of Agnes's hand on her cheek.

Cora shuffles a little closer to Agnes. Her touch grows more insistent—she is gripping Agnes by the hip now. And when she looks up, Agnes's lips are parted, though there is no sound of breath. Agnes is still, waiting.

When Agnes finally moves, it is to take a single finger and move it down the side of Cora's neck, and along the line of her collarbone.

"We can be slow," Agnes says softly. "I don't want you to . . ."

Cora shakes her head.

"Me want . . ." she says. Because there is the truth. She wants and she wants and she wants. She does not have words for what must come next, but it is written in her body, which anticipates it, shivers for it, and Cora knows there is no other time but now, and no other way but this. Both her hands move under Agnes's shirt, resting against bare skin, feeling somewhere underneath the fluttering of a pulse.

The puzzle of Agnes is that she can be, in some things, so cautious. Almost hesitant. And yet, in others—in paddling out to sea, or drawing her bow to fell a moose calf—so sure.

There is no uncertainty in the way Agnes touches Cora now.

They shed clothes, layer by layer, until there is nothing between them but skin, and even that seems somehow too much. They must find openings—ways to be closer. Their movements grow more urgent. A little clumsy; they are not practiced. But they find their rhythm. They smile a little, sometimes laugh, and Cora has never known joy like it—has never felt simultaneously so present, each moment slow enough to savor, each moment comprised of a thousand smaller moments, so that time has become infinite and this coming together of their bodies will never end. But also she has never floated higher, been a mind more untethered—carried away by desire so she hardly seems to be a body at all but a ball of pure light.

Outside, the first frosts have formed on the autumn ground—fractal blooms, glittering white on hardened earth, catching the rays of the dawning sun. The morning smells of winter. But inside, they keep each other warm.

The Trial

January 1798

There is no escape from the unforgiving chill of the courthouse except into memory, and so Thursday thinks of a different room, far less grand, in a dilapidated Virginia barn sweaty with the heat of bodies. A preacher shouting to be heard over the gathered crowd of slaves, voice shaking with righteous fury as he recounts every kind of sin.

Thursday a young boy, lost in the thicket of legs. He cannot see, can only hear. Much of what is spoken of he does not understand. But it awakens something in him, the tenor of the preacher's words, if not their meaning. A faith that has been by his side ever since.

Over the years, he has met many who chafe against the religion he learned that day, who see in it only shackles of a different kind. The plantation, too, had its commandments, had the whip for penance. Even free there is no escaping it—Blackness itself a sort of sin, upon which punishment is heaped by all from the smallest men like Farmer Nash to the mightiest kings. Why turn, some ask with scorn, toward the white man's god to bind you further?

Thursday remembers his mother, who kept her own gods but understood and respected his. She said to him once, *Every god got they own price. But they got they own rewards to give, too. That there is the difference.*

And she was right, of course. What he heard in the barn that day in Virginia, what moved him, was not fear but a promise. In this life, what does it get him, following the plantation's law, accepting Farmer Nash's will, enduring all the suffering and pain and loss? It allows him to avoid being beaten, starved, jailed, killed—nothing more.

But the idea that, in spite of this, there is another moral force in the universe, another set of laws; that, in the next life, it will all have been worth it, that he and his father and his mother and sister might walk once again, side by side . . . That is an idea that can sustain him. That has been his solace through the hardest, leanest Nova Scotia winters.

His life, of course, littered with broken promises. Perhaps the doubters are right; perhaps God's promise is just another. But to take that thought into his soul, Thursday knows, would kill him. He does not need paradise in all its splendor, does not need a heaven of abundant bliss and riches. But he does need to know that his suffering has had a witness. That God has seen all, is merely biding his time.

———

On the benches of the courtroom, he says a prayer for Cora, not the first one he has said for her this past year, but perhaps the most fervent. And as always, when praying for her, there is a slippage, the features of her face becoming, for just a moment, his mother's, before settling on his sister's. Or, more exactly, his sister's face as he imagines it. The game he has always played, counting years on his fingers, taking the lost time and adding it to the age she was when she died. It was the biggest difference between him and his mother, this need to propel Hannah into the future, continuing her life after death. Efe's instinct was to preserve Hannah intact, just as she was; his mother's natural quietness and gentleness giving way once, abruptly, when Thursday tried to engage her on the question of how Hannah might have grown up in the intervening years. Efe had snapped at him, pained—

You stop that and let her be.

But he can't. A child himself when Hannah died, he cannot hold on to her past as tightly as Efe did, and he cannot release Hannah to a void of nothingness. So it is a private ritual for him, marking the person Hannah would be had she survived the whipping, the brutal blow to the head. How tall would she be now? Would there be lines starting to crease the corners of her eyes? Would the childhood lisp have stayed or softened; would she wear her hair long or short? Would memories of Efe, their mother, be better preserved when held by two rather than one? The years after Efe left for Sierra Leone were the time he most often tried to bring Hannah to life, as a witness to the grief; as the only other person in the world who might have understood his actions, have reassured him of their rightness. A comfort.

When Cora barreled into his life, all those months ago, running from the forest and straight into the side of Abel, he took her in—height, hair, lively eyes, the right age with skin the right shade, and he did think it was Hannah. Not for long, but long enough. It doesn't matter if you witness the death, see the body, touch it, lower it into the ground. There's always a part of you that does not, cannot, take the death in. For a moment, Hannah lived, and she was right there in front of him, before death reasserted itself and Hannah flickered back out of existence and a stranger stood before him. He knew then, he would walk beside her a while in the snow-covered forest. He could not have known their path would lead them here. The courthouse. The trial.

What is justice? Thursday wonders. Justice is the law that said his mother was bound by Farmer Nash's lie, the piece of paper she could not read that named the terms of her indenture. Justice the judges that will hear a lie from a white mouth but not the truth from a Black one. Justice the overseer who walked free after Hannah died at his hand.

Thursday has never been sure of miracles. Accepts in his religion only the promise of the good things to come, gratification deferred. Has seen no evidence of a god that would work at the level of a single day, a single moment, reaching down into a small life in a small place to reshape the world.

And yet . . .

There is no sign of the shining light of faith from anyone else in the room, least of all the accused. But Thursday has no choice. He keeps praying.

WINTER

1797–98

24

Come December, the ground hardens, the leaves shrivel, and Cora learns that while summer in the forest is abundant, winter is a lean time.

For a while, she and Agnes are carried along on the magic of new love. But the freshness of it lasts only a few weeks; they are already too familiar to each other, have spent months now just in each other's company. Passion flares up from time to time, on cold nights when they must huddle close together. But, before too long, it is easy to see what has happened not as a breach, a rending of the fabric of the universe, but rather as a natural part of the pattern of their lives. Days take on the same shape as before. Agnes grows thoughtful, a little subdued. Cora feels, little by little, that love is not the center of their world— the center is survival.

The first snow of the year comes overnight, blown in by a bitter wind, leaving the forest eerily quiet when they awake. Agnes, who has spent the last weeks fashioning Cora a pair of snowshoes, nods, relieved that she has finished the work in time.

"Beautiful," Cora says, looking out at the snowfall—partly because she means it, partly to try to lift Agnes's mood, to get her to see something other than privation and danger in the frozen world outside. But Agnes just chews on her lip, worrying the chapped skin there until she draws out a bead of blood. And Cora knows Agnes's head is filled with thoughts of food, of fish living in frozen lakes and where the ice is thin enough for them to cut holes and cast a net below; of ax-heads grown too blunt to chop firewood, and where she will find the best stones to sharpen them; and of animal hides, and which trees are best placed to stretch out fresh pelts so that they can dry and be cut into blankets, coats, and muffs.

It has been half a year since Cora left Preston. Her hands are calloused now, her fingers nimble. Her body leaner, more used to work. But as the world turns white and strange, Cora feels a shiver of fear—feels as if she has just now, this very moment, wandered from civilization. She is aware of how unprepared she is to help Agnes, still unable to work the traps, still clumsy with a bow, still lost sometimes in the winding paths of the forest. She knows what it is to want Agnes—to desire her. But now Cora realizes she *needs* Agnes. Would die out here without her.

It is a lonely thought. It gets into the gap between them, the inches between their hands that do not touch, and widens it, until Cora might as well be standing miles away.

She tries to harden her mind, her heart. She resolves, then and there. She will not be a burden to Agnes. She will not sit at home and wait while Agnes hunts, or watch while Agnes shapes fresh tools unaided. She must do her part to help them survive.

———

Even in the bleakest parts of December, there is still beauty.

When snow falls, flakes of it catch in Agnes's hair, resting white against her coils before they melt—and Cora cannot believe she is here, with this woman she loves; cannot believe the magic of Agnes, snow covered and smiling. Cora tilts her head to the sky, letting snowflakes settle on her own face, and Agnes comes to her and uses her lips to gently warm where each little piece of cold has landed.

They are happy.

But they are also exhausted, scared, and bitterly, bitterly cold.

And so, when the traps break, it is easy to see why they break a little, too.

———

Cora's doze is interrupted by the sound of Agnes's approaching snowshoes. Cora has been in the wikuom since Agnes went out at first light, curled around Patience for warmth. She comes outside in time to see Agnes shake the snow from her shoulders, sit down on a boulder, and put her head in her hands.

"What is it?" Cora asks.

Agnes does not raise her head. Her answer is muffled—she has to repeat it.

"Deadfall and three of the snares all broken. Deadfall wood rotted right away, need all-new logs for it."

"Oh," Cora says. And hates herself a little for saying it—feeling that helplessness descend again, and it makes her sick of herself. Sick of being useless.

With great effort, Agnes raises her head. Her face looks gaunt and her eyes are black holes in the center of her face, no sparkle in them now. Suddenly, ridiculously, Cora remembers summer—remembers warmth, being out on the waves, and the whooping joy of seeing the whales dance in and out of the water. A fleeting memory, soon replaced by her body's insistence on returning to the present, where Cora's fingers and toes are already beginning to numb.

"I'll fix them," Agnes says. Sounding resigned. "Take a few days. Still one working snare, but empty today . . ."

She trails off. Cora thinks she knows the cause of Agnes's worry. They have almost no food left—a few cuts of moose put in a tree hollow to freeze, a little away from their camp, and no guarantees that foxes won't raid their stores. If Agnes has to check the final trap each day just so they have enough to eat, then fixing the new ones will have to be done slowly, after dark, with fingers made clumsy from the cold. It may take weeks until they have three working traps again. Can they afford to wait so long?

"Me can check the snare," Cora says. "Tomorrow. The next day. However long it take."

Agnes shakes her head.

"It's a long way," she says. "Not easy to find your way back."

"Then let me fix the others. The ones that are close."

Agnes looks at Cora, exhaustion in her eyes.

"You don't even know how," she says softly. It feels like a rebuke. Cora is growing agitated, almost angry.

"Let me help," she says.

Agnes lets out a long breath.

"We can go to the snare together," she says.

"No." Cora's voice rising as Agnes's stays the same volume. "That just gon' waste time when you could be fixing the rest of them."

"It's not safe alone."

"You do it alone."

Cora is warming to the argument; it is as if old, tired muscles are coming to life, ready for conflict that she and Agnes have not yet had, all the heady days of summer and autumn. It has been so long since Cora has had to fight like this. But Agnes just shoots her a pleading look—wanting, at all costs, to avoid confrontation.

"Cora," she says.

Cora lifts her chin, a stubborn set to her jaw.

"Me gon' go," she says. "Tomorrow."

It's all they speak of for the rest of the morning. They are losing precious light, and Agnes has to sharpen the axes, hunt for the right wood, and chop it, all to prepare for the job of fixing the traps. Cora fetches them fresh water from the river— because of the current, not yet frozen, but there are patches of stagnant water near the banks that have an icy film over them, a reminder that everything will only get harder and harder. They are not yet even at the darkest day of the year.

When night falls, they eat. They talk little, and when they do, they talk around their fight, no mention of what will or will not happen when the sun rises again. A gibbous moon rises in the sky, sometimes hidden by cloud, but at brief moments uncovered, shining bright.

Cora watches Agnes, made silver by moonlight, feeding scraps to Patience and giving the dog a scratch behind the ears. Some instinct tells Cora to wait, to stay quiet, and so she does.

Agnes looks up. Sees Cora watching her. Sighs.

"Something you should know," Agnes says. The fire between them has turned to ash; even bundled in furs as they are, they won't be able to sit out much longer. But the cold night air brings sharp clarity—brings truth. As soon as they enter the warmth of the wikuom, things will become easier to obscure.

"Tell me," Cora says—though gently. With kindness. Leaning forward a little, showing Agnes she is eager to listen.

"I've been . . . alone," says Agnes. "Since Pa died."

A moment's silence, Agnes grasping for the words.

"Did you know," she says, "that we wanted to go? To Africa. When the men came and asked people to sail away. We heard about it all through the Indians. And we wanted to go."

A cloud passes across the moon. Agnes's face is hidden by the darkness. Cora reaches out, gropes, and finally finds Agnes's hand to hold it.

"In the winter, Pa got sick," says Agnes. "And he . . . he didn't rest. He kept working. He wanted to look after me. He got sicker and sicker and then he died."

Silver strands of smoke rise from the fire, curling around their wrists and intertwined fingers. Cora squeezes Agnes's hand hard.

"Agnes," she says. "Me not sick."

"I know," says Agnes. "I know."

Cora thinks of Elsy, and of hurts held inside you, misplaced blame, anger and grief like hard stones that cannot be shifted, that lie weighing down your soul. She knows what Agnes must feel. Some of her irritation from the morning slips away—but her determination stays. Agnes was not thinking clearly when she said Cora could not help. Was thinking of her father, and of unfounded fears of harm.

"Tomorrow," says Cora. "Me gon' go to the trap. You stay here. Fix the others."

She leans forward, bringing her lips to Agnes's hand, brushing a light kiss over Agnes's knuckles.

"Yes," says Agnes, her tone weary. "I guess you will."

25

The night brings a bitter chill, cold enough to freeze the snow into hard, slippery ice. Cold enough that, reaching the lake that lies about a mile from their camp, Cora sees that it is frozen, too, covered in snow to produce that eerie white wasteland, just like the place where Cora saw Agnes for the first time. Patience is with her. On this, Agnes insisted. And by the time she is an hour's walk or so from home, Cora is glad of it, because it is extraordinary how much the forest swallows sound, creating a thick, absorbent quiet that makes Cora feel achingly, desperately alone.

She reaches out a gloved hand to give Patience a pat. Not much farther now.

Cora's feet feel heavy and clumsy in the snowshoes. She remembers how Agnes moved across the ice, back when Agnes was just an unknown shape in the snowy forest. Cora is sure she will never have that quickness.

They are near the snare—near enough to see it through a gap in the trees—when Patience stops abruptly. Cora stops, too, unease creeping over her.

A tiny streak of movement, close to the ground. Well hidden, its winter coat pure white against the snow, a hare is moving around the trap. It stops, sensing their presence, and raises its head—ears twitching.

Cora holds perfectly still. She doesn't even breathe. Beside her, Patience is also frozen—mesmerized, they both stare at this creature, which, satisfied that it is alone, begins to hop around the undergrowth again.

Cora feels a tangle of emotions. There is a kind of primal excitement—an imagined smell of blood in her nostrils. Perhaps, with Patience beside her, Cora is catching a little of the dog's predatory instincts; the hare in their sights, neither can look away.

Then there is a cooler, more rational desire—the hare will mean food, will mean less pressure on Agnes, and so Cora watches its winding path around the trap with anticipation. Surely, just a few hops more, and the hare will be caught.

But there is also another feeling that runs counter to both these things. There is an affinity—a connection forged in that first sight of the hare, in the appreciation of its beauty, its perfect adaption to the winter around it. And so, a small part of Cora's heart cannot help but will this creature away from danger—cannot help but wish for it to escape. Because what are any of them but animals in the cold trying to survive?

They wait. Patience is taut—ready to pounce. But, with a hand on the dog's back, Cora keeps her at bay.

The hare comes toward the trap. Stops, as if considering it. Its body ready to spring, toward the snare or away, Cora cannot know.

Cora moves her foot. The snowshoe wrenches free from the snow with a crackling sound. The hare takes startled flight, a barely visible streak of white, soon lost from view. Patience bursts forward in pursuit but bounds only a few dozen feet before concluding it is a lost cause. The dog trots back to Cora; they exchange a glance, but it is free of disappointment. Cora even shrugs, as if to say, *That's how it goes sometimes.*

Secretly, below the layers of her coat and undershirts, her heart is pounding—and her mind is with the hare, racing away to freedom, sharing in a little of its relief at such a narrow escape.

When the magic fades, and Cora's rational self regains control of her mind, she finally feels a sense of loss, even of frustration. Cora looks up at the sun, which shows the day to be around noon. She imagines going back to Agnes empty-handed and hates how powerless the idea makes her feel.

She looks at Patience.

"What you think?" she asks the dog—her voice ringing out clear through the woods. "We gon' stay?"

There are still a few hours of daylight. Another hare might stray close to the trap, or a fox. Cora pats her pocket; she has a knife there, should she need it. The thought of being a hunter, a provider—of sitting out of sight and awaiting prey, so she can bring something home to Agnes—is a seductive one.

Patience cocks her head, and Cora takes it as assent. She searches around the trap until she finds a place where two trees, growing close to a large boulder, have created a natural hollow.

Crawls into the space and gently pulls Patience in beside her. Here, they are concealed from the view of any animals passing by. Sheltered from the wind, the hollow is not even too cold. It smells damp and mossy. Cora leans back against the rock.

"Well," she says aloud. "Now we wait."

She fixes her eyes on the forest, imagining herself an eagle, a wolf, a bear. Feeling as though she will catch every rustle of branches, and every slinking thing that tries to crawl close to the ground, unseen. She feels powerful. Not one small creature among many, in these woods. She feels, for the first time, master of everything out here in the wilderness.

She watches and she waits.

———

Cora jerks awake to the slobbery sensation of Patience licking her face, cracking her head against a tree trunk. Sore and disoriented, she takes a moment to understand where she is. The world is swirling white; outside the hollow, the wind roars. Squinting into the blizzard, Cora realizes how late it has grown; she cannot see the sun, but the only light is coming from low in the sky. She has dozed off and the afternoon has slipped by.

She is so cold she does not realize she is cold at first—has moved past the point of shivering. But she starts to panic when it hurts to breathe.

"Oh no," she says. "Oh no, no, no."

She crawls out of their hiding place and scrambles upright. Stamps her feet and claps her gloved hands to bring feeling back into her extremities. Snow settles on her arms; icy flakes blow into her eyes. She turns, trying to orient herself. The trap—wherever it is—is hidden by the flurry.

Alarm fades to embarrassment. She half expects to see Agnes at any moment, emerging from the woods and chiding Cora for her carelessness. But of course, Agnes was most likely gone all afternoon, chopping wood. She never would have known that Cora was away so long. And now the snowstorm— Agnes could be waiting it out somewhere, thinking Cora is home alone. . . .

Night is coming. Already the white clouds have a gray tinge and the forest is full of shadows. If she tries to spend the night out here, she will freeze.

A shudder passes through Cora—her body coming to life.

She doesn't let herself think about it—doesn't let the fear return. Instead she says—

"Come on, Patience."

And off they go.

———

The paths are lost under fresh snow. Cora tries to orient herself by the sun, knowing that she walked north from the wikuom to reach the trap, but the slanting light of evening seems to come from all around her.

Even Patience is lost. The dog runs where Cora trudges, dashing one way and then another, going in circles, pushing her nose against the ground. But the snow has destroyed the scent trails, too.

"Stupid," Cora mutters to herself. A bitter wind blowing flakes against her face; she uses her hand to shield her eyes against them. "Stupid, stupid, stupid."

It's frustration she feels, more than anxiety. Walking has warmed her a little, putting the fragility of her body out of her mind. Instead she is thinking of Agnes—how cross she will be, when Cora returns late and empty-handed. Or worse, as the darkness draws in, Agnes might even go looking for Cora, might be worried something has happened. . . . In her head, Cora is already rehearsing the argument they will inevitably have, when she and Agnes are finally reunited.

The blizzard thins—then stops. Night has fallen, and without the movement of falling snow, the woods have a ghostly stillness to them.

Cora looks around as best she can in the low light. The trees around her seem tantalizingly familiar—surely she has passed that crop of three pine trees before, leaning into one another like old friends? But whether that was on the way out to the trap or mere minutes ago, she cannot say.

Patience lets out a whine.

"Is all right, Patience," Cora says, in a voice designed to soothe herself as much as the dog. "Is all right."

They move on through the gathering dark.

————

When she sees the lake, Cora lets out a breath of relief. She knows the lake. Can orient herself now. Home about half an hour's walk away. Patience barks in happy recognition, and Cora gives the dog a hearty pat on her back.

They begin their slow walk around its edge, and soon the heady relief of reaching it fades, leaving Cora's limbs heavy with exhaustion. She glances up, looking longingly over to the far banks, to where they will pick up the path that leads them home.

What if . . . ?

For the second time that day, Cora remembers Agnes out on the ice. The snowshoes feel solid, have cut easily through the freshly fallen snow. And on the way out, when the ground was frozen hard, they served her well. She lifts one foot and then the other, testing them. . . .

What seals it is a gust of wind, so cold as to be painful, finding every tiny opening in her clothes, around her neck and wrists. She will save precious time going across the ice. It is dangerous, after all, to be out too long in this weather; how often has Agnes impressed this upon her, insisted that in winter, exposure is death?

Cora walks slowly to the edge of the lake. It is uncanny, the way the snow makes it look like flat, solid ground.

She tests the ice—puts one foot over the bank. It sinks into snow, then hits the hard surface beneath.

Gingerly, she applies more and more weight until almost her entire body presses down. Nothing cracks. There is not even a creak. The ice holds her with ease.

Another step. Her second foot caught by the ice without trouble.

With bended knees, Cora walks. Careful of the slipperiness—but the snow makes the passage easier. She can feel herself relaxing, settling into a rhythm of movement. She turns back to look for Patience—not yet beside her, but watching apprehensively from the bank, now a good few feet away. Cora lifts a gloved hand and beckons. . . .

The crack, when it comes, is not the sound Cora is expecting. Not thunder, not a gunshot. More a series of crunches—she thinks of bones, ground underfoot. The noise travels—it runs from under her feet outward, unseen patterns swirling across the surface, hidden under the snow.

Cora has time to think—

Oh.

And then the ice is gone from underneath her and she is falling.

————

Through the brutal shock of cold, her mind notes, dimly, that something is wrong. She should be in water, but she is in ice—encased in it, unable to move. Limbs heavy. Not sinking or flailing, but perfectly still, held in darkness.

It is almost peaceful. Timeless. She might have been here many hours already, in this place without movement or light or sound. She could stay here, frozen, forever. . . .

Except, of course, for breath. She becomes aware, slowly, of this problem. Of the air knocked out of her lungs by the fall, and the way they ache in protest. She must breathe—the knowledge has a dull urgency to it. And yet, she does not move.

She is frozen. She is ice. She will be ice forever.

————

A noise like a dream, faint and far away. But something in Cora's mind tells her to seize on it—to hold it like a rope.

It is a dog. Barking.

Why is there a dog barking?

As if in conversation with herself, Cora answers.

It's Patience. Barking because you fall through the ice.

The voices in her head are slow and sluggish.

No. That can't be right.

Focusing on the barking makes it seem closer. Close enough to reach out and touch . . .

Open your eyes.

But it is her nose and mouth that want to open, want to suck in breath and ease the tightness in her throat. It feels like there is no way to open her eyes and not the rest of her; she has to stay closed, a fortress against the awful cold.

Open them. Now.

There is light. Just above her, a pool of silver. The moon. And a shape against it, distorted by water.

Still the barking sound. Patience. Up there. The hole in the ice.

It makes an awful kind of fragmented sense, and Cora starts to panic.

She is not at peace, lost in some comforting eternal darkness. She is in the lake. And she is drowning.

The cold of the water, which has been a deadening force, lulling her to stillness, suddenly becomes sharp—pain jolts through her entire body and shocks her into action. She flails, sodden clothes weighing her down, the snowshoes clumsy on her feet, but slowly she is rising, rising, toward the light.

Her head breaks the surface; she chokes and splutters, and air floods her lungs. Hands, shooting out, clutch against the jagged edges of the cracked ice, which breaks further as she tries to get purchase. Over the sound of her gasping breath, she can still hear Patience barking—and dimly feels something on her face, Patience licking her—but the world is very far away, any sensation shut out except the agonizing cold.

Shuddering, Cora clings to the ice, but it is too slippery, her body too heavy and useless. She cannot pull herself up. She tries to push into the ice, toward land, breaking a path, but the ice is unyielding. Panic again threatens to overwhelm whatever small part of her mind is not frozen. She can't stay in this water. It will kill her.

In the end, it is Patience who saves her. Grips her jaws around one of Cora's arms and pulls, Cora kicking weakly, and together, they drag Cora from the water. On shaking limbs, Cora crawls, the ice groaning underneath her. She crawls and crawls until she reaches the bank, the lip of it rising above her, a seemingly impossible height. All strength has left her now. She has started to shiver violently—teeth chattering so hard she bites her tongue and tastes blood. The thought of resting here a while is so comforting—she could just gather her strength before ascending the shore. . . .

Patience noses insistently into the side of her face.

"Yes," Cora murmurs. "Yes, me know."

Because Patience understands what Cora's mind is too muddled to see clearly—that lying, cold and wet, on the ice is a death sentence, too. Slower than the one that would have come for her in the water, but no less fatal.

Cora breathes as best she can when her chest feels like iron. She summons whatever energy she has—the corners of her vision go dark and her focus blurs, as reserves of strength stored in her senses rush instead to her limbs. She scrabbles for purchase on the shore, hands sinking into the snow until they find stony earth. Supporting herself this way, she is able to get to her knees. From there, she falls forward—or this is how it seems to her, gravity doing the last bit of work to get her to land.

And she has done it. She sprawls onto the shore, her face

pressed to the snow. Somehow, it doesn't feel like a victory. She wonders whether she could simply lie here until the snow buries her. How peaceful the idea seems. How soft the ground . . .

Pain returns again, sharp and insistent. Her whole body shudders. She sits up with a gasp. Time turned strange—how long was she lying there? The moon seems in a different place from where she remembered it last, now clear of the treetops, heading toward the crest of its arc across the sky. But maybe what she saw before was an illusion. She has the sense that she cannot trust herself anymore. Cannot trust her instincts or her thoughts.

She is cold.

You need to walk.

Still on her knees, she tries to stand. Stumbles, and on all fours lets out a groan.

It is only then that her mind catches up to the fact that Patience has gone. She looks around as much as she can; her neck, like the rest of her, is stiff. But the dog is nowhere.

Did she imagine that Patience was here with her? It is hard to summon the memories, or the feeling of Patience dragging her out from under the ice. In that moment, she is almost ready to believe Patience is entirely fiction—that she has never existed, and that Agnes hasn't either. That Jamaica is a figment of her imagination and that Leah was only a dream.

She is so cold.

She starts to crawl. Almost blind, the world gray around her, just snow and looming trees. But the last of her instincts for survival keep her moving—pressing onward, toward home, though home now is less a concrete direction than an idea, a fading hope. Since her eyes are closed, it might be right in front of her—she imagines she can see the flickering fire, feel the warmth. . . .

How long she has been crawling, she does not know. Cannot mark time, her mind too addled and the surrounding woods too similar. The lake is no longer beside her—but that could mean she has come around it and found the path to the wik-uom, or that she has gone badly wrong and is headed in the opposite direction. But the imagined warmth of the fire at home—that begins to feel real. A pleasant heat at first, but soon grown awful—she is sweating under her furs, finding it hard to breathe.

She sheds her gloves first. Her bare fingers in the snow, and still they feel too hot. Next, her coat—shrugging it off and leaving it on the ground, but though she feels the wind on her exposed skin, she cannot feel the chill.

Her arms give out underneath her. She can crawl no farther.

Lying there, on the ground, shuddering and feverish, she looks her own death in the face. Feels no fear, only a sense of annoyance. How stupid, to lose Agnes—to have wasted her love.

The world around her is losing its material reality. It shimmers and swims. Uncanny visions dance around her—bears and wolves and moose with glowing eyes, and animals that are not really animals at all, that walk on their hind legs and have the limbs, heads, and horns of different beasts. British soldiers with guns. Elsy and Benjamin, chasing each other and laughing. Her own mother, clapped in irons but smiling and singing as Leah leads her back to her plantation to face her fate.

To close her eyes would be the easiest thing in the world. Would be to rest—and all she wants is to rest. But something keeps them open.

Just a little longer, she thinks.

And the last thing she sees before she finally closes her eyes is a dark shape rushing toward her, and it might be Agnes or it might be Elsy or it might be Leah or it might be an angel.

26

What Cora does not see—

Agnes, reaching the trap through the blizzard, panicked after Cora did not return before dark. Battling with everything she has against the fatalism in her heart, belief in the inevitability of death—some force of the universe determined to keep her alone, striking down everyone cursed by the fact that she loves them.

Agnes, standing in the empty forest. If she could kneel, she would, but the ground is too snow covered. If she had faith in the goodness of God, she would pray.

Then, from the trees, Patience—bursting forth, barking, a greeting and a warning in one. Agnes understands at once. She follows, light on her snowshoes, almost at a run. The urgency of Patience gives her hope, but the hope is a fragile thing. Images flash across her mind, each more awful than the last. Cora dying. Cora dead. A red streak in the snow, the body gone—dragged off by some creature to be consumed.

They find her lying on the ground, face up, eyes open to the moon. Coat abandoned beside her. Still. Agnes stops running, stops as suddenly as if she has walked into a tree. Cannot bear to come closer. But then a great shudder runs through Cora's body.

Alive.

Agnes, hoisting Cora from the ground. Cora feels small and breakable in her arms. She is shivering and fevered. Agnes holds her close. She walks.

———

In the wikuom, Agnes, rubbing Cora's frozen feet and hands. At the moment of rescue, Agnes was all considered action. It is only now the fear comes. She trembles so badly it is hard to hold the spoon of bone broth to Cora's lips.

Sometimes, Cora's eyes close. At other times they are open; she looks around with a sense of urgency. Agnes murmurs soothing words that Cora does not seem to hear.

Finally, Cora succumbs to a deeper sleep. Agnes hunches over and cries.

Outside the wikuom, Patience stands sentinel; she will keep the dark, dangerous world at bay, as penance for the fact that she could not protect Cora.

It is too late, of course. The danger no longer outside, but within.

———

Cora's fever is getting worse. Agnes, like a statue, remains by her side. In her heart, she has given up. And yet cannot bear to give up. Inside her, the two forces struggle. She accepts death and yet she rails against it.

Not this time. Not this one. Not when she has, for the first time since her parents died, known a deep, reciprocated love that has eclipsed all else.

Out in the forest, Agnes is many things. Hunter, builder, crafter of axes and arrows. But she is not a healer. Beyond basic salves, she knows nothing of what might help Cora now, what would banish the fever, get the chill from her bones, make her well again.

A gray dawn breaking. Agnes, resolved. She goes outside and readies the wooden sled—not used for weeks now, not since she last managed to fell a moose and had to drag the meat back across the forest. She piles onto it every fur she has—her own coat, the rug from the floor of the wikuom, the bedclothes. She carries Cora out.

Agnes whispering words Cora will half hear in a dream—
I love you. Don't leave me.

Four miles' walk to a place Agnes once called home.

It is faintly snowing. Light flakes, like motes of dust, small in the sky and yet together, on the ground, a thick blanket.

Agnes starts to walk. Dragging the sled behind her. Head down, each step a strain, each step an act of faith. Each step taking her closer to Shelburne, taking her away from her years of solitude.

———

The quiet forest. Snow-covered pines watch their progress. Agnes's tears freeze hard on her cheeks, little diamonds made of salt water. But still, she walks. Cora, motionless, almost invisible in the pile of furs. Patience, by Agnes's side—as she has been since they found each other, and as she will be until the end.

———

Shelburne. Reaching the outskirts after dark, Agnes slow and panting with exhaustion. She falters—the endless walk, the dragging of Cora on the sled, was enough to numb her fears, but now, here, she is uncertain. This is not her world. She knows the woods now, not this. The smoking chimneys, the candlelight flickering in windows. Streets empty but the sound of people, closer to the town center. She shrinks into the shadows.

What now?

Agnes leaving Cora, Patience standing guard, hidden in an alleyway. Circling the streets, keeping out of sight, slinking, afraid. She goes from window to window, searching for some sign—a doctor, though how she would know one by sight she cannot say. Even a kindly-looking family would do, someplace she might knock and leave Cora safely on the doorstep, knowing she would be helped by those inside. The cold settles within her, sharp and painful. Cora, unmoving, will be colder still. Panic, now, in the way Agnes moves . . .

Agnes reaching a tavern, the glass fogged from breath inside. The murmur of voices within. A figure comes so close to the window she has to duck away, but as he stares into the night his features come into focus through the pane. She knows him. . . .

Agnes straightening. Letting herself be seen, or half seen

in the dark. The figure at the window meets her gaze. Recognition.

The opening of a door. Agnes holds herself, fearful but determined.

Thursday steps into the night.

"Cora," Agnes says.

The smallest change in his expression, but it is sufficient to convey heartbreak.

"Dead?" he asks.

"Sick," Agnes says. "Very sick."

A brief silence between them. Then—

"Please," Agnes says.

Thursday following Agnes to the sled. He peels back one of the blankets. Sees Cora within—eyes closed, breathing labored, a sheen of sweat over her face despite the cold. He touches a single finger to the side of her cheek—a soft, brotherly kind of tenderness. Then he takes her into his arms.

Agnes, waiting. Crouching between two houses, in the darkest shadow she can find. Patience by her side. Two pairs of eyes that watch as strangers pass, hunched against the wind, thinking only of the warmth of their homes.

Thursday returns. He stands on the street corner and looks around, frowning. Agnes, still hidden, knows he is thinking she has gone—slipped away. And she could go. The safest thing would be to go. Thursday seems harmless, but there have been many people who seemed harmless right up until the point they did her harm. . . .

She steps out into the moonlight. She has to know.

"Is she . . . ?"

"Dr. Mann," he says. "He'll take care of her." A small shrug—that might, to those who do not know him, seem careless, seem an expression of a small feeling, but that masks a deep pain. "We wait and see."

Silver trails of breath from both their mouths, rising to the point where they curl together and become one. Agnes, staring at the ground, thinking of the long walk home. Thursday looking at Agnes.

"You're tired," he says.

Agnes shrinks back, afraid to be looked at, to be seen.

"No," she says.

"I got a room at the inn," he says. "Seeing old friends. Used to live here, come back when I can. Meant to start the journey back today. But the snow—couldn't leave."

Agnes has stepped away, but he continues, undaunted.

"Stay."

"No," she says.

"In the morning, we'll know more. About Cora."

His voice deep and gentle, a hum felt in her bones. And she is tired—of course she is.

She brushes fingers through Patience's fur, as if this will provide an answer. Makes a choice, the decision written on her face and in the uncoiling of her body, no longer poised to flee.

Thursday nods, satisfied. He turns to walk away, knowing she will follow. And so she does—a few paces behind, every step cautious, her eyes skirting the houses, the darkened windows, looking for danger, but finding none.

Some dangers, of course, unseen. Some dangers are eyes in the darkness, shapes at the darkened windows, watching the slow progress of this young woman with a wild look, and thinking—

Could that be her?

———

Morning. No more snowfall. A hard, slate-gray sky and a bitter wind. Thursday, returning from the doctor to the small room where he and Agnes have spent the night.

"No change," he says.

Agnes wrings her hands together, looking stricken.

"That means no worse," Thursday says gently. "Doctor says she needs time."

Agnes nods. Her eyes out the window, her mind miles away, agonizing over what to do now.

"I have to go," she says, more to herself than to Thursday. "It's not safe." And yet she does not move.

Thursday's arm twitches, as if he wants to put a reassuring hand on her but thinks better of it.

"I can come back," Thursday says. "Have someone send word if she . . . Well. I can keep an eye on her. And if—when she's better. She'll come back to you."

The last words spoken sadly. Agnes glances at him, assessing him. Trust not something that comes easy to her.

"The waiting will kill me," she says. But in a resigned sort of way. They both know she will go. She will hide in the forest and she will hope, and there will be days when that hope fades to almost nothing and she will cry herself to sleep, but the hope will be like the birch trees in winter, bare and hardy, ready to bud again when the world thaws.

Agnes and Patience, slipping out into the cold morning.

Agnes, thoughtful, focused inward on the turbulence of her feelings and the difficulty of all that is to come. Not scanning the world as she usually does. A momentary slip of awareness. She does not see the soldiers waiting.

———

Two of them. Red-coated, rifles over their shoulders. Rubbing their hands to keep warm. When the girl appears, they move easily—they are not afraid. Though they have been told she may run, if she can. But two more of them, out of sight, around the corner, just in case.

———

When Agnes finally sees them—too late, much too late—she freezes.

"We're looking for someone," one of them says. His voice casual—deceptively so.

Agnes is hardly breathing.

"From the Dalton land," says the other.

This is when she starts to run. The name unleashing in her something primal—a complete terror that sends her stumbling away. But here, in town, she has none of her usual grace and speed.

She slips on the icy ground. Lands awkwardly with her hands out, trying to break the fall. A cry of pain—and they have her, seizing her by the arms and dragging her upright.

———

Patience. Until now, the dog has gone unnoticed, crouching low to the ground, ears pinned back, making no sound except the softest of growls.

But when the soldiers put their hands on Agnes, Patience leaps.

A snarling streak of fury, teeth bared, her jaws snapping left and right, tearing cloth and biting down into flesh . . .

One gunshot. Another.

"No!" Agnes cries, but her refusal is meaningless. They march her away, one soldier limping, trailing drops of scarlet from the wound in his leg as he goes.

———

All is quiet. The residents of Shelburne, peeping out of their windows at the sound of trouble, turn away, shaking their heads. But their days must go on. It is none of their business.

Thursday, who has seen all from the inn, curses himself for his inaction but knows, deep down, that there was nothing to be done. Sometimes, the cruelty of the world must be accepted as it is. It is not the first time he has learned this lesson, nor will it be the last.

On a pallet bed in the back of the doctor's house, Cora sleeps fitfully, cursed by strange and unsettling dreams.

———

And in the middle of the road, a little body, gray and limp, soon to be covered by falling snow.

27

The case is brought up from Shelburne to Halifax for convenience's sake, one of the parties having sailed into Halifax and planning to sail out again as soon as the trial has concluded. He had, of course, not expected a trial at all, this man who claims Agnes. This is what Cora struggles to understand. That Agnes—her Agnes, whose fierce will for survival has sustained her all these years—was not going to fight. Instead, it was all Thursday—steady, quiet Thursday. The world, in many ways, turned on its head. By the time Cora's fever broke, it was done, Thursday's petition placed before the magistrates.

"There was this woman, Mary," he said to Cora, sitting in the dark room of the doctor's house. "She lived here, years ago. A man tried to sell her. She went to court, said she was free. Maybe Agnes can do it, too."

They sat in silence. Thursday looking pained, unhappy at

the grief he had caused Cora in telling her of Agnes's arrest, unaware that all her anger and sadness was turned inward. For all this, she blamed herself.

When he stood up to go, Cora finally found her voice.

"She win?" she asked in a hoarse whisper.

"What?" said Thursday.

"The woman. Mary. She win?"

Thursday looked at her a long time, then turned and walked away. Which was answer enough.

———

Agnes looks the same. Cora was not expecting this; it stuns her. She stops, half-risen from her chair, and watches Agnes be led to the dock—the same body, the same face, the same close-cropped hair.

"Agnes."

Cora realizes she has spoken without meaning to. How could she hold back the name, when Agnes looks just as she remembered? And Cora's love is undiminished—pulls her toward Agnes like a connecting cord.

The heads of all those at the front turn toward Cora—the lawyer, gray-haired and stooped, a sheaf of papers tucked under his arm, and his client, strikingly dressed, in a bottle-green frock coat, not much older than Cora, with a thick head of blond hair and an upright bearing. But she does not see; sees only Agnes raise her head, and the way her lips part. They had tried to send word, when Cora woke up. But they were not sure anything got through, and now Cora knows it did not, because Agnes is looking at her with relief.

Maybe that is why she did not fight. She had thought Cora was dead.

Agnes looks away first, dropping her gaze to the floor. Cora, unsteady on her feet, almost falls back into her chair—but Thursday is there to catch her, to help her into her seat. When he lets go, she reaches out to take his hand. Knows she will need to hold it, to get through what is to come. Her legs shake. Her chest is tight, her lungs not yet returned to what they were, before the lake and the ice. Though even if there had been no illness, she would still tremble here, still struggle to breathe.

After she woke up, after she hitched a ride on a cart going north, came and slept, hidden, in Thursday's hut on the farm, they spoke of Agnes.

Cora said, "Me love her."

Thursday said, "I know."

Cora said, "You don't understand. Me *love* her. In all the ways."

Thursday said, "I know."

And that was all they needed to say.

The judge is ruddy-faced and middle-aged. His bulky body looks like it would make more sense on a farm than here; he lacks the refinement or fastidiousness that is present in the other men of the court, the lawyers and the clerks. He seats himself at his desk and perches a pair of spectacles on his nose, the better to examine a piece of paper in front of him.

"To begin," he says, his voice carrying with ease, "the court acknowledges Mr. Dalton, and expresses its condolences at the recent loss of his father." The judge, with a pause, looks over the top of his glasses at the young man in front of him. "Good to see you back, Henry," he says, in a warmer, less official tone.

The young man in the green coat—Henry Dalton—inclines his head. "Justice Matthews," he says.

The judge collects himself, lets the fond half smile slip from his face. He turns to his clerk with a curt nod that indicates the trial may commence.

The clerk opens with the bare bones of the case. Thursday's claim is that Agnes is being kept against her will, and may be transported from the colony, when in fact she is free. Mr. Dalton alleges that Agnes is his rightful property.

Mr. Dalton sits at the front of the courtroom, relaxed and easy in his chair, arms folded across his chest. Cora tries not to look at him. Any time he catches her attention by a slight movement—a bending to speak in his lawyer's ear, or a tilting back to gaze up at the ceiling—she is overcome with a powerful hatred.

Instead, Cora's focus is on Agnes—standing motionless, head still bowed as if in silent prayer. Cora notices everything— from the way Agnes's eyes drift closed and then snap open again to the way her left hand twitches every time Dalton is named. She looks resigned. She looks defeated and afraid. And it is this, more than anything, that terrifies Cora. Because the truth, something pure and unsullied by the evils of human cruelty, is that Agnes is free—belongs only to herself, and perhaps in parts to Cora, a belonging freely given and rooted in love. But there is another, darker truth, forged by human hands in the hellfires of conquest and bondage, written in blood on a page and made law, enforced by those with the power to forge the world as they see fit and keep those other, purer truths at bay. Cora fears that, according to this law, Agnes is a slave. That she belongs to this man, Dalton—was indeed, as he alleges, brought over from Virginia by his father, who settled in Nova Scotia. That she ran away. And that Mr. Dalton, who is now established on a sugar plantation in Jamaica, but has returned to Nova Scotia to settle the affairs of his father after the latter's recent death, intends to reclaim on behalf of his family what is rightfully theirs.

When Jamaica is mentioned, Cora does not even notice at first. Thursday nudges her, and she glances questioningly at him.

"Jamaica," he says.

It sounds like another language, like the name of a forgotten god from a long-dead civilization. The word takes time to find the part of her mind where it has meaning, where there are memories she has kept locked, that have lain untouched since Agnes and the forest and the promise of a new life.

There are some words that, when heard, light up their partner in your mind. *Mother* and *love* or *snow* and *cold*. There was a time when, for Cora, *Jamaica* and *home* were a pair, perhaps the strongest pair of all. But no longer. *Home* has found a new match, and it is *Agnes*, and it throws things out of joint to have *home* and *Agnes* and *Jamaica* all together. To think of Agnes sent to Jamaica, enslaved there, creates a profound anguish, a tangling of the proper relations between the things Cora has loved.

The clerk reaches the end of his summary, and Mr. Dalton's gray-haired lawyer is on his feet.

"If it pleases the court," he says, in a reedy, unctuous voice.

"Mr. Dalton wishes to address it on certain particularities of this case."

The judge spreads his hands, an invitation to speak. Mr. Dalton stands. Glancing once behind him, as if to assess his audience—his eyes, briefly, find Cora's but slide quickly over her, unseeing and uncaring, before he turns back to the judge.

When he speaks, it is with a certain rhythm, a certain showmanship. An arrogance. A voice and pattern of speech honed through practice, through many years of being listened to as the utmost authority.

"For me and my family at this time," Mr. Dalton begins, "it is important to clarify something of the personal importance of the matter before the court, and of the character of the accused."

Mr. Dalton, of course, technically the accused—accused of the theft of a person. But why should he care for such details as these?

"I do not need to belabor the point, Justice Matthews," he continues, "of the great upheaval and uncertainty of that period of war that brought my family to this province—your own family having followed the same path as ours from the state of Virginia to here. We arrived, like so many, with but a modest share of the property we had left behind, and my late father was determined to rebuild on these new shores."

Mr. Dalton holds the court in rapt attention. The clerk, in glancing up too often, loses his place in his notes and has to hunch over and scribble down what he has forgotten to record. Mr. Dalton's lawyer nods approvingly. The judge's eyes dart behind his spectacles, following every move of Mr. Dalton's smooth white hands as he gestures broadly to emphasize his speech.

Cora alone watches Agnes. Watches the slow, almost imperceptible change in her face—a grim set coming over it, jaw tight, a flash of fierceness in her eyes. Signs that the fight might not be all out of her yet.

"In a few years, our farm here prospered," says Mr. Dalton. "And yet, when all seemed tranquil after the hardships we had suffered . . ." He pauses. The clerk, pen hanging loosely in his hand, leans forward. "Tragedy struck."

Mr. Dalton had been standing in place. Now he moves forward a pace—closer to the judge, but also closer to Agnes, and Cora sees the way Agnes flinches.

"As part of our property, brought from Virginia, we had three slaves—a man, a woman, and a young girl," Mr. Dalton says. "Treated by ourselves with nothing but care, offered a new life in Nova Scotia after all the horrors of war. And yet, they repaid us by running—the man and the girl disappearing one night. This was their first crime. Then, not long after, the woman—" He breaks off abruptly. Turns his head away from the front, and Cora can see something dark in his expression, a flash before he gathers himself and turns back.

"My sister was killed," he says. The words plain, unadorned, and hinting at some ghastly pit of rage, lurking just beneath his controlled veneer of normality. Cora shifts in her seat. She feels, for the first time, not contempt but fear—because what has come before has been pure performance, but this is raw. This is real.

She glances at Agnes, who has raised her eyes for a moment

from the floor. Something like shock in her face—but it is quickly shuttered away.

"Poison," Mr. Dalton says. "The case never heard before any court, seeing as the murderer died herself soon after. Judgment from God, perhaps, if not from the law of this province."

He turns, for the first time, to Agnes. Addresses her with a cold precision, though nominally his remarks are still for the judge.

"It feels pertinent to the facts of the case," he says, "that the accused is the daughter of a murderer—is from a family of murderers, who conspired to do great harm in an attempt to steal their freedom from us."

He pauses. Draws a breath—seems to be the only one in the courtroom still breathing, the others mere statues awaiting his every word.

"After the death of my sister, we searched, of course," Mr. Dalton says. "But my father soon gave up his missing slaves for dead. I left for Jamaica, to live with an uncle there, and we believed that to be the end of the sorry affair."

He smooths back his hair—his voice regaining some of its former quality, back to being an actor on a stage rather than a man barely concealing the force of his wounded, grieving fury.

"How fortunate, then," he continues, "that I happened to be in the province to settle the affairs of my late father at just the time when rumor surfaced that, perhaps, one of the slaves had survived after all. Fortunate for myself—of course—but fortunate also for the province. To have such a dangerous individual at large would, it goes without saying, be of grievous risk to the good people of Nova Scotia."

Mr. Dalton fixes Agnes with one final glance—cursory, cold, and dismissive.

"It is my sense of duty, above all, that drove me to relay the full story of my family's tragedy, and to inform the court of the particular history of the accused."

Mr. Dalton resumes his seat beside his lawyer. The court-room feels like a gun has been fired—the air thick and heavy and the silence ringing.

The judge removes his spectacles slowly.

"Mr. Dalton," he says, "it sounds as if you intend to bring a case not of ownership, but of being an accomplice to murder. A very different, and very serious charge."

Mr. Dalton makes a small movement with his shoulders—almost nonchalant, as if to say that it does not matter, that in proving one he can avenge the other, once he becomes the sole arbiter of Agnes's fate.

"My client is content for proceedings to continue as intended," Mr. Dalton's obsequious lawyer says. "He just wished to set out certain matters before we come to the question at hand."

The judge nods. He is frowning, and the effect on his large, round face is severe.

"Of course," says the judge. "I quite understand."

He glances over at Agnes, who still stands motionless, hands clasped in front of her, head bowed. A pose of devotion, of prayer.

"The court invites comments from the plaintiff, should she choose to make them."

Agnes does not react. Either she does not hear, or she does not understand, or she has nothing she wishes to say. Cora sees

Mr. Dalton and his lawyer exchange a triumphant glance and her blood boils afresh at the sight of it.

The judge makes a small upward movement with his eyebrows, as if to say—

Well, this will be brief.

And while Mr. Dalton is still the center of Cora's rage, she is beginning to hate this judge, too, this vast man all dressed in black, who purports to represent justice and yet greets one of the parties in his court by his Christian name.

"Mr. Dalton," the judge says. "You have, I assume, the bill of sale."

His tone suggesting this is a mere formality. But there is a pause. When Mr. Dalton replies, he sounds faintly puzzled.

"Not with me today."

The judge has returned the spectacles to his nose, the better to sit with his pen poised over his papers. He looks up in surprise, his eyes made larger by the glass as he blinks at Mr. Dalton.

"I see."

Mr. Dalton's lawyer steps in. "The document exists, of course, sir."

"Of course," the judge replies. But says no more—leaving an awkward silence, with the expectation that someone will fill it. Mr. Dalton looks at his lawyer; there is an irritation radiating off him now.

"And of course, we would be pleased to present it before the court," the lawyer continues smoothly.

The judge seems mollified.

"That would be most helpful," he says. "There are procedures to be followed." He gives Mr. Dalton a somewhat apologetic glance. "I'm sure you understand."

Mr. Dalton says nothing. His lawyer says, "We do, sir. Of course."

"An adjournment of a few days will suffice, I hope, to locate the document?"

"Absolutely, sir," the lawyer says. "More than enough time."

Cora exhales. She does not know what would be worse—to hear the news now, today, that Agnes is gone from her forever. Or to hold on to a sliver of hope another few days, the futility of believing the outcome will be different if they only wait a little longer.

The judge stands to make his exit. Mr. Dalton and his lawyer stand, too, and Cora watches as Agnes lifts her eyes toward where Mr. Dalton sits. There is an intensity to the way that she looks at him; it stops Cora's heart a moment, though she is not the target of it. The expression on Agnes's face suggests a tangle of things; if Cora had to describe it, she would say it was Agnes's way of communicating that there are other moral codes than the ones held up in this courtroom, ones not written into law. Codes of survival, more intimately acquainted with matters of life and death . . .

And Cora, suddenly and unexpectedly, thinks of her mother. Covers her eyes with one hand, to try to banish the unwanted image.

"Cora?" Thursday says gently, close to her ear, his tone concerned.

"Nothing," she manages to reply. Opening her eyes to find Agnes hanging her head again, as if that brief flame of resistance might have been a dream. "It's nothing."

In the public viewing area, a floorboard creaks behind

them. Strange; they are alone. Cora turns in time to catch the back of a figure, retreating quickly out the door.

Another dream—because the back of the figure could be Leah. But Cora blinks until her eyes recognize the impossibility of this. Her mind merely conjuring ghosts of the past—Leah, her mother—in response to the day's dissection of freedom. The question—what would you do to be free?—proving to be one that has haunted her, followed her, from Jamaica to here.

———

They walk out into the winter light. Cora's head aches and she is exhausted. She looks around, as if Agnes might be there, waiting for her—though she knows, of course, that she will not.

"Me need to see her," she says to Thursday.

He gives her a thoughtful look, like he knew this was coming.

"Not easy," he says.

Cora stares back at him, her expression hard. Sitting silently in that courtroom has left her spoiling for a fight, ready to shout all the things she wasn't able to shout at the odious Mr. Dalton and his slippery lawyer and the ineffectual judge.

Thursday sighs.

"You cold?" he asks.

"No," Cora lies. Halifax is frosty, and a biting wind blows through the streets. The Citadel rises like a frozen guard over the city.

Thursday doesn't believe her but doesn't have it in him to argue.

"Wait here," he says. He trudges off, round the side of the courthouse and out of sight.

As soon as he is gone, Cora feels smaller—weaker. She starts to shiver. Tries to move her weight from one foot to the other to keep warm blood flowing around her body, but she is clumsy—worries she might fall.

Finally, Thursday emerges from the gap between the court-house and the jail.

"Five minutes," he says quietly. "Come."

28

At the door, Thursday hands over money. In another time, or another world, where Agnes was still free, Cora would object to this—to Thursday losing something of which she knows he has so little. But because Agnes is behind that locked door, she says nothing. Hardly even notices he has done it.

Thursday touches her hand.

"You need me?" he asks, in a tone that suggests he knows the answer.

Cora shakes her head.

The guard opens the door, just a crack, revealing the darkness within. Cora, careful on the uneven stones of the threshold, makes her way inside.

Her eyes take time to adjust to the absence of light. It is freezing outside, with the wind blowing fiercely, but in here there is a different kind of cold—a cold that hangs, unmoving, in place, one that promises it will linger, come what may.

Against the far wall hangs a pair of shackles, their chains

looped through an iron circle driven into the stone. Cora stops dead at the sight of them. All her life, freedom and unfreedom have been abstract things, have been glimpsed in days spent wandering the mountainside in Jamaica with sugarcane lands laid out below, or brushed up against that day in Halifax when the man demanded her papers. This is the roughest, clumsiest, and most unforgiving rendering of freedom—of its absence— that Cora has ever seen.

Agnes sits quietly below the chains, her wrists held half-aloft by them. She does not seem to have noticed Cora enter. And Cora realizes what is wrong with the picture—beyond the horror of the chains, beyond the awfulness of Agnes confined like this, stripped of her normal context of forest or sea and open sky. It is the fact that Agnes is alone. The space beside her, where Patience should be.

(Thursday saw it all. After the soldiers went, he told Cora, he went down to Patience. He brushed the snow from her and he took her into the woods and he broke the frozen ground with a pick, swing after swing, until he could dig a shallow grave and bury her.)

"Agnes," Cora says, when she finally finds her voice.

Agnes looks up slowly. Disbelieving at first—perhaps Cora has visited her already, in shadows and dreams. But there must be something in the way Cora stands, not yet daring to come closer, that convinces Agnes she is real, flesh and blood. Agnes's eyes begin to fill with tears.

"Thought you died," she whispers.

The spell is broken; the sinister cold that has kept Cora lingering close to the threshold loses its power, and she rushes to Agnes's side. Cora touches Agnes—her face, her hair. But then—the clang of metal on metal. Agnes has raised her hands to Cora and found that the chains do not quite let her reach.

The harsh sound makes Agnes slacken with a different kind of sadness. She draws her legs in close, shrinks away from Cora.

"You should go," she says quietly.

"Agnes . . ."

It hurts so much to see her like this; especially when hanging over it all is the idea that it is all her fault, Cora's. That if it wasn't for her, Agnes would still be in the forest, living free.

Cora is trying to summon the strength and courage to broach this idea, to try to atone, when Agnes lifts her head.

"It's true," Agnes says, her voice hoarse. After she has said the words, she seems shocked, appalled, as if the only thing standing between her and believing this was speaking it aloud. She takes a breath that is half a sob, her eyes wide, and when Cora reaches out to try to touch her face, she flinches back.

"What you mean, true?"

Agnes can't look at her now. She is twisting away as best she can with the cuffs, her face almost buried in her shoulder.

"I ain't know it," Agnes says. "I ain't know it before."

"Agnes." Cora is growing distressed at the sight of Agnes's pain. She catches herself before trying to touch her a third time, holds her hands together, twisting, and tries to stay calm. "What you mean?"

She has to wait for the soft sound of Agnes's crying to ease, replaced by silence. For Agnes to turn back, not looking directly at Cora, but staring hollowly at the wall behind her.

"We killed her. I killed her."

Cora takes a step back. She doesn't mean to; it happens before she can stop it. And Agnes sees it and looks ready to break apart all over again. But then her expression shutters, as if she will not even give herself the small comfort of feeling. As if she must stay blank and cold, encased in a hard shell. In that look there is a little of the dark-eyed stare Cora remembers from almost a year ago, when she and Agnes first came face-to-face in the frozen forest.

"Tell me what happen," Cora says. And she is cautious, too. Guarded. It can't be true, can it? That Agnes is a murderer?

"I mixed the poison," Agnes says, in a dull, flat tone. All the work of the months together, the slow unraveling of the tight knots of her, teaching her to love again—it now seems gone.

Cora is hugging herself, afraid of Agnes in this moment. Afraid that the person she loves will not come back.

"Mixed it for Ma," Agnes continues. "It was meant for the master. Ma was sick, had been sick since winter. Too weak to run. But if he was dead, we thought maybe she could join us after we'd gone. Before we left, I got the herbs."

Agnes leans back, rests her head against the wall. Looks up at the ceiling, where frost blooms across the stone.

"Ma never came. We ain't know why. Thought she died before she could use it. They were searching for us—men and dogs. We couldn't come back. Couldn't see what happened."

Agnes closes her eyes. A tear leaks out, runs down her cheek.

"Now I know. She used it. Made a mistake. Killed the little girl."

A heavy silence follows her confession.

Cora's mind fumbles to understand how she feels after hearing this; the cold and the lingering illness make the thoughts come slowly, clumsily. And the longer she waits to speak, the more resigned Agnes grows. Cora, whose moral code has always had clear, bright lines between right and wrong. Who grew up hearing stories about slave revolts put down by the Maroon army, accepting that even though slavery was not right, killing the white people was wrong enough to make keeping the slaves where they were a necessity.

But what have these last few months with Agnes been but a lesson in ambiguity, in all the things that exist beyond those lines?

She thinks, for a moment, of those creation myths again. One man, one woman. An instruction on how to love that leaves no room for anything else. Have not Cora and Agnes shown the lie of this? The world is more complicated than she once knew.

A sharp knock on the door makes both of them jump. Five minutes have slipped away without Cora realizing it. The scrape of the door against the flagstones as it opens, letting in a beam of sunlight. Their time is up.

It is a risk—but Cora darts forward, counting on the darkness to protect them, and brushes her lips against Agnes's. A kiss of forgiveness. She feels how Agnes trembles, wishes she could stay to be sure that Agnes will now forgive herself.

When Cora pulls away, she says, "No perfect choices."

And she walks out into the light.

29

Thursday is restless. He paces the hut as Cora looks on—worn-out, she longs for sleep, but she will not for as long as he stays awake. She owes him that much.

It is four days since the courtroom. Tomorrow, they will return. Thursday has been in Shelburne, hitched a ride down but had to walk most of the road back, returning long after dark, his face grim.

"No one will do it," he says. He watches his feet as he paces—not hurried, frantic steps, but slow ones. Almost thoughtful. "I asked around, if someone would come and say she was free. But no one will do it."

"No one gon' lie," says Cora.

"They scared," Thursday says, continuing as if he hasn't heard her. "I told you about Mary. The last time, a trial like this. People got their houses burned."

Cora is slow to take in his words—her mind, as usual, half-absent, half of it still with Agnes, in her cell, hoping that by some miracle she can bend the laws of physical space to open up a gap in the universe and slip through to touch her. But she finally comprehends what Thursday is saying.

"Wait," she says. "Burned?"

Thursday is not listening. He makes his way along the length of the room again. Head bowed, brow furrowed.

"Thursday," Cora says, with more urgency. "What you mean burned?"

He finally looks up.

"Tomorrow," Cora says. "You gon' speak for her?"

"Yes," says Thursday.

"Then you gon' be in danger?"

Thursday shrugs.

Cora feels the pieces of her beginning to pull apart. Because she will do anything to keep Agnes. But the idea of Thursday in danger hurts her, too. A sudden, vivid, horrible flash—a white mob with torches. And at the head of it, Mr. Dalton, with his terrible smile, the white blond of his hair glinting in the light of the flames.

"Thursday," Cora says. "Agnes not gon' want that." Because this is the truth.

Thursday fixes her with a look. He can see her—really see her.

"But you want it," he says. Not a question. "And so I'm doing it."

There is a little awkwardness in the ensuing silence. Cora searching his face, to try to understand the nature of his love for her—because, deep down, she fears there is a price to it, that he will expect repayment in kind. But she should not have doubted him. She sees only unconditional kindness. Is reminded, in the most painful way, of little Benjamin. This is familial love without blood—two people entangled for good, come what may, and no one is keeping score.

Thursday sits down heavily next to Cora, their backs against the wooden wall.

"You should know," he says, speaking slowly, weighing each word, "that I ain't scared. There ain't nothing they can do to me. They already done it all."

He turns to her and there is fire in his eyes and now it is Agnes Cora thinks of—but an Agnes that keeps flickering from one moment to the next into Leah, into the look on Leah's face that awful night when she confessed what she had done to Cora's mother.

"You understand?" Thursday asks.

Cora cannot speak. Only nods. But it is not a lie. She faces them all—Thursday and Agnes and Leah. She understands.

———

Cora is not usually one given to despair. But that night, she feels it blanket her, a suffocating sense of powerlessness. She feels as if she has glimpsed a truth of the world—that none of them are free, not really. That their lives move along predetermined paths, and that ultimately, nothing can be done to change them. That any god or gods in this world are as cold and remote as the stars glittering in the distance, a beautiful distraction but unable to alter the course of things.

With despair comes a kind of acceptance. There is nothing she can do—to help Agnes, or to help herself. She embraces, wearily, this heavy truth. Perhaps, she thinks, this is the closest they will ever come to freedom—because there is liberation in the idea that she is a cog in the universe, that her life is out of her own hands. Freedom is the death of the illusion that it could be any other way but this. . . .

She has fragmented dreams. Elsy is in them—her dead, unblinking eyes. Benjamin beside her, covered in blood—though in the real memory, there was no blood, and from a distance Benjamin and his mother looked peaceful, resting beside each other. In the dream, it becomes a cursed image, an image of horror, though Cora has lost her voice and cannot scream. Then Thursday's mother is in the dream; or rather, Cora's imagined idea of her, working the land, walking, like Thursday, behind the plow, where the oxen Cain and Abel—the forefathers of the present Cain and Abel, and of all the Cains and Abels yet to come—trudge with their horns swinging slowly from side to side. In the dream, Cora comes forward—offering herself in Thursday's mother's place. But it is not Thursday's mother anymore. It is Cora's own. And the oxen are gone and the sugarcane sprouts until it towers over her, blocking out the sun, and she is afraid—and she wishes, selfishly and hopelessly, that she could take back what she has done.

A rustling of cane. Leah emerges—and hands Cora a cane bill. They must work together, side by side.

Cora lifts the bill. Swings it, the movement slow, like moving through water—because she is in water, cold water, as dark and murky as the frozen lake. But her hand is still swinging, until the blade makes contact with something solid, presses into it; she feels the give, and there is blood in the water and Patience's little body floats away into the darkness—the current carrying her out to sea, toward distant shadows that might be whales or might be some other creature, more menacing and more hideous, and Cora is alone and exposed in the green-black water, the knife no longer in her hand, and she tries to fill her lungs but there is no air—

———

She wakes to darkness and a cold that will not leave her, that is under the skin and won't come out again.

And she cries—because the overwhelming sense that the world is predetermined has left her in the night, and now she is left with the crushing thought that she is free, can act, can shape things according to her will, that the right set of moves will bring the right outcome and bring Agnes back to her, but she cannot see the way forward. And that is a much more hopeless thought.

———

Thursday has cut his hair, close to the skull, shaving off the tight curls he had let grow long over the winter. He wears his best clothes. Cora watches him outside the courthouse, as they wait to go in—the nervous way he tugs at his collar, a little too tight around his neck—and although her overwhelming feeling is one of dull exhaustion, she cannot help but care for him, love this man in a too-small Sunday shirt, his slow movements, the faraway look in his eyes.

They take their seats on the public benches again. Everything the same as before. Through the side door, Agnes is brought—the strain starting to show on her face now, a haggardness and vulnerability that make Cora's heart ache.

The judge, still as improbably large and solid as ever, sits behind his desk and surveys the room.

"I believe we can commence," he says. "Mr. Dalton—you have the bill of sale?"

Mr. Dalton is in navy today. Strong winter sunlight shines through the windows and brings out the white gold of his hair.

"I do," he says.

His lawyer approaches the bench, a piece of paper in hand. The judge inspects it, nodding slowly, then looks up.

"Well, gentlemen," he says. "There is a matter that has come to my attention that deserves a hearing."

Mr. Dalton shifts in his seat. Beside Cora, Thursday twists his hands in his lap—neither of them knows when the judge will call on him, and this could be the precursor to it. Cora feels a tight knot in her chest—evidence that, for all the cold despair she has felt these past few days, she has hope left inside her yet.

The judge looks down the room, toward Thursday—who starts to rise from his seat, with one last tug on his collar. But there are footsteps from behind—Cora and Thursday turn together, to see who could possibly be making their way down the public area and toward the judge's bench.

Leah does not even look at Cora as she passes. And the shock is so acute that Cora has no time to speak, to interrupt what is to come, before the judge says—

"Your name is Leah Jones?"

Leah replies—a slight tremor to her voice.

"It is, sir."

Agnes lifts her head. A small frown on her face—whatever this is, she has not planned it.

"You came to the province last year with the other Maroons from Jamaica?"

"Yes, sir."

Cora's mind is rushing through possibilities, each worse than the last. Could Leah know? Could she understand what Cora and Agnes are to each other? Is she here to use their love against them, to add it to the weight of evidence that Agnes is dangerous? But Thursday's hand on her—along with some more diffuse quality in the air of the courtroom, a presumption toward silence, a weight of occasion within these walls—keeps her from calling out, from trying to stop what is now in motion.

"Leah Jones," the judge says, "would you share with the court what you told me yesterday?"

Leah hesitates. Cora cannot see her face but notices the slight movement of her head—as if she is unsure of where to look, of whether to address the judge, Mr. Dalton, or Agnes herself.

"There has been a mistake," Leah says. Each word spoken carefully—she is straining to erase her accent, the Jamaican lilt of her speech and the older, African tones that come through sometimes, Cora knows, when she is excited or angry or on the rare occasion when she tells old stories, memories and myths from home.

Agnes and Cora briefly lock eyes, united in their confusion.

Mr. Dalton's lawyer is on his feet.

"What is the meaning—" But he is cut off when the judge raises his hand.

Leah continues.

"This girl here is named Agnes. But she is one of us. She come here by ship in July last year."

Leah turns; she is now facing Mr. Dalton.

"This girl is not your slave," she says.

There is a pause, a collective hesitation. The courtroom

scene arranged like a painting in its stillness—Thursday and Cora, close together, hands held; Leah, standing at the center of the room; Agnes, one hand on the railing of the sheriff's box to support herself, her expression one of disbelief; Mr. Dalton's lawyer, mouth open without sound; and Mr. Dalton beside him, his face not yet taking on any sign that it understands what has been said. And finally, at the front, the black-robed judge, a picture of careful neutrality.

Cora cycles through astonishment, exultation, and something close to anger, so quickly they become almost one feeling.

It is Mr. Dalton who finally breaks the silence.

"This is preposterous." He sounds unperturbed, but there is a hint of strain in his voice that suggests this is a deliberate attempt to mask his disquiet.

The judge looks at him without speaking. A slight incline of his head, as if inviting him to speak further. This irritates Mr. Dalton; when he speaks again, it is with a little more exasperation.

"You have the bill of sale in your hand."

The judge makes a face that might be sympathetic and might be apologetic as he brandishes the bill of sale.

"Forgive me, Mr. Dalton," he says. "But this is a bill of sale for a woman named Zilpah."

"Her mother," says Mr. Dalton, with an angry gesture toward Agnes. "Of course. Because she was born . . . We don't . . ."

He trails off under the unwavering gaze of the judge. Meanwhile, Leah still stands, straight-backed and immobile, hands clasped behind her.

The judge puts the bill of sale down slowly, carefully, on his desk. Looks from Mr. Dalton to Agnes. And there is just the smallest shift in his facial expression—a sort of hardening of his eyes. And suddenly the bulk of him seems intimidating—gone is the man who greeted Mr. Dalton by his Christian name at the beginning of the trial, this stranger left in his place.

"Mr. Dalton," he says. "May I clarify? If this indeed is the woman you think it is—"

Mr. Dalton makes a strangled sound of outrage, but his lawyer seizes his arm.

"—your last sight of her would have been more than ten years ago, correct?"

It is the lawyer who answers.

"Yes, sir."

"At which point you would both have been not much more than ten years old."

The lawyer looks at Mr. Dalton, who gives a tight nod.

"Yes, sir."

"Well," the judge says. "You perhaps see my difficulty. On the one hand . . ." The judge lifts his left hand, palm facing up. "We have the testimony of Leah Jones here." He nods toward Leah. "And on the other . . ." Out comes his right hand. "We have a bill of sale for someone else, and a memory from childhood."

The judge mimes weighing these two things between his hands, as if the scale is in fine balance—no one knows which way it will fall.

Mr. Dalton has risen from his seat. Even from behind him, Cora can feel the force of his anger.

"You can't be serious, Matthews," he snarls.

The facade of pleasantness that was just about still fixed to the judge's face falls away. He gives Mr. Dalton a warning look.

"Inside these walls, Henry," he says coldly, "it is *Justice* Matthews."

Mr. Dalton, on his feet, fists clenched at his sides, says nothing.

"Leah Jones." The judge turns to her. "You are certain of your claim? The girl here is a Maroon, one of those whose freedom is guaranteed by the British Crown?"

"Yes," Leah says.

"And Mr. Dalton. You are testifying before the court that the woman you see here, a woman whom you have not seen for over a decade, can be none other than the girl once owned by your father? Without a doubt?"

Cora leans forward. She still can see nothing of Mr. Dalton's face. She sees the way his head turns, toward Agnes—who quickly lowers her gaze.

And Mr. Dalton hesitates. For the briefest moment, which in the chill of the courtroom feels like an eternity, he hesitates.

The judge marks Mr. Dalton's silence with a small nod. Mr. Dalton comes to life, spluttering with rage. "Of course I'm certain, damn it!"

But the judge, ignoring him, gets to his feet and smooths down the front of his robes.

"We will retire briefly to consider the case that has been brought before us."

Mr. Dalton turns on Leah; finally, his face is revealed to Cora, and it is twisted with anger. Unmasked, civility stripped away, because what is all their civility, Cora thinks, but an illusion, a cheap trick? This is the face of an animal, a bear defending a carcass.

"You—" he begins, but his lawyer throws a restraining hand across to check him. On the threshold of the doorway that leads to his chambers, the judge is still standing, watching. His face unreadable in shadow, but the stance of his body clear. A warning.

Mr. Dalton takes a deep, rasping breath. He gazes around the room—from Leah, his eyes move briefly, almost unseeingly, across Thursday and Cora, before finally coming to rest on Agnes. He makes a noise of disgust, turns on his heel, and storms out of the room.

Before Cora can move or speak, Agnes looks at Leah.

Agnes nods her thanks. Leah, with a slight bow of her head, accepts it.

30

When the judge comes back in, he doesn't even glance any-
where but at Agnes—not toward Mr. Dalton, now returned and reseated; not toward Leah, who still stands where
she stood and testified.

"The court can only apologize for this inconvenience," he
says, with surprising gentleness. "You are free to go."

There is a moment as the words sink in, before Cora leaps
to her feet and calls Agnes's name—when Agnes simply stands,
blinking, disbelieving—her right hand rubbing the raw skin
around her left wrist, where the shackles had been and will be
no more.

———

Cora forgets everything but Agnes. Forgets Thursday in his
Sunday best, forgets Leah—forgets even the lingering illness
that still saps her strength. Today, she shows no weakness.

Out into the winter sunlight—a clear afternoon, the air

sharp with cold. Ice gleaming on puddles in the street. A color-less world of gray and white, but to Cora it is the most beautiful thing in the world.

She has Agnes by the hand, pulling her away from the courthouse, away from all this. Has half a mind to run straight back to the forest. Will the wikuom still stand, empty, after all this time?

"Wait," Agnes says.

She looks back. Leah has followed, stands a few paces out-side the courthouse. She looks from Cora to Agnes, her gaze dipping briefly to where their fingers are still intertwined. Cora drops Agnes's hand too quickly, and in doing so marks what has come before all the more clearly, the fact of their hand-holding standing out as stark as a drop of blood on white, untouched snow.

"Cora," Leah says.

"We're leaving," says Cora.

But Agnes repeats her name, quietly. The meaning clear—
You owe her that much.

Agnes and Cora exchange a glance. Then Agnes turns and slips away—a few steps and she is no more than mist and shadow.

Leah looks over Cora with careful sadness. They do not em-brace. But Cora is shocked, almost appalled, by the physical response of her body. The ease with which the love returns, a feeling of warm familiarity that pushes up against the pain and betrayal, threatening not to overwhelm it but to mix with it, to produce some new and more complex emotion that can contain the hurt and the love side by side.

Light flakes of snow fall from a white sky. A few passersby who pay them little mind, each person a player in their own drama that does not touch this one.

Leah looks tired, thinner than before. Cora knows that she herself still bears the signs of the long illness—hollow eyes and pallid skin.

Cora is going to ask—

Why?

But it is Leah who speaks first. Cautiously, with care.

"Silas gone."

Cora, whose whole life has been Agnes, the trial, and before that the demands of food and water and shelter to make it through winter in the woods, cannot make sense of this at first. It is so far from what she wants to know, the words evoke no feeling.

"The colonel send him to England," Leah continues, "with a petition for the king about leaving this place."

"He coming back?" Cora asks.

Leah shrugs.

"Sometime. Not soon."

Cora is amazed that she feels a little relief. That she has held inside her some of the fear from months ago, that Silas still had some power over her. But now he is gone.

There is more; Cora can see it on Leah's face. The small frown, the hint of worry. It is an expression that Cora knows well, because Leah's is the face she has known best her whole life. It is the way Leah looks when there is something she must say, but the words will not come easily, and she is afraid she might not find them at all.

"Him was the one who . . ." She trails off. Tries again. "You was gone. We all worry. Little Benjamin, him don't say anything at first, but in the end him say a name. Agnes."

The mention of little Benjamin causes Cora pain. She looks to the frost-hardened ground, listens to the rest of Leah's story with her head bowed.

"It was Silas who start telling others, folk in Halifax. Word get around about this girl Agnes living in the woods."

She does not need to say more. It all falls into place, what Thursday has told Cora—the soldiers waiting. Dalton must have gathered them when he heard, ready for a search; what luck, for them, that Agnes appeared in town, sparing them the long march through the wilderness.

Cora looks up. Her eyes find Leah's; she is still trying to understand. Is this why? Leah here to pay Silas's debt.

"Why you do it?" Cora asks. With a heaviness that is part resignation and part a hint that Cora is carrying so much, and might be ready to lay it all down.

Leah's dark hair dusted with white, flakes melting on her skin. She looks at Cora and tries to convey something beyond words. Something beyond Cora, beyond *Come home*—because Cora can see that Leah did not do this for her, not really.

In that look is the shape of an answer. It's Leah coming in secret to the first day of the trial, probably just to see Cora, to try to understand where she has been. Leah seeing Agnes—and somehow both seeing through her, seeing her as a representative of something, a dark figure, head bowed, the marks of shackles on her wrists, standing for the freedom that Leah has lost and gained and bargained for and traded her whole life.

But also, seeing Agnes as she really is, the singular nature of her plight, standing for no more and no less than herself.

Leah did it for Agnes.

Leah did it for the men and women who came before. Cora's mother and who knows how many others, their desperate grasps for freedom doomed to fail, Leah holding their chains.

And, most of all, Leah did it for herself. Cora can see it in her eyes. Because what better measure of freedom is there than to help others rise? It was always built on shaky ground, their freedom in Jamaica, resting on the back of the plantations; they made their deal and shook white hands and they knew not to look too closely at the price. For some, like Cora, it was easy enough, not seeing, because they had never known different. For Leah, not seeing was survival; it was running from the past; it was the long hurt of slavery written on scars across her skin; it was visceral, the need to never go back. Only here, across the ocean, one freedom lost—the freedom of home, the freedom of long, warm evenings and never having to think about all the ways that cold can kill—could she see a freedom gained, the freedom to break others' chains.

Justice has no scales. Cora cannot place her mother on one side and Agnes on the other. Leah would not want her to. Leah is not engaged in an act of erasure; she is the sum of everything she has done, and one act cannot replace another.

Cora nods, slowly. Has an impulse that she keeps in check to tell Leah the truth, that Agnes really did help kill that girl—an ugly impulse to push Leah's newfound morality to its limits. But she owes it to Agnes to keep it secret, cannot risk Leah rescinding her testimony. So she keeps quiet.

Leah takes Cora's hand; Cora lets her.

"Cora," she says. "We miss you."

It is hard to hear the way her voice wavers. Cora realizes that all these months in the forest, the numbing effect of working hard and the distraction of falling in love, it didn't take anything away, the mess of emotions surrounding Leah and her mother, it just buried them deep, and all it takes is a touch and they are unearthed. She is trembling now. Leah takes her own shawl, wraps it around Cora's shoulders with gentle care.

"Little Benjamin still ask for you most nights," Leah says. That hurts. Cora closes her eyes, can almost feel the weight of him in her arms. How much will he have grown since she left?

She looks to the road Agnes has taken. The one she knows Agnes will follow, to the edge of the forest, where she will wait. Cora imagines going. Asking her—*Come with me.* To Preston, the hut with a fire burning, holding back the darkness. She is so exhausted. The winter is so cold.

But there is a memory. One night of many lying in each other's arms, when Agnes said to her—

I'm not ashamed. Took a long time. I regret lots of things. But not this.

And she gestured between the two of them and the strength of her conviction shone like firelight from her dark eyes.

"Agnes," Cora says. Her throat is tight; she touches it. The words threaten to lodge there, and she needs to get them out. "She . . . We . . ."

Cora swallows. Thinks how free she will feel, how unburdened, if she can just find the right words. Home, Preston, Leah, Benjamin, Agnes. She can bring them all together, if only she can say this.

"She is my—"

But Cora breaks off abruptly. She sees the way Leah's shoulders tense. Sees, in her face, the warning.

Leah waits, braced. When she realizes Cora will say no more, she nods once. Decisive, relieved.

Cora removes her hand from Leah's. The dark clouds of her mind part, the fog of confusion. A ray of sunshine—an image of the two of them, her and Agnes, out there in the forest.

To be known entirely by another.

She steps back.

"Cora," Leah says. A quiet plea.

If she turns away now, she turns away from all of them. Benjamin, too. He is the hardest part of it. There were promises, not spoken aloud but still understood between Elsy and her. When Elsy died, little Benjamin became hers. She forgot that once already.

But then the love between her and Elsy. Everything left unnamed. The two of them in the river, floating, ducking under the surface, opening their eyes against the sting of the water, sunlight piercing through right to the riverbed, their bodies, faces, hands shimmering—everything moving, the current drawing them together, almost to touching, but then carrying them apart. Cora heard Elsy's mother once. *Careful with that girl.* And for a while Elsy touched her less freely, kept a gap between them when they walked side by side. . . .

I'm not ashamed.

Cora turns. She hopes Elsy would understand.

———

Frost-covered forest paths, sparkling with moonlight. They move quickly, Agnes ahead—her movements graceful, familiar.

Cora behind. Her heart cracking—with pain, yes, but cracking also because throughout the trial it has been encased in ice, frozen, and out here among the trees, something is thawing. The crack must let the hurt come in, for all that she leaves behind, but with it comes relief, too. And also love.

She stumbles, but Agnes is there to catch her. Take her hand. Guide her onward, deeper into the wilderness, the winter silence, a silver world that they slip back into as easily as the whales slip back below the ocean's surface. It calls them home.

The Trial

January 1798

A heavy tread on the wooden stairs as William Matthews, respected magistrate and longtime resident of Halifax, climbs up to his rooms above, ducking his head to avoid hitting the low beams of the ceiling.

In his bedchamber, he settles himself into an armchair with a weary sigh. Tilts his head back and closes his eyes.

The creak of the door as it opens. And still, after all this time, there is a moment of false hope—a moment when it could be Patrick.

"Sir?"

The voice is, of course, not Patrick's. William Matthews opens his tired eyes. His manservant hovers in the doorway—a young lad of not much more than eighteen. With a wave of his hand, Matthews dismisses him. One of his idiosyncrasies, his tendency to ready himself each night for bed alone, without the help of a servant.

Tonight, he sits a while in the chair, unmoving. Staring

vacantly at the opposite wall, his mind on the trial. There may be trouble from it. Not from Dalton himself, bound back to Jamaica already, no doubt cursing this province and all the hurt it has caused his family, most likely never to return. But trouble of a more diffuse kind—word getting round about the decision. Fellow magistrates looking at him askance. Perhaps fewer cases. A month or so where the governor sends no more invitations to dine. But it will pass. His unblemished career speaks for itself. And people here have short memories. It's the winters, he is sure of it. Each cycle of the seasons is a fresh start; when spring comes, people are quick to forget. They don't want to dwell on the cold, or on any of the rest of it.

The corner of his mouth twitches—a small, private smile. Perhaps it was Patrick who said that about the winters here. He can't remember. He has many thoughts and feelings, even now, of uncertain origin—that might have been Patrick's or his. And there is a sweetness to the ambiguity. A sense that there might be tiny fragments of Patrick with him still.

Matthews gets to his feet, pushing on the arms of the chair to help him stand. It is always strange to him how, at the core of himself, he feels ageless, the same man that he was ten or twenty years ago. But his body tells a different story, his joints a little stiffer every year. He begins the slow process of undressing, and as he does so, he imagines himself as someone else—as some distant acquaintance. Tries to see himself through their eyes, and marvels at how little they would know.

He imagines the talk around a dinner table, somewhere far across town.

He had that servant, didn't he?

Did he? I can't recall.

I'm sure of it. Can't remember the name but they were together many years.

Oh, now you mention it, I do remember something. . . . Came from Virginia with that man, didn't he?

And so on. An illusion, of course, that anyone would speak like this at all. Because here, the memories of Patrick proved the shortest of all.

Matthews lies in bed and listens to the sounds of the house. Soft footsteps, somewhere below. Hushed voices. And then— after a time—silence.

When the quiet has lasted long enough that Matthews can be sure all his household are asleep, he rolls onto his side. Feels under the pillows until his hand closes around the familiar oval. Pulls it out and holds it, for a moment, to his chest, before lifting it up to the light cast by the candle still burning on his dresser. A miniature, in a simple, unadorned frame. The brushwork clumsy and amateur, done, in fact, by no great artist, because to most, the man in the picture—with his dark curly hair, crooked nose, and shy smile—had no reason to be depicted. Was not worthy of capturing and preserving in paint this way.

Matthews remembers the feeling of the tiny brush in his fingertips. His frustration with the work, and how the fine lines he pictured in his mind would not come out on the canvas, his fingers too large and their movements too indelicate—opening up a chasm between the portrait as he wanted it to be and the portrait as it was. Remembers how Patrick—always gentle, always kind—made him put down the brush until he was calm again. Taking each of his fingers and kissing them gently. With Patrick, he had felt that every part of him was precious—that despite his size and his awkwardness, he might, in fact, be delicate and beautiful in Patrick's eyes. The portrait was painted in the early days, the Virginia days. At the heady point where they had tipped from closeness into something deeper—the first sprouting of a love that, over time, promised to grow as tall and sturdy as an oak. It felt so urgent, then, to capture Patrick exactly as he was—youthful, quietly charming. They were at that age where it felt like they might live and be young forever. But somehow, still, Matthews sensed it—that the moment would pass, as all moments did, and that painting it was the only way to try to fix it in time forever.

There are tears in his eyes tonight, as he brings the miniature to his lips and kisses it gently. This is unusual—the taking out of the portrait such a ritual that it does not make him cry like it used to. What makes today different?

He supposes it is the trial. He cannot help the image of the girl flashing across his mind—standing in the dock, her downturned eyes. When he first saw her, he thought of Patrick, despite all that separated them, because the question before the court was freedom—her freedom. A question settled for Patrick by force, by a gang of sailors seizing him on a street near the harbor and bundling him onto a ship.

The reality of war, so they said. A stream of men needed to fight against the French, and not all of them would have the luxury of going of their own free will.

Matthews holds the miniature out again. Studies the face. People here forget winters, but he will not forget Patrick. That was the vow he made.

The greatest regret of his life is that, when Patrick was pressganged, he did not do more to find him. He was scared, that is the truth of it. Scared that his reaction would be seen as disproportionate—the loss of a servant, after all, meant to be an inconvenience more than a heartbreak. By the time he finally wrote to his cousin, an admiral, to try to trace Patrick, it was too late. He had already been dead a year, killed in an engagement with the Spanish in the Caribbean.

Strange that he was a magistrate so many years before he really knew injustice. An abstract thing became real for him, the day he lost Patrick.

William Matthews is no radical. He is no campaigner for abolition. He keeps his abhorrence for slavery, found late in life, to himself. He did sign, once, quietly and unobtrusively, a petition to ban the practice of press-ganging, little more than state-sanctioned kidnap. Otherwise, no one would notice the change in him; he might be any other man from Virginia, cast out after the revolution and left to build a new life for himself elsewhere. A man who never thinks of freedom, because freedom is only ever felt in its absence. When you have it, you experience it as a fish experiences water, encompassing everything and seemingly without end.

This trial was the closest he has ever come to laying his private feelings bare.

It was not the girl. Not really. As he drifts to sleep, Matthews is no longer thinking of Agnes, nor will he ever think of her again, except for in a vague sense. He will not remember her features—soon will forget her name. But he will remember what she stood for. Over time, it will become as if freedom itself was on trial that day, briefly embodied in the form of a slender, nameless, dark-skinned girl.

SPRING

1800

31

Soft spring sunlight filters into the wikuom. Cora, for once, is awake first—and uses the time to watch Agnes's sleeping face. Taking joy in the study of something as familiar to her now as the forest, its slopes and stones, its hidden parts and its places of astounding beauty. A sense that life is, at once, out there, almost infinite, the vast expanse of woodland and out to the open sea; but at the same time, is in here, is no more and no less than the steady rise and fall of Agnes's chest and the fluttering of her eyelids.

A day lies ahead of them like any other. Predictable in its tasks, the things to which they must attend. It doesn't get easier, living out here alone. But it grows more natural—and every spring, they grow a little brighter, Agnes less forlorn, Cora less impatient, because spring means sunshine and rain and buds on the birch trees. Thawing ice, the little canoe on the water—lakes, rivers, and even the sea. Waiting, always, for the day the whales will come. Too early for it now, but Cora marks the passing of each year by their first appearance. Feasts and celebration days that might mean something in the other world, the world over the hills in Halifax, fade to nothing here. But the whales still mean something—the same family of humpbacks, their numbers sometimes thinned out, perhaps by hunting, but last year there were more than ever and Agnes wept to see it, trying hard to make Cora understand why it moved her so much, this little sign of resilience in a sometimes unforgiving world.

Agnes stirs, wakes. A smile coming slowly over her face, a rising sun. Cora leans over to kiss her—the sort of gentle, easy kiss of two people settled in love, where there is nothing to hurry. Where passion has become quiet companionship, the depth of a life shared together.

Outside, the gentle whines of a dog—Faith. She can always sense when they are awake, and hates the idea that they are in there without her, talking and laughing. She always wants to be included in all things, a touching loyalty that is as strong as and yet somehow so different from Patience. They have not had her long; a year at most. Agnes was reluctant to get her at first, seeing it as a kind of disrespect to Patience's memory. But to Cora, Faith is not a replacement for Patience. She is a new companion, completely her own creature. And it is, of course, practical to have a dog out here. Faith came to them from the Mi'kmaq to the west—they are less cautious, now, about trading with them, and with some border peoples in small towns on the edge of the province. But they still avoid Halifax and any other large settlements. The old fear has never quite gone away for Agnes. And besides, the world does not understand them. Cora knows their love is better kept out here, in the wilderness, away from prying eyes.

It does get lonely sometimes. Not for Agnes, who seems hardened to it, who spent so long by herself that just having Cora is a wonder, a blessing for which she has never ceased to be grateful. But Cora grew up with more.

Sometimes, she still dreams of Jamaica—though her sense of the place has long since faded, the heat and the humidity and the smell of its soil. She dreams of Elsy, Benjamin. Leah.

But they are just this—dreams. They do not touch the reality of her life. In waking, she has time for work and time for Agnes. It is a simple life. They are happy with it.

———

From the water, Cora squints to shore. Certain she can see, on the rugged coast, in among the rocks, a figure. Standing alone—too far for her to tell which way they are facing. But she feels, or imagines she can feel, the eyes of this figure on them.

She nudges Agnes.

"Someone there?" Cora asks. Nodding toward the cliffs.

Agnes peers over. A frown—the ghost of old concerns. They exchange a wordless glance, and Cora reads in Agnes's face their choices. Paddle wide, evade whoever might be waiting on the shore. Or get a little closer, see who is there—if there really is anyone at all. They are far from the main towns here. The strange figure may be one of the Mi'kmaq, may even be someone known to them, no danger at all.

Before Agnes can speak, Cora decides, curiosity getting the better of her.

"You can go closer?"

Agnes paddles. The wind is strong enough to whip up white-caps on the waves, but Agnes navigates the boat without fear, and it is a long time since Cora last felt unsettled by the movement of the water. She trusts Agnes too much for that now. Salt spray hits her face, bracingly cold. In between her and Agnes, Faith lifts her face to the sky—she seems delighted by the sensation of wind in her fur, and when a wave breaks against the boat she snaps playfully at the water as if trying to drink it from the air.

With the sun in their eyes, it is hard to see much more than a silhouette. Cora is on the verge of saying they should turn back—an uneasy feeling creeping up inside her at the way they keep getting closer and closer and can see no more of this person on the shore than a dark shape—when suddenly, she understands. The breadth of the shoulders. The calm, steady stance—unmoving as they paddle toward land.

Could it be . . . ?

Cora, feeling a rush that pushes her into the risky move of half standing upright in the plunging canoe, coming down off the crest of a wave, raises her hand.

"Thursday!"

On the shore, the figure lifts his hand in return. The movement of the boat almost knocks Cora off her feet; Agnes shoots a hand out to grab her. But Cora is laughing, exhilarated, turning to Agnes with a grin. Who would have thought that the sight of another person—a friend—could produce a sensation so strong?

"Let's land," Cora says. Because sometimes, it is only when wounds heal that you can realize their severity—only once the pain is gone that, in its absence, you understand its size and strength. And until now, Cora had not realized how much she had missed Thursday. It feels wrong to admit—a disrespect to Agnes's love. But perhaps it is not enough, just the two of them. As they move toward the shore, Cora leaning out the better to get a glimpse of Thursday's face—he is making his careful way down the rocks to meet them in a small cove, with calmer, sheltered water—she realizes that this is what she must have been craving all along. The company of others.

Cora scrambles onto rocks that are slick with seawater, but, surefooted, she does not fall. She comes barreling into Thursday, throwing herself into his chest, and his arms surround her in an embrace.

"Cora," he says, as she grips him tightly. She hears the warm smile in his voice.

Cora hears the sound of Faith snuffling around Thursday's ankles; feels as the dog's little body circles him and her, the beat of Faith's wagging tail on their legs. Faith has never quite taken to being a guard dog, not like Patience was. She has no caution around strangers.

Pulling back, Cora is better able to consider Thursday's face. Just over two years since she last saw him—she cannot tell if he is changed or if her memories have not stayed faithful in all that time. He seems bigger than she remembered, but surely it is impossible that he has grown in their time apart. And his face seems more careworn; the eyes set a little deeper in his face, the fine lines at their corners more pronounced.

Thursday looks over Cora, too. She wonders what he sees. She thinks of herself as the same, but there must surely be differences. A body that is firmer, muscles formed from the hard labor required in the wilderness. A face that is thinner—and, she likes to think, that seems more wise. But what would she know of the way her face has changed? The only glimpses of her reflection are pictures scattered and distorted by the rippling water of puddles and lakes.

Cora pats Thursday on the arm, checking the solidity of him again. But he is really there.

She hardly knows where to begin, releasing a tumble of words. "What— How— But you— Why?"

This makes Thursday laugh, a deep, rumbling chuckle that floods Cora with pleasant warmth.

"Good to see you," he says.

As quickly as the first sight of him filled her with joy, a cloud passes over Cora. She draws one hand across her chest, catching her left elbow with her right hand.

"You never come before."

The charge is not really a fair one; Cora has never ventured into town to see him. But she realizes that the hurt is there. That somehow, all this time, she has been expecting him.

Thursday doesn't answer. Just shrugs, his expression giving little away. The gesture might mean—*I didn't know you wanted me to.*

Cora turns. She had, for a moment, almost forgotten Agnes, tying up the canoe and now standing, watching the two of them. A look of caution on her face. But still, she nods to Thursday.

"Listen," Thursday says. "Can we talk?"

A wordless glance between Cora and Agnes. The look of two people used to each other, almost able to see through skin to the souls underneath.

Cora's eyes ask the question.

Agnes's reply: *Go.*

Cora falls into step beside Thursday as they follow a path along the coast, close enough to still smell the sea. This part of the coastline is a rugged place—rocky outcrops jut out of the sea, bashed against by fearsome waves. It is the reason it is quiet, almost untouched—at least for now. You need Agnes's skill to move boats between those rocks that wait, like teeth, to drag unsuspecting sailors down. Only their little canoe, nimble as it is, can pass through some of the gaps, in search of fish that live here, undisturbed by larger nets.

Faith has followed them, ears pricked up, a sign of happy alertness. She noses into his hand, swinging by his side as he walks, and licks it.

Thursday laughs, scratches the dog behind the ears, then looks sideways at Cora and cannot help a smile.

"Been a while," he says.

"Yes."

After these brief words, an easy silence. Brought on not because there is nothing to say; Cora has plenty of questions—about town, and about the lives people are still leading over there. But Cora had forgotten how Thursday always had this effect on her. A calming steadiness to him that encourages moments like these—pauses, a quietening of her otherwise busy mind.

"How are Cain and Abel?" she asks. With a slight teasing note to her voice, an acknowledgment that she is starting with the most inconsequential topics first.

Thursday gives one of his little half smiles, the corner of his mouth tugging upward.

"Wouldn't know," he says.

Cora frowns.

"What you mean?"

"Suppose that's my big news," he says. "Old Farmer Nash died. No family to inherit. The place is being sold. But it means I'm done."

The words take a while to sink in. Then Cora stops in her tracks. Grabs his hand, open-mouthed.

"Thursday!"

He chuckles, a little bemused at her reaction.

"You're free," she says, elated for him. But he merely shrugs.

"I reckon so."

"That's wonderful." Cora is still holding his hand, looking at him in amazement.

"Well," says Thursday. "You can't eat freedom."

"Out here you can," Cora says—almost without meaning to. Just thinking of the feeling of being out at sea, the vast expanse of water, a sense of the world opening up before you—a fish on your line, pulling it in, already salivating at the thought of the taste of it, grilled over an open fire under a black night sky that is filled with stars. But then, quite suddenly, an idea takes her, and she squeezes Thursday's hand hard.

"Thursday . . ." she says. But before she can say more, he shakes his head.

"No, Cora," he says gently.

"You could—?"

Cora's imagination deals best in abstractions—in the feeling of having Thursday out there with them, how nice it would be. Not in particulars, like the loneliness he would surely feel. The little frictions that might arise, as soon as there were three of them. Imbalances as two took one side against the other. Cora cannot picture those things. She can only see the vague outline of life, an image made of fire smoke or droplets of salt spray. A sense of happiness and companionship.

"No," Thursday says again. A man of specifics where Cora is a woman of dreams. "I can't."

Cora drops his hand, hiding her disappointment. They walk on, passing a pair of weather-beaten thornbushes, the only things growing this close to the sea.

"So," Cora says eventually, with artificial brightness. "You gon' get some work?"

"Yes," he says. "Looking now. For something on a ship. Not much going. But might know one leaving soon . . ."

Cora waits for him to say more. But when he speaks again, it is in a different tone. A little somber.

"Listen," he says. "I came because . . . Well. Leah asked."

Cora's reaction is not immediate. The change of topic so abrupt and unexpected she cannot fit all the pieces together. But then she stops again. A look of reproach on her face.

"No," is all she says, though what exactly she is refusing is not clear. Perhaps the very idea of Leah herself, in her entirety.

Thursday holds up a placating hand.

"She's got a message."

"*No*," Cora says again. Louder. Turning and walking back down the cliff path, back toward Agnes.

(Because how can this life of hers be maintained except with a separation so total that she never thinks of it, never dwells on what has been lost? She suppressed the ache long ago and that was the only path to happiness.)

"Cora." Thursday comes after her. "Please. Wait."

Cora hesitates. Does not speak, but with a tight nod signals that he may continue.

"She wants to see you," he says.

"She know where to find me."

"No one knows where to find you."

"She can look. You did."

"Took me a while."

Cora, lips pursed in frustration, tilts her head back, trying to find calm in the passage of the clouds across the sky. The ones overhead are scattered and white. But in the distance, they are gray, heavy with rain.

"Why?"

Thursday is slow to reply, so Cora repeats herself.

"Why she want to see me?"

Thursday looks uncomfortable.

"Maybe you should hear that from her."

"Me not gon' see her unless me know why."

Thursday hesitates.

"Well. You'd find out soon enough. They're leaving."

Whatever she was expecting, it was not this.

"What?"

Her mind jumps to the impossible—Jamaica. And a wound she had long thought healed reopens. An ache for the island— her island—fills her.

"Home?" she asks, in little more than a whisper.

But Thursday shakes his head.

"Africa."

Cora has to turn away. Now she is angry, hurt, and confused all in one, and none of the feelings will yield to the others, so is she left feeling them all at full strength. A swirl of pictures in her mind—of Leah, of Jamaica, and of a place that has no clear features, but that contains within it a set of vague ideas and stories and imagined things. A lost home, a lost hope. A place that people prayed to visit in death.

Cora can see, farther up the path, where Agnes waits for her—a small figure in the distance.

From behind, Thursday asks—

"So. Will you see about her?"

Cora does not know. But opens her mouth anyway, waiting to see what words will form.

32

Leah is smaller. Thinner and shrunken, with lines on her face. Had she looked the same as ever, the same as the memory held static in Cora's mind, frozen in time these last two years, then perhaps Cora would have held herself back. But the change is so stark that, almost without thinking, Cora falls into Leah's outstretched arms and they embrace. Leah smells the same—like cooking oil and sweat—and when they pull apart, Cora is crying. She lifts her hand to rub the tears away, but Leah catches it at the wrist and holds it still, her eyes following the path of the teardrops down Cora's cheeks.

"Daughter," Leah says. The word seems as much of a surprise to her as to Cora. It is both the best and the worst thing to say. It reminds Cora of everything that binds them together, of the fact that Leah raised her, the years of love and devotion that can never be erased. But it reminds her also of the truth in her blood—of who her real mother was.

Cora pulls herself gently free of Leah and stands back. For a while, neither of them speaks.

"So," Cora says eventually, breaking the silence. "You gon' go home."

"Not Jamaica," Leah says. "Africa."

"Yes. Your home." Cora speaks with a gentleness that she did not expect in herself. All the bitterness she felt on the way to Preston has fallen away. The overwhelming sensation, standing here before Leah, is of the futility of anger. Of a past that is fixed and cannot be undone.

"Well," says Leah. "Me come from a different place. Inland. But close enough."

"You . . ." Cora takes time to find the words. "You looking forward to it?"

Leah shrugs. But then, just for a moment, a light comes over her face. Makes her features younger. Just a flicker, then gone.

She says, "Yes." Then, with a weak smile: "Not so cold."

The question not yet asked hangs over both of them. Cora waits patiently. The kindest thing she can do is wait.

Finally, Leah says, "You could come?"

She sounds resigned. Tired. But, heartbreakingly, there is a little hope there. Cora hears it. And, although she came here knowing her answer, that hope gives Cora pause. She can't look Leah in the eye, her eyes instead moving toward the ceiling of the hut: the uneven grain of the beams, the pots that hang from hooks, the cobwebs in the corners.

"Me can't," Cora says.

She hears Leah sigh.

"The girl?"

At this, Cora looks back at Leah. Feels a flare of the anger she carried with her all the way here. Because if her mother was the original sin, Agnes was the other infraction. Complicated, of course, because Leah saved her. But then could not hear that they loved each other. Cora's mother is an idea from long ago. Maybe, one day, she could forgive. But Agnes is here and now, living and breathing. That is why Cora cannot forget.

"Yes," says Cora. "Agnes."

Cora did ask. She won't tell Leah this, but after Thursday left them, Cora said—*We could go.* Leave behind Nova Scotia and all the unpleasant memories and the risk of recapture. They could take a boat halfway across the world to a new life, a promised land. Even as Cora asked, she knew it was a dream that would not survive contact with reality—that they would have to hide what they were to each other. That they would live with fear of a different kind, be alone together in a different way. But Agnes did not speak of any of that. She spoke of her mother and father, dead and buried in this soil. She spoke of the line of her family, torn from one place and then another, up-rooted again and again until their roots shriveled and died and they were left with nothing. Nothing but the dead—the small, unmarked mound in a clearing in the forest that Agnes visits every spring, as soon as the wildflowers bloom and she can pick a bouquet to lay there.

As good a home as any, Agnes said. And so, it is impossible. Agnes will not go, and so Cora will not go either.

Cora watches some internal struggle in Leah that manifests as a quivering at the corners of her mouth. Leah's eyes close, then open.

"Me wish . . ." Leah searches for the words. "Me don't understand it," Leah continues. "But . . . me can forgive."

It is clumsily worded, and for a moment Cora bristles, ready to say that there is nothing to forgive. But Leah spoke a different tongue, long ago, and may not have the right way to say what she really wants to express.

Cora thinks she knows what Leah means. Because she has felt it herself—it has been inside her these last two years without her realizing, and now she sees it clearly. It is how she feels about Leah and her mother, the mother Cora never got to know. She does not understand why Leah did what she did—not in terms of really being able to feel what Leah felt, imagining herself in the same position and making the same choice. But she can accept it. She can forgive.

They are not sure where to go from here. Leah reaches out and pats Cora's shoulder—an old gesture, familiar, and a brief source of comfort. Cora gives Leah a tired smile.

A noise near the door. Cora turns and—

"Oh."

The boy on the threshold is taller than she remembers. But of course he is. She had forgotten how much children grow. Time has changed Leah—but it has transformed little Benjamin, almost beyond recognition. Not so little now. On the cusp of being a man, and she sees more of Silas in him than before, when it often seemed he was all Elsy.

Benjamin lingers on the threshold, shyly.

"You remember Cora?" Leah says. The question is a ridiculous one—of course he remembers. See how his face is overtaken by memory. Cora can see it all in his expression. The love he had for her—may have still. But now tempered with a sense of her abandonment. Because he is too young to understand. At that age, his world begins and ends with himself, so how could he imagine Cora doing what she did in spite of him? It must somehow have been because of him. And he carries that hurt with him still, Cora can tell. Maybe he always will.

"Hello, Benjamin," Cora says, her voice cracking.

Benjamin nods but does not speak.

"Me was telling Cora about Africa," Leah says gently.

Benjamin looks between the two of them. His face changes, shines.

"She coming?" he says. And his voice has not broken yet— it sounds just the same.

A memory. Holding Benjamin, the smell of his hair—the past asserts itself so vividly that Cora's arms feel the weight of him, as if she has been transported back to that moment, the present fading away to nothing. The whispered promise.

We gon' be together. Always.

"Me can't," Cora says.

He is hurt but tries to hide it.

"Oh," he says.

His is the harder goodbye, Cora knows it. Leah has been in her life longer. But Leah is old—seems older now, the last few years of Nova Scotia cold withering her and showing her age. As she enters the twilight of her life, Cora will always have been her sun, burning bright in her memory. But Benjamin—he has his life ahead of him. The years they spent together will fade, until they are little more than a shadow, the brightest years still to come. Who will he grow into, on the shores of Sierra Leone? Cora will never know.

That afternoon, she stays a little longer in Preston. The day takes on a strange familiarity—but the familiarity of an echo, distorted as it bounces off the stone walls of a cave, more than the familiarity of the original sound. She sees Silas, returned from England, now married to one of the other young women— exchanges a few, stilted words. She sees others: Old Joe, Dido, Venus, Sarah, Bessie—all much the same and yet somehow changed, the differences less perceptible than those in Benjamin. Nevertheless, it is always present, the feeling that life here has passed on without Cora. That, when the sun sets and she must make her way back to Agnes, it will carry on, still. There is no stopping it—and she imagines their lives diverging and forging onward, like a river that forks into a dozen smaller streams.

There is comfort in this moment, spending some time with Leah, with Benjamin, with them all. But at no point does she doubt her choice.

As night draws in, Cora leaves them. Dry-eyed, she and Leah embrace. It will not be until later that Cora weeps, as it finally sinks in that this is the last time she will ever see the woman who was mother to her almost all her life. Cora parts from little Benjamin last of all, taking his still-small body into her arms and holding him. He fits there, the memory of him strong in the way her limbs surround him. When they break apart and she starts to walk away, she feels the ghostly presence of him, tucked under her chin, hands clasped behind her back. Knows she will always feel it, will always carry him with her.

The path through the forest is narrow. It is hard to see what lies ahead. Twisted roots threaten to trip her; she must proceed with care. But the moon is bright and the night is full of stars, and with crisp air filling her lungs it is hard to live in memory too long. The present calls to her—its sounds and smells, the shape of the trees. And, somewhere ahead, unseen but felt as a growing warmth in her heart, is Agnes. Home.

August 1800

The ships glide out of the bay, toward the rising sun. From this distance, they are no bigger than the stone heads Agnes shapes for their arrows. Hard to believe they contain people— six hundred of them. Almost everyone Cora has ever known. The Trelawny Town Maroons, now bound for Sierra Leone.

It is one of those warm days that contain no hint of winter, that make the snow from only a few months before seem impossible. From their vantage point on the cliffs, Agnes and Cora watch the passage of these ships in silence. Faith at their side, pink tongue lolling from her mouth, panting in the heat. A line of spruces stand guard; behind them, an open plain; and behind this, the forest, trees growing thick together, hiding a whole other world, where bear cubs splash in streams and eagles circle the skies and foxes hunt, their eyes gleaming. Everything living as if the summer will last forever and the cold will never come.

Agnes rests her head on Cora's shoulder. Knowing that

there are no words that will help with the mess of emotions Cora feels at the sight of her people sailing away. But Cora is glad of it—can breathe in the smell of Agnes's hair and remember why she has made her choice. Agnes is letting it grow a little longer, has promised that Cora can braid it soon. The first braids Agnes has had since her mother died.

Light pools across the surface of the sea, silver and gold. Close to shore, it is unmistakably water, but out on the horizon, near the ships, it looks almost solid—like they might step out and walk on it. An illusion, of course. Cora's feet stay where they are.

They did not come yesterday, to see off the other boat—Thursday's. Bound for the Indian Ocean. A whaling ship. He came to deliver Cora one last message—the Maroons' date of departure—and let slip that he was leaving, too. He did not tell Cora what kind of vessel, but he did tell Agnes, when she walked him a little of the way back to Halifax. When Agnes returned with the news, Cora was enraged. There could be nothing more repugnant, to her mind, than a killing mission of this kind.

Agnes did not feel it so deeply.

No perfect choices, she said. With a smile.

Cora did soften then, but only a little.

No, she replied. *But some choices bad and some better.*

This made Agnes laugh. Both of them trying to move the other toward their point of view over the years. Sometimes failing, and sometimes succeeding. Cora cannot think what Thursday has done is right. But for her, freedom has no price. It is a state she has held since birth, and she knows that colors her way of thinking. So she has tried, these past few weeks, to wish him well.

On the cliff tops, Agnes points toward the ships. Her breath catches.

"Look."

In their wake, the whales are dancing. The humpbacks—the whales Cora and Agnes look for every summer. They throw their bodies from the water, not much more than small dots in the distance, framed against the pink morning sky before they fall back into the sea.

Cora cannot believe it. The tightness in her chest might be the beginning of laughter or of tears. But the main sensation she feels is of the world turning—of the years since she first saw the whales from Agnes's canoe. She closes her eyes. Tries to imagine Leah and Benjamin, wills them to look back, just once, and see the animals follow them. There is so much ahead, she knows. Their minds will be on all that is to come. But one glance back and they can share this wonder with her, just for a moment. They, too, can be touched by its impossible beauty. Its fleetingness—there for a fraction of a second, and then gone. When Cora opens her eyes again, the whales have disappeared beneath the ocean's mirrored surface, hidden in the depths. The ships slip over the horizon one by one, until they are out of sight.

Cora and Agnes stay watching a while, though there is nothing to see but the ocean. The occasional gull that circles overhead. The slow climb of the sun through the sky. Resting against each other, taking slow, even breaths.

A whole day ahead of them. Much to do. But not yet.

Author's Note

The seed of this novel was planted by Adam Hochschild's *Bury the Chains: The British Struggle to Abolish Slavery.* As an overview of abolition, it is global in scope, acknowledging the contribution of Black as much as white struggles for freedom, a welcome correction to hagiographic accounts of William Wilberforce and the like. Parts of the book focus on the founding of Freetown in Sierra Leone, which ended up bringing together free Black people from Britain, the United States, and the Jamaica Maroons—the latter two coming by way of Nova Scotia in Canada.

I have always felt a particular affinity with histories that transcend national borders, in both fiction and nonfiction (one of my favorite novels, Annie Proulx's *Barkskins*, a multigenerational epic about the destruction of the North American forests, constantly draws together unexpected places like seventeenth-century

Canada and China, or nineteenth-century New England and New Zealand). This is partly for political reasons: I resist the idea that we should learn history in national silos, largely because European imperialism constructed a global system. Our ancestors wouldn't have recognized a strict distinction between these places, and nor should we.

But it is also personal. My own family history involves migration from the tropical islands of the Caribbean to the gray shores of England. Some of the most resonant stories of my grandparents that I have heard over the years are those that highlight this temperature change, like the fact that my grandmother had never seen fog before she arrived. I grew up wondering, What is it like to move from a warm place to a cold one? And so the story of the Jamaica Maroons, in particular, drew me in.

This was a community I was already familiar with from my studies of Caribbean slavery, compelling as a symbol both of resistance—they were one of the only groups of runaway slaves to achieve formal recognition of their freedom by the British—and of complicity—that freedom came at the price of serving as defenders of the plantation system itself. I wanted to learn more about their years in Canada: their experience of cold winters, but also their close proximity to another group in the Black diaspora, the former slaves from the American South who had won freedom in the War of Independence. How did these groups, whose experiences of colonialism and enslavement were so different, relate to each other? Thus, the story of Cora and Agnes and their exploration, together, of what it really means to be free, was born.

In the course of researching this novel, I spent some wonderful weeks feeling out the landscape of Nova Scotia: the winter snows and the frozen lakes, and the summer whale watching on a misty, ethereal day much like the one Agnes and Cora spend together when Cora sees the humpbacks for the first time. I have to give credit for the sentiment Agnes expresses in chapter 15 to our guide on the Adventure Bay Whale Watching Tour out of Tiverton—it is humbling to see these animals that can only be seen in the water, their home, and are only seen when they want to be.

I would also like to acknowledge Carrefour Atlantic Emporium, the Millbrook Cultural & Heritage Centre, Shelburne County Museum, the Black Loyalist Heritage Centre, and the Black Cultural Centre for Nova Scotia, all of which were invaluable in supporting my quest to capture the historical texture of Nova Scotia, especially the strange contradictions of freedom for the province's Black population. One particularly poignant detail from the Black Loyalist Heritage Centre that informed the novel was the story of Lydia Jackson. Like Thursday's mother, Lydia was a Black Loyalist who could not read and signed a contract as an indentured servant that she believed was for one year; really, it was for thirty-nine. The trial of Mary Postell, which Thursday alludes to before Agnes's trial, was also a real event, where a Black Loyalist woman tried to prove her freedom in court, and white people burned the houses of some of those who testified on her behalf. Mary was ultimately sold back into slavery and separated from her daughters, showing just how precarious Black freedom in Nova Scotia could be.

This is also a book about love. Specifically, queer love,

so often hidden or expunged from the historical record. The confusion between friendship and love is a well-worn trope when it comes to relationships between queer women: not just the willful misreading of queer love as friendship, but also in the experience, shared by so many of us, of looking back on intense adolescent friendship dramas and realizing that, in hindsight, there was something not quite straight about the whole affair. . . .

It will therefore never fail to amuse me that, when I first conceived of this book, I imagined a story of female friendship. Having told, in *River Sing Me Home*, a story of motherhood, I was interested in moving on to bonds of love beyond family. What came to me first was the idea of three women, not related but whose lives would become deeply intertwined. I puzzled out their relationships, starting with Leah and Cora, an adoptive mother and daughter. I then imagined Cora and Agnes in the shape of a story similar to this one—a meeting in the woods and Cora being drawn out into the forest. It was only once I had mapped out the whole story and started writing that it became obvious to me what was missing. Cora and Agnes weren't just friends. They were in love.

Writing about queerness through history is never easy, especially where it concerns women, whose sexuality is subject to intense erasure. I was grateful to have as a guide *Sapphistries: A Global History of Love Between Women* by Leila J. Rupp and *Boy-Wives and Female Husbands: Studies in African Homosexualities*, edited by Stephen O. Murray and Will Roscoe. Any queer historical story like this one, that is not (or not solely) characterized by misery and persecution, will always open an author up to charges of anachronism. All I can say in response is that our imaginations have failed us if we think the queer people who came before us never experienced joy. We should not forget that they were demonized and punished. But we should also not forget that, sometimes, they simply loved.

Acknowledgments

Thank you to my brilliant, brave, funny, wise, and kind sibling, Cal. I miss you and wish so desperately we'd had more time. For as long as I have ink left in my pen, anything I write will be for you.

Thank you to my agent, Laurie Robertson, for your unfailing support. Thank you to my editors, Sherise Hobbs and Kate Seaver, for stewarding this book with such care. Thank you to everyone at Headline and Berkley for everything you do to take this story and share it with the world.

To Jennifer Schaffer-Goddard and Indyana Schneider, I couldn't be half the writer I am today without you to inspire me. Thank you. May our writers' group last forever!

To all my friends, who helped me through the darkest of times, I am unbelievably grateful.

To my parents, who gave me and Cal everything. None of it would be possible without you.

And finally, to Charlie. Even if I filled every page of every book I've written and ever will write with all the reasons to love you, it couldn't be enough. Thank you.

RAISING READERS
Books Build Bright Futures

Dear Reader,

We'd love your attention for one more page to tell you about the crisis in children's reading, and what we can all do.

Studies have shown that reading for fun is the **single biggest predictor of a child's future life chances** – more than family circumstance, parents' educational background or income. It improves academic results, mental health, wealth, communication skills, ambition and happiness.[1]

The number of children reading for fun is in rapid decline. Young people have a lot of competition for their time. In 2024, 1 in 10 children and young people in the UK aged 5 to 18 did not own a single book at home.[2]

Hachette works extensively with schools, libraries and literacy charities, but here are some ways we can all raise more readers:

- Reading to children for just 10 minutes a day makes a difference
- Don't give up if children aren't regular readers – there will be books for them!
- Visit bookshops and libraries to get recommendations
- Encourage them to listen to audiobooks
- Support school libraries
- Give books as gifts

There's a lot more information about how to encourage children to read on our website: **www.RaisingReaders.co.uk**

Thank you for reading.

hachette
UK

[1] OECD, '21st-Century Readers: Developing Literacy Skills in a Digital World', 2021, https://www.oecd.org/en/publications/21st-century-readers_a83d84cb-en.html

[2] National Literacy Trust, 'Book Ownership in 2024', November 2024, https://literacytrust.org.uk/research-services/research-reports/book-ownership-in-2024